THE SCOT'S DECEPTION
HIGHLAND SWORDS BOOK 5
Published by Keira Montclair

Printed in the USA.

Cover Design and Interior Format by
The Killion Group, Inc

THE SCOT'S DECEPTION

HIGHLAND SWORDS 5

KEIRA MONTCLAIR

THE GRANT FAMILY TREE

ALEXANDER GRANT and wife, MADDIE

John (Jake) and wife, Aline – both deceased
Alasdair and wife, Emmalin—John and Ailith

James (Jamie) and wife, Gracie
Elshander and wife, Joya
Alaric
Jowell
Merelda
Maryell

Kyla and husband, Finlay
Alick and wife, Branwen
Paden
Broc
Chrissa

Connor and wife, Sela
Dyna and husband, Derric-daughter Tora
Claray (half-sister)
Hagen
Astra
Morgan

Elizabeth and husband

Maeve and husband

PROLOGUE

1314, the Highlands of Scotland

ALEXANDER GRANT CLOSED HIS EYES, hoping he'd be blessed with a visit from his wife, who had passed on before him. She came to him in his dreams, something that happened no more than twice a moon. He treasured each instance, holding the feelings close to his heart.

A mist appeared at the opposite side of his chamber, and he climbed out of bed, praying it was his wife.

"I'm here, Alex."

Her voice came to him in a soft whisper, the same voice she had used with him in bed after their lovemaking, talking quietly so as not to awaken the bairns down the passageway.

"I miss you so, Maddie." Her voice, her scent, his memories…they nearly undid him.

"Alex, is that a tear? Oh, Alex, do not cry. 'Twill not be long now, I promise."

"Maddie, when will you trust our bairns and grandbairns to do battle on their own, to see Scotland move ahead with the skills and sense we've raised them with? I'm nearly eighty summers, love. My bones pain me daily now, and I can no longer use my sword. My movements are slowing."

"But you can still use your mind. Do you recall long ago when your mother spoke to you about the fae?" She moved closer and reached out to brush the wetness from his cheek. Her gown was the heavily brocaded green one she used to wear at the holidays, gold thread stitched into the bodice. She even carried the scent of the pine boughs she used to carefully arrange around the great hall.

Forcing himself to listen, he thought back to his mother's stories. "Aye, she always told Brenna and me that the fae would help protect this land from evil, but they would sometimes need a wee bit of help from us."

"And do you recall Avelina's power?"

"Aye, she was chosen by the fae to wield the power in their relic, the sapphire sword, and to protect it until she passes it on."

She stepped into his arms, her finger tracing his jawline. "You are as handsome now as ever, Alexander Grant."

As soon as she touched him, his aches and pains disappeared. Wrapping his arms around her, he kissed her slowly, savoring her. She was the one who pulled away, a look of regret on her face. "Alex, the time has come for Avelina to pass along the protectorship of the sword. She will bring it to you. 'Tis up to you to choose who will hold its power."

"Tell me who should wield it, and I will see to it, Maddie."

"You must determine that. I cannot do it for you, but I trust your judgment." Her expression turned solemn. "The sword will be needed soon. A big battle is coming, Alex. If all goes well, King Robert will finally send the English back home. You'll finally understand our grandbairns' power."

She moved back until their gazes locked. "But you're needed for something far more important to me. Please be patient, husband."

"Anything for you. What has you worried this time?"

"There are two more problems. One is that an evil force plans to overtake Grant Castle, and the other problem is much, much worse."

"What could be worse in your eyes?" he asked, cupping her cheek and rubbing the pad of his thumb lightly across her soft skin.

She leaned into his touch and sighed. "Soon, Alex."

"But our descendants are completely capable of protecting our castle, of attacking any force that tries to overtake our castle. You know that."

"I believe you are correct. You've done a fine job training our clan."

"We, Maddie. We trained our clan, our bairns, our grandbairns. We did it together."

"Aye, but this new threat is too awful for me to take a chance."

"What could possibly be worse than the last battle for the Scottish Crown or someone trying to overtake our castle?"

He watched as tears flooded her eyes and spilled down her cheeks, something he hadn't seen in a long, long time. "What is it, Maddie?" He kissed one of her tears away. "I'll do it, whatever 'tis. Just stop crying."

"The Ramsays and Grants will attack each other."

He froze, simply because he hadn't expected that answer at all. She was right that it was the worst outcome he could imagine. Their descendants dead at the hands of Clan Ramsay? His descendants killing the sons and daughters of his friends? His head hurt from the implications. Stopping his soft ministrations to his wife's smooth skin, he cursed. "I didn't think there was anything that could make me wish to stay, but you've done it."

"You must stop it from happening, Alex."

She stepped away, moving backward, parts of her image flickering into nothingness as she moved.

He couldn't argue this time.

He had to stay.

"Soon, Alex," were her last words.

CHAPTER ONE

Late May 1314, The Highlands of Scotland

DROSTAN MADE HIS WAY TO the lists, a smile crossing his face as soon as he saw the lasses walking ahead of him. Dyna, the laird's daughter, was leading a group of archers to the practice range, and the sight of Chrissa Grant in her leggings and tunic always made his day a wee bit brighter. The way the garment molded against her bottom when she aimed at her target enticed him, but not as much as watching her let loose a succession of perfect shots, her arm and leg muscles rippling with the movement. He enjoyed watching her amazing ability, even in the practice field.

His interest in Chrissa went far beyond all the hours they spent together honing their fighting skills, but she had a warrior's spirit, fierce and independent. She wasn't the kind of lass who would be impressed by pretty words or gifts.

"Chrissa, do you think you can better me today?" Dyna asked.

Chrissa's sister-in-law, Branwen, who was several months pregnant, said, "Even I could beat you, Dyna. You've been sloppy lately. Too busy watching your husband's arse."

Chrissa giggled and Dyna said, "Guilty. Guilty of that every single day. And I'll not apologize for it."

Would Chrissa reveal whose arse *she* liked watching? Could he dare hope it was his?

At two and twenty, he was ready for marriage—part of him felt it had to happen this year—but he had no idea how to go about changing his friendship with Chrissa. He'd hung back for fear of losing her. Because if marrying someone else was an unacceptable thought, losing her was an even less desirable outcome.

Chrissa said, "I've been practicing. I think I can beat you *and* Branwen."

"You only need to worry about me," Dyna said. "With Branwen's big belly, she'll be lucky if she can shoot anything. Think you she can keep still long enough to nock an arrow? Or will she fall over and roll down the hill?"

Branwen threw her head back and let out a belly laugh.

"Be careful," Dyna called out. "I'm not bringing that bairn into this world."

Alick Grant came running past Drostan, making his way through the group until he reached his wife. He kissed the back of Branwen's head. "Come on, wife. Show them who is the best archer."

She laughed and tilted her head toward Chrissa. Alick quickly said, "Sorry, sister. I was just teasing.

You'll probably be able to beat her. For now."

Chrissa's brother was a fierce warrior with a massive chest and a wide set of shoulders. Surely he'd expect any of Chrissa's suitors to be equally fierce. And then there was her grandsire, who used to be known as the fiercest warrior and best swordsman in the Highlands.

To court Chrissa, he'd have to be fierce and strong.

Practice, practice, practice.

It was the only way he could prove himself to her grandsire, sire, and brothers. Of course, he would still have to find some way to earn the esteem of her mother, the bold sister of the lairds, something he suspected would be even more difficult.

Although it was tempting to watch the lasses' archery practice, he continued on to the lists. Alick had gone ahead of him. Two of the very best warriors were leading the practice—Connor Grant, one of the lairds, and Dyna's husband, Derric Corbett.

Corbett barked at him as soon as he entered the area. "Chisholm, you will go against Alick."

Hell, but he'd be well challenged. He nodded in acceptance and moved over to the area Alick had claimed, lifting his sword over his head to loosen his muscles.

They'd only taken three swings at each other when a sound rent the air that sent both Alick and Drostan running toward the archery field. Chrissa let out a squeal and yelled, "Leave me be!"

The front of the archery field was next to the

lists, though the archers shot far out. If she'd been attacked picking up arrows, they never would have heard her.

Drostan had no idea who had dared to touch her, but he'd break every single one of the bastard's fingers, if necessary. He bounded over the pile of straw surrounding the archery field, his gaze landing on the tall, lanky man close to Chrissa. The man looked much older than he'd expected, and he stood next to a wolfhound and two pups. Something about him was vaguely familiar, but he had no desire to stop and chat with him, especially since he'd dared to touch Chrissa. And he wouldn't allow the details about the pups to give him pause. His impulsive nature was propelled by the memory of Chrissa's squeal. She wasn't a lass prone to complaining.

Drostan launched himself at the old man, throwing a fast punch at his jaw, but his target anticipated the blow and dodged it. He stepped away from the dogs, grabbed Drostan's arm, and flipped him onto his back in a flash.

"Drostan, what are you doing?" Chrissa yelled. "He's my cousin." She stood over him, her bow tossed to the side and her hands on her curvaceous hips.

Drostan said, "He touched you. No one can touch you."

Chrissa growled, a most unladylike sound, and said between clenched teeth, "He didn't. The dog jumped on me. Oh, and just to let you know how foolish you are, meet my cousin Torrian, chieftain of Clan Ramsay. He came along with my cousins Maggie and Molly for a wee visit."

Hellfire, but he'd gotten himself into a bind again. He knew that clenched jaw of Chrissa's would have something to say later. And he would deserve it. Why couldn't he learn to control his impulses? Drostan didn't know how to get out of this situation without looking like a complete fool.

Alick, who'd come to a stop right behind him, said to Torrian, "Let him be. He and Chrissa have practiced together since they were young, so he's a bit overprotective of her."

Torrian laughed and let him up, offering him a boost to his feet. "I hope not to have hurt you, lad, but I'm a wee bit old to allow someone to beat my face."

The other archers had fallen in around them, along with more observers from the lists, and Drostan felt himself blush a deep shade of red. One of the pups jumped up on his leg, its tail wagging, so he bent down to pick up the wee beast.

What else could he do?

"Chrissa, forgive me. My lord, my apologies. I thought someone was hurting her. I mean you no harm."

He took in the crowd he'd drawn, his face growing hotter, before his gaze descended to the grey-haired pup in his arms.

"Looks to me like you've won yourself a pup for your foolishness, Drostan," the Ramsay chief said with a smirk. The dog stared up at him as if to say, "Please?"

"You don't want your puppies?" he asked Torrian, hoping the man would say he'd been jesting.

Torrian chuckled and said, "We brought a litter along, looking for homes for them. My wife, Heather, has the others in the courtyard. Looks as if you've been chosen as a companion. Be kind to her now, will you please? Her name is Sky because her fur has a bluish cast to it."

Drostan sighed, but he couldn't see any way out of it without embarrassing himself further. So he sauntered off with a wee dog clasped in his arms, yipping and licking his chest.

The pup looked at him with wide eyes, tongue hanging out. "Are you thirsty, Sky? I'll find you some water. Will you be a good dog if I take care of you?" He'd heard that dogs loved their owners unconditionally.

If he could only be lucky enough for Chrissa to love him like that.

With that thought came another: how could he be a powerful warrior and take care of a wee pup?

Once Drostan was far enough not to overhear them, Chrissa muttered, "My apologies for my friend."

"Friend?" Maggie said. "I doubt a *friend* would have reacted so quickly from such a distance."

Molly added, "I'd say he has quite an attachment to you, Chrissa."

"Nay, there's naught between us," she whispered, staring after Drostan. "We've practiced together for years. He's just overprotective."

But even as she said it, she second-guessed her words. Had something changed between her and Drostan? Lately, she'd found herself thinking about him more and more, yet she had no idea why. Turning back to Molly and Maggie, two of her many idols, she flipped a couple of her dark braids over her shoulder. "Will you watch us practice? Your opinion means a lot."

Molly and Maggie were the adopted daughters of the famous archer Gwyneth Ramsay, the woman who'd trained Dyna, and although Dyna did not lack for skill, they had many more years of experience. Their cousin, the chieftain of the Ramsays, had headed back to the keep to speak with Connor and Jamie.

Dyna shouted over to her. "'Tis your turn at the target, Chrissa. Shall we see how you're doing?" She gave her a challenging smirk. "Can you prove to our friends you've learned something new?"

Chrissa narrowed her gaze at Dyna, who'd always understood how to push her to better her skills—by making her angry.

She fired off a slew of arrows from her quiver, hitting near center with each one.

Molly let out a slow whistle. "King Robert will be pleased to see your skills."

Dyna applauded her performance and joined them opposite the targets. "Always pleased to see you two, but what brings you to Grant land?"

"Mama wanted us to help you train as many archers as possible before the battle at Stirling.

Gavin, Merewen, and Gregor are working with our archers, so sent us here with Torrian. Word has it that King Edward has gathered tens of thousands of men to head this way, though they're gathering in Berwick at present. They intend to destroy Robert the Bruce once and for all. If Edward has his say, we'll never be free of the English."

"Do your parents think we can beat that many?"

"Papa is convinced Bruce's force will tear the English apart. He expects 'twill make Robert's position as our king unassailable. This could be the last battle in the war."

"I hope Mama allows me to go. I'm more than old enough to travel with the Scottish army. You will both go?" Chrissa asked Molly and Maggie.

"Oh, we'll be there," Maggie confirmed. "All of our best archers are coming. I just hope Mama isn't foolish enough to try joining them."

"But she's still such a fine archer."

"Mama's shoulders are not what they used to be, and I think he'd rather see her stay home and protect the castle. He's adamant that we need many strong warriors to stay home. If King Edward loses, he could take his anger out on the Lowlanders. Any castle he passes on his way back from Stirling would be in danger of an attack. Papa himself is coming to the battle, of course. He's slowed down too, but he wouldn't miss it. Our husbands will be traveling with the warriors Clan Ramsay sends to King Robert." Maggie glanced at her sister, and Chrissa suspected she knew why. From what she'd heard, and she was *always* listening, Molly was feeling her years too. Her muscle pains were bad enough that they sometimes kept her from leaving Ramsay land.

Dyna narrowed her gaze and looked straight at Chrissa. "You'll be going for certes. You, Lora, Branwen, Maggie, Molly, and as many others as we can train."

Chrissa nearly squealed with delight. She'd longed to prove herself in battle for years, but no one had allowed it…all because she'd snuck off Grant land and followed her grandsire after her mother was kidnapped. True, she'd been little more than a child at the time, but no one could convince her it was anything but an overreaction.

Dyna smiled. "'Tis time to end Edward's cruel monarchy over the Scots."

"And I'll be there!" Chrissa said with determination. "We deserve to have our own king. I want to fight for that right, every step of the way." She'd grown up on stories of her aunts and uncles and ancestors fighting for Scotland. Some of her favorite stories were about the clan's role in the Battle of Largs against the Norse, but she also loved hearing about the role the Ramsays and Grants had played in shutting down the Channel of Dubh, a network of smugglers who'd stolen lads and lasses and shipped them across the seas. Maggie and her husband, Will, had led that effort. "I wish to prove myself like you and Will did when you fought the Channel of Dubh, Maggie."

Maggie tilted her head. "Be careful what you wish for."

Chrissa nearly snorted. "But you won, did you not? You crushed them, and the clan still speaks of it!"

"Aye, and the memories of winning are wonderful. But we didn't save all of them, Chrissa, and the fear in those bairns' eyes haunts me, all these years later."

Molly squeezed her sister's arm. The two had been mistreated when they were young, sold into servitude by their parents. Mayhap that was why Maggie's memories still haunted her. Chrissa would only come away from this battle with Edward with fine memories.

"'Tis because bairns were suffering," Chrissa said, her hands firmly planted on her hips. "This is different. We will defeat the English. I don't know how a memory of fighting them could haunt anyone for years."

Maggie just gave her a look. It wasn't the first time Chrissa had gotten that look from someone; she recognized it well. *Someday you will learn*, it said, *and you'll not like the lesson.*

CHAPTER TWO

DROSTAN HEADED TOWARD HIS FAMILY'S cottage, carrying the pup in his arms. "No pishing on me, Sky."

Since he had no idea what to do with a dog, he'd decided to bring the animal with him to check on his sire. Mayhap the man would take to the beast. Looking after a dog would give him something to do other than his constant ale drinking.

His sire had imbibed too much ever since an injury had put an end to his days as a Grant warrior. A deep slice to his sword-arm had severely damaged his muscles. He'd taken the wound in one of the clan's battles against the English, and he'd never been able to move on. His whole identity was wrapped up in being a warrior, something he could no longer do, and so he'd wallowed in drink instead of finding a new purpose. He'd even turned down an offer to train new warriors in the lists.

The amount he drank had increased each year, his temperament changing with it. While he'd never hit Drostan or his mother, he had a violent temper when in his cups. The smallest things would make him bellow or throw furniture. Everyone around him had suffered for his misery, especially Drostan's mother, who'd run off three years ago.

She had finally tired of his drinking and his temper—of his habit of blaming others for his own problems. Drostan couldn't fault her for leaving… or at least he wouldn't have if she'd *told* him. She hadn't even said goodbye. She'd told his father she was leaving for England, where she'd been born, and then disappeared, leaving Drostan in charge of his father.

He took care of the man as best he could, but he dreaded his visits to the cottage, preferring to spend his time with the warriors in their building.

Still, the man was his father, and he loved him and recognized his duty to care for him. No one else would. Besides, the man wasn't all bad. The father he loved was not the man who spent his afternoons and eves drinking to the point of stupor, but the one who tended to his small garden and discussed the situation with King Robert with his neighbors, something he never tired of. The war was of great interest to him, enough so that it temporarily roused him from his stupor. It was from him Drostan had heard all the tales of Clan Grant's prowess against their enemies. Those stories drove him to train harder, fight better.

Someday, he hoped it would be *his* name his sire heard the clan members discussing with pride. He had the foolish wish to make his father proud.

Still, his father was two men—the drunkard *and* the man who loved his clan and country—and often Drostan's visits to him were not pleasant. It had been a while since he'd last been home. No matter. It was nearing the noon meal, so he hoped his father was still able to carry on a conversation.

Sky gave a whimper, as if understanding his quandary, and licked his nose. He smiled at her as he opened the door. The stench of ale and unwashed clothes nearly made him choke. "Good morrow to you, Papa."

"Where you been, you ungrateful cur? All those years I worked to feed you, and you don't have the decency to visit your own sire? Did you bring me another container of ale? I'm nearly out." His father stood up from the table in the middle of the cottage, but the movement had been too abrupt, and he leaned over to catch the side of the table to keep from falling over.

Hellfire, but he was already in his pots. "Papa, you need to eat before you drink. Have you eaten yet?"

"Nay, you bring me naught. Or have you now? That creature in your arms has a look of something I can skin. Leave it here for me. I'll make a fine stew of it."

Drostan couldn't stop his wide-eyed stare at his father. "This is a dog, not a rabbit. You'll not be skinning her for the pot."

"Don't leave it here or I will." He tried to glare at Drostan, but he was so tossed that he swayed on his feet and couldn't keep his eyes focused on one thing.

Drostan groaned inwardly. "I'll go to the keep and find you a loaf of bread and porridge as soon as we've talked." He'd had another purpose for coming, and he wished to explain himself before the man was so deep in the ale he couldn't stay awake.

"Don't bring me any porridge. Bread and a bone to chew on. 'Tis all I need. And a pitcher of ale would be nice, too." He swayed as he moved back to his chair. "Where did you get the dog and why would you want one?"

"I won her in a challenge." He moved to the table, pulled out the chair and sat down, which his father took as an invitation to unload all of his troubles.

"I used to be a fine warrior, lad," he moaned. "They should take good care of their warriors, bring them all the food and drink they need. I shouldn't have to go to the keep for food. At least, my neighbor had the consideration to bring the last pitcher of mead. I fought for Clan Grant for years." He hit the table with a loud bang. "Someone should bring me what I want every day."

"Papa, you are completely capable of going to keep for the daily meal. You shouldn't need to be waited on. You're far from helpless." How he hated the way drink transformed his father into someone lazy and miserable, completely unpleasant to be around.

His father scowled and flung an arm out toward the door. "Don't sit your arse in one of my chairs until you bring me some food." He swung again, wildly, and the back of his hand caught Drostan's face, his ring striking him in the eye. "What the hell, old man? Look what you did!" His hand went up to his eye for protection.

For a moment, the shock transformed his father. His eyes held genuine regret. "Forgive me, Drostan," he said. "I did not mean to hit you." The apology was sincere, but the look faded into a murky glower. "'Twas an accident and you know it. Get me some food."

"Fine, you muddled old fool. I'll get you some food, then I'll leave you and not return for a moon. I came early so we could chat, but once you start drinking, there's no point in staying."

His sire tried to follow him, but Drostan caught his arm and maneuvered him back into his chair. "Sit, Papa. You might hurt someone, including yourself."

"I was a fine warrior not long ago. You'd not be treating me like this…"

He opened the door and slammed it behind him, ignoring the rest of his father's rant. He glanced down at Sky, shaking in his arms. "Don't worry, I'll not allow you to be roasted in a pot, wee beastie."

Sky licked his face again.

Chrissa stood over by the hearth that night after the evening meal, not far from her grandsire. He had his own large chair close to the fire. Though he didn't move around as much as he used to, his mind was as keen as ever. They all took turns sitting by him so they could help if needed. It was her turn.

"Chrissa," he said, his gaze settling on her, "do me a favor and ask Torrian Ramsay to sit with me a bit. I wish to talk about King Robert."

"I'll find him for you, Grandsire."

She approached the table where Torrian sat with her parents and uncles and aunts. Her mother glanced up, arching a brow as if she expected trouble, and Chrissa leaned down to whisper in her ear. "Grandpapa would like to speak with Chieftain Ramsay."

"I'll go with him." Her mother stood. "Your time at the hearth is done. Go enjoy yourself for a bit."

She nodded, then quickly left, heading over to a group of young girls. Her favorite cousins were Merelda and Maryell, Uncle Jamie and Aunt Gracie's daughters. Though they didn't practice archery, they were the closest to her in age, and the three of them enjoyed gossiping about lads. Chrissa was the eldest at nine and ten, then Merelda at eight and ten, while Maryell was a year younger than her sister.

Then there was the thorn in their sides: Astra. Dyna's younger sister was a terror at three and ten. Her favorite activity was tattling—any activity to anyone. The three did their best to stay far away from her, but Astra had an uncanny way of being everywhere, especially where she was least wanted.

As soon as she was close to them, Merelda leaped up off the bench and tugged her off to the side, giggling. "You must tell me about Drostan fighting over you." She giggled, glancing over Chrissa's shoulder to make sure no one else was listening.

Especially Astra.

"It was naught," she said, wishing everyone would forget about that unfortunate episode.

"You said before that there was no fighting after Drostan tried to hit the chieftain. So why does Drostan have a black eye?"

"What?" She spun around, her gaze searching the area, but Astra had stepped up behind her and blocked her vision. At three and ten, she was nearly as tall as Chrissa. She towered over many lads her own age, but then again, she was Uncle Connor's daughter.

Her cousin's nearly black hair shone in the torch-light. "You hit your boyfriend? 'Tis what they're saying."

"I did *not* hit him! You better not spread lies."

Astra wriggled her nose and said, "Fine. I'll tell them what you said. Who hit him? Someone did a fine job discoloring his face." She laughed at her own jest.

"Not funny, cousin. Shall I punch you in the face and see if 'tis funny to you?"

Astra took a step back as she said, "You'll not catch me." Then she ran, yelling back over her shoulder, "Ever."

Chrissa clenched her jaw. "Someday that lass is going to get her just due."

"She's harmless," said Maryell, the calmer and more serious of the sisters. "You acted nearly the same at her age."

"I. Did. Not." She sent her most intimidating gaze at Maryell, but it didn't work because Merelda was already agreeing with her.

"Aye, you were," Maryell said, a big grin on her face. Then her cousin grabbed her arm, her eyes sparkling with delight. "Drostan's coming." She gave a short moan. "He's so handsome. You should let him know you like him."

Chrissa scowled at her. "Who ever said I did?"

"You've practiced with him forever. You should be married to him by now."

Maryell nodded her agreement. "She's right, Chrissa. You were meant to be together. 'Tis in the stars."

"And how would you know?" she asked, planting her hands on her hips.

"Ask Dyna. You know she's a seer. I'd wager she sees Drostan as your husband. Soon."

Chrissa didn't like the direction this conversation was going. She hadn't come over to talk about Drostan. However, she couldn't deny that her feelings for him were changing. She'd been thinking about him ever since their encounter that morning. The way he'd stood up for her. The look in his eyes when he'd taken on Torrian. Mayhap he *did* have deeper feelings for her and, more startling, mayhap she was beginning to return them. Their simple friendship, so long and enduring, had twisted around and changed.

But into what? If she were two years younger, she'd have dared to ask him. Now she wouldn't dream of risking such a thing. Maturity, it seemed, had stolen some of her boldness.

She glanced over her shoulder at him, her belly fluttering in an odd way. But she refused to admit to her new weakness for him. "Just because we've practiced together doesn't mean we should marry. I helped him with archery, and he taught me how to use a dagger. 'Twas a simple trade." The two girls cast the same impish grin as they turned away from her. Moments later, Drostan approached them with the wee pup cradled in his arms. The sight brought on more of that strange fluttering sensation. Had he kept the pup since his confrontation with Torrian?

He didn't wait for any word from Chrissa, instead launching into conversation with her. "Are you going to fight with the Bruce on Midsummer's Day? They say this could be the last battle in the war."

"Aye. I think so."

"You don't know?"

"My cousins told me I probably would be going."

"But you've yet to receive approval from your parents?" A teasing smirk crossed his face, and Sky looked up at her as if she were awaiting the answer as much as Drostan. He just loved to rib her about how overprotective her parents were over their daughter leaving the keep.

She reached for the wee wolfhound and cuddled her against her chest, petting her fur, which was much softer than an adult dog's coat. "Papa will allow me to go because he'll be going."

"Your sire intends to fight? I didn't think he'd

leave the keep."

She should agree with him because she was surprised her sire had said he'd be going along, too. But lately, her instincts had her disagreeing with almost everything Drostan said.

She couldn't help but wonder what that meant.

"He will for this. King Robert wants as many of us as possible. My sire is still a fine swordsman, and Uncle Connor will go, too, so I'll be fine. Grandsire thinks the whispers are true. He believes this battle, if it happens, will decide everything."

"Will you make sure I can go with the cavalry? I wish to fight alongside the Bruce."

The excitement in his gaze told her he wished to go as badly as she did. Or perhaps nearly as much as she did. No one wanted to fight in this battle more than Chrissa. "I'll talk to them. From what I heard, if you've any sword skills, you'll be going. I wouldn't worry about it." She shifted her attention to his bruised eye. "Who hit you?"

"No one," he said, but his gaze dropped to the ground. "I tripped over the dog and fell into a branch."

She knew he was lying. His father had lost most of his sense to the ale he drank. She knew it was the reason his mother had left. "I think your sire did it. Has his drinking gotten worse? Has he progressed and started striking you for no reason?" His sire had been drinking too much ever since his injury, but to her knowledge, he'd never hit anyone when he was in his cups. Had that changed?

If so, he needed to tell someone.

"Nay, I fell. 'Twas just as I said."

She leaned toward him, handing the pup back, and whispered, "Your sire hit you. I can tell. Did you hit him back?" One look at his flushed cheeks was answer enough. "Nay, you wouldn't. If you'll not defend yourself, I can tell someone he's turned abusive. You know what that word does to my grandsire." She tipped her head as if to challenge him, crossing her arms.

His cheeks flushed. "You'll say naught. 'Twas an accident. He lost his balance when he was bellowing in one of his rages. If he'd done it apurpose, I'd have stopped him, but he didn't. Worry about your own problems. If you tattle, you're no better than Astra."

"I'm nothing like Astra." She gave him her fiercest glare and leaned toward him, not that it would work on him.

And it didn't. He simply spun on his heel and left.

She wished to stomp her foot, but not with this many witnesses. Instead she turned away, heading toward the trestle table closest to the hearth where her mother and father, Torrian Ramsay, and Grandsire now sat, surely talking about the upcoming battle.

Now that she knew she'd be joining them, she wished to hear all the details. And she would push for Drostan to go along.

She glanced over her shoulder at the annoying man, not surprised to find him looking back at her. But the look he gave her was not the sort of attention she wished to get from him. Perhaps she'd been a wee bit harsh.

His glare at her was harsher than the one she was giving him.

CHAPTER THREE

DROSTAN WAS UPSET THAT CHRISSA had figured out the truth. He didn't want anyone to know about his sire's heavy drinking either, especially not the lairds. Most knew he drank, but he didn't think they knew how bad it had become.

How he prayed she wouldn't say anything. The last thing he needed was for Chrissa's relatives to regard him as a victim—a warrior incapable of standing up to his own father. It would surely ruin his chance of traveling with the Grant cavalry. And of wooing her.

As Chrissa had suggested, King Robert would probably allow anyone to fight, but he wished to fight on horseback. He was better at controlling animals than most. It would make his father proud, he was sure…proud enough, possibly, to put aside the ale for a few nights.

Will he even notice?

His small lies about his sire did no one any harm. No one but him, and he could take it. Because even if his sire was a mean drunk, he was still the man who'd taught him how to throw a dagger, how to hunt and fish in the loch, how to use a knife to whittle. He even recalled the first time his father had brought him to the keep for a festival. The finery and large hearth had amazed him, and the meat pies and fruit tarts were better than anywhere.

It had been a long time since they'd done any of those things together, but it didn't matter. He couldn't desert his father the way his mother had left them both. On a good day, early in the morn, he enjoyed his father's company. It was his own fault for going so late in the day. The next time he'd go way before the sun was highest.

Shaking the thought away, he found a position at the far end of the hall, paying close attention to the Grant lairds and the Ramsay laird near the hearth, openly talking about King Robert, that bastard Edward, and who knew what else. Chrissa had joined them, bold as you please, even though her mother had disappeared. She'd tell him what she knew later, but she tended to cut straight to the point, leaving out the sort of details Drostan craved. She had no idea how fortunate she was to be privy to such conversations.

He wished to know everything that was transpiring in Scotland. It could be difficult to judge which tales were true and which were the inventions of wagging tongues.

Someone bumped his arm, nearly knocking Sky down, but she lifted her head to stare at the intruder with big, beseeching eyes, always anxious for new people to smother her with love or hugs.

"Excuse me. No bother, but may I make a request?" It was a young red-haired lad with freckles dotting his cheeks, and his demeanor was most serious.

"Who are you?" He wondered what youngster would dare poke the arm of a Grant warrior. How he loved that reputation. His pride in being one of them made him understand, to some extent, why his father struggled so, although he would never be able to fathom his other choices.

"My name is Hendrie, and I want more than anything to squire for a warrior for the battle on Midsummer's Day. I've been faithfully watching in the lists and you're the best fighter." He stopped and imitated a parry with an opponent, ending it to step closer. "I saw you fight the laird. You did a fine job. Have you been placed on the battle list? Will you get to ride a horse into battle? Be part of the cavalry?" The lad paused with an audible sigh, his eyes huge with hope as he stared up at Drostan. It almost made him laugh. The lad had to be daft to think Drostan had done anything but embarrass himself this morn. Mayhap he'd simply come to the conclusion that Drostan was the most likely to accept him…and he had to admit, the possibility of a squire held merit. While he'd never fought in armor, he'd heard their lairds had ordered many sets to be made for their warriors in the front lines, along with helms. Truth was he had no idea how to don armor and could use help. He'd heard it was a difficult task.

"I hope to join the battle. Before I accept you, I must see how talented you are. Join me in the lists on the morrow, and I have a challenge for you now as well." Drostan scanned the table by the hearth again, trying to decide if he dared to attempt what he had in mind.

"Anything, master." The lad's eyes widened with excitement.

A smile twitched on Drostan's lips. When had anyone called him master? He might like having a squire.

"How old are you?" he asked.

"One and ten, master," the lad replied, a look of wonder on his face.

"Do you see the group gathered around the table near the hearth? The one where Alex Grant is sitting?"

"Aye."

He nodded with such exuberance that Drostan laughed, he just couldn't keep it inside.

"Take the pup and meander over to an open spot near the hearth. Settle in and then call me over. I wish to hear what they are saying," he explained, not worried the lad would reveal him.

Hendrie scowled. "I'll not get in trouble with the lairds, will I? I just arrived on Grant land three moons ago. I wish to stay here, become a Grant warrior."

"Lad, if they were worried about people listening, they'd be in the solar. Now, can you do it?" He held Sky out to him to see if he would accept the challenge. "And don't call me master over there, just Drostan."

The lad took off without looking over his shoulder. A few moments later, Hendrie had found a place by the hearth and was waving him over. "Please help me with the pup, Drostan."

Drostan sauntered over, his walk a swagger he hoped Chrissa would notice. She was seated not far from her grandfather, pretending not to notice him. Well, hopefully she was only pretending. He thought her feelings for him might be changing, like his had for her, but he wasn't sure.

Kneeling down, he petted his pup and lifted her into his arms, his ears attuned to anything said by the Grant and Ramsay contingency.

"Do you think King Robert will go through with the battle, Torrian?" Alex Grant asked. "I have this fear he'll back out in the end because 'tis not the way he prefers to fight."

"I think he has no choice in the matter. His brother made the arrangements for him. 'Tis an overly civilized approach to war to my mind. Although the king may have wished to settle things differently, without giving the English so much time to prepare and plan, he believes he has no choice. The matter is settled."

Alick asked, "Why wouldn't he want to fight? I've heard the same from others and I don't understand. King Robert has never been afraid of a challenge."

Derric, who'd spent a considerable amount of time fighting with Robert the Bruce and William Wallace, stood up from his spot to stand behind his wife, still seated in her chair. He unwound her long plait and started massaging her scalp, much to her apparent delight. "Here's what you need to know about our king and why he is so strong."

Drostan knew a moment of confusion—did he mean Robert or Edward?—then he recalled what Chrissa had said to him once when he'd said King Edward. "Don't call him that. He's not our king, Robert is," she'd barked.

From then on, he'd assumed they spoke of Robert whenever they used the word "king."

"Robert believes cunning and stealth are far better than face-to-face fighting. He prefers outthinking the enemy to using brute force."

"Exactly," Alex added. "Which is why we took Edinburgh Castle back with only thirty of our best men. We didn't need a thousand men."

"The English are fools," Dyna said flatly. "They're slow and lazy. 'Tis not difficult to use stealth against them. King Robert would have continued on in that manner if not for his brother's loud mouth. Now we'll have English everywhere trying to spy. They'll want to know how many we have, which weapons we'll use, and everything else they can find out. Be on the lookout for spies." She tipped her head back and closed her eyes, her husband still playing with her hair.

Drostan could not understand why such a powerful warrior was playing with a woman's hair in full view of everyone. He watched with interest, glad that no one seemed to pay him any mind.

He'd never once seen his sire touch his mother, much less try to please her in front of everyone. Of course, his father had made no secret of his belief that Chrissa's father, Finlay, spoiled her mother by giving in to her every whim.

Drostan thought they appeared happy, much happier than his parents had ever been. And Derric and Dyna had never made any secret of their passion for each other. Was this what love looked like? 'Struth, he'd like nothing better than to stroke Chrissa's hair, and if she let him do it in front of everyone, he'd be proud rather than embarrassed. He knew what his father would likely think of that, yet if the conduct was unbecoming of a Grant warrior, then surely Derric and Finlay wouldn't act as they did.

Alick's wife held her round belly and said, "I wish I could go along on this one. I could shoot from a distance."

Alex said, "You have a more important duty at the moment, Branwen." He nodded toward her belly.

This was something else Drostan found interesting about the Grants. The most renowned warrior in the Highlands spent every eve fussing over his great-grandbairns, telling them stories from picture books. He treated their arguments about who got to sit closest to him or earn the honor of sitting on his knee as seriously as he did the war with the English. Not that Drostan had ever sat by the hearth to listen to the tales, but he'd seen the gatherings. Sometimes Chrissa even joined in. On rare occasions, Alex sometimes invited all of the bairns on Grant land to participate.

Drostan's sire had oft said bairns were women's work, but his mother hadn't seemed inclined to agree, which had resulted, more often than not, in Drostan being alone.

Dyna and Derric's youngest daughter, about a year and a half old, toddled into the middle of the group as if she belonged there, followed by two of her cousins, who were apparently watching over her. She'd been named after the god Thor as a tribute to her grandmother's Norse heritage. Tora could do nearly anything she wished, or so it appeared to him. She was hard to miss because her hair color was so light, like her mother's.

The lassie liked to pretend she was shooting arrows like her mother, and Drostan had witnessed her aiming them at her cousins in the past. When she did that, Alex Grant didn't hesitate to chastise her, although he did it with an indulgent smile.

This time her great-grandsire lifted her onto his lap and turned her around to face the group, never pausing in his discussion about the upcoming battle.

The wee one's smug smile gave Drostan the urge to laugh. "What think you, Sky? Can they not see she's got what she wishes?" His sire would never have done such a thing.

For a moment, Drostan had an image of himself sitting near the hearth in a small cottage, a wee dark-haired lassie on his lap, Chrissa sitting next to them. A feeling of longing unfurled through him, more powerful than he'd expected.

If they had children, he'd do all he could to make

them feel happy, he decided. Because he knew how much it hurt not to have that.

Connor said, "Jamie, I'd like to send a messenger to King Robert to find out more about his needs. Perhaps we can send out a group to train with him, and another one to root out spies. I agree with Dyna. There'll be English roaming everywhere, looking for information, and we must do what we can to ferret them out before they can return to Edward. But he probably has multiple patrols out already, and we don't wish to duplicate his efforts."

"Agreed," Jamie replied. "We'll meet in my solar once the messenger returns. When do you expect the English to begin marching this way, Torrian? Have you seen any evidence of them yet?"

"Nay, the last we heard was that troops are gathering at Berwick Castle, where Edward is at present. 'Tis the only Scottish castle of any worth he still controls, besides Stirling. When they plan to advance, I don't know. Uncle Logan is making his way toward Grant Castle. He was planning to visit Aunt Avelina and then come here. I suspect he'll be looking for evidence of the English along the way."

"Papa thinks Edward will have ten or twenty thousand by mid-June," Molly added.

That brought silence to the group as they all considered the ramifications of that many men. Drostan had no idea how many Scots King Robert had at his disposal, but he intended to be chosen for one of the Grant patrols.

Hendrie whispered, "Will we patrol, master?"

Drostan waved his hand to shush the lad, but he couldn't blame him for asking what he'd been thinking. In fact, he'd noticed Hendrie had an impressive ability to intuit his thinking.

An invaluable skill to have in one's squire.

"Your guess, Corbett?" Alex asked. "How many can Robert train?"

Derric scratched his head, halting his ministrations to his wife, who sighed loudly enough for everyone to stare at her. "I'd say three or four thousand trained. He's calling for any Highlanders to join him, and he cares not how well trained they are, strictly because we're known for our heart and our strength."

"'Tis true," Alex said, rubbing his chin. "I'd like to be involved in this discussion. Once we've heard more about what King Robert wants, we'll make our final decision. Until then, let us enjoy our clan."

Drostan took that to mean he needed to step away. He looked at Hendrie and said, "Lad, you're hired. Be at the lists at high sun on the morrow."

"You'll not regret it, master." His eyes lit up with such joy that Drostan had the sudden inkling that he'd just made one of his best decisions ever.

He and Hendrie would be a powerful force together.

Though he'd rather be part of a team with Chrissa.

CHAPTER FOUR

LOGAN STOPPED HIS HORSE, GLANCING over his shoulder at his sister and her husband, Drew Menzie. "Does this look like the correct location?"

"Aye," Avelina said, "over there." She pointed off to the left of their path to a burn that flowed over sets of rocks. With all the rain they'd had of late, the water flow was strong, the sound glorious to Logan's ears. Although he loved his clan, he'd always felt most at home on the land. Outside.

There were several guards with them, but Logan sent half out to patrol so the men wouldn't see exactly what Drew and Avelina were here to retrieve.

"Enjoy your memories," Logan said to the two as Drew dismounted, then helped his wife down. The two walked off toward the burn, their gray hair standing out in the near dark.

Logan pointed to the rest of his guards. "Find a cave for us to sleep in. We'll have to spend one night." Off they went. One stayed behind, his gaze following the older couple with obvious curiosity. Although they'd lied about their purpose, telling the guards the Menzies wished to return to the place where they'd met, they hadn't convinced all of them. "Can you not hear me?" Logan bellowed. "Go!"

Though Logan was an old man now, there was still power in that bellow. The man turned his horse around and hurried away, leaving Logan with an uneasy feeling in his gut as he stared off into the horizon.

He'd learned to pay attention to those feelings over the years, so this one weighed on him.

Something was not as it seemed. Evil hung in the air, thick and dank. If Gwynie were here, she'd sense it, too. He'd left Gavin home to watch over her and Brigid, though Brigid's husband was more than capable. He never had to worry about Sorcha, not with Cailean nearby. The two were to join up with him once they headed north after Drew to return to Menzie land.

He snorted at the thought. His fair-haired daughter had chosen well. Cailean's fiercely wild temperament and sword skills guaranteed no one would come near her. He'd also protect Gwynie, simply because Sorcha wouldn't leave her side. Of course, no smart man would dare to anger his wife or any of his daughters—they could skewer a man's bollocks with an arrow at a moment's notice.

Still, it comforted him to think of how well his children had married. He felt confident Clan Ramsay would carry on his and Quade's legacy.

Torrian and Heather's eldest was sharing the lairdship, and Lachlan was proving to be a quick learner. They'd all carry on just fine without him.

Once this mess is done.

Because he wouldn't consent to leave before it. Though he guessed he'd go down with a fight, no matter which way the Lord chose to move him onward.

On the morrow, Drew would go home to protect his keep and land from all the English marauders. He had been fully supportive of Avelina's mission. The faerie queen had visited her in the night, informing her it was time to retrieve the sapphire sword, hidden so many years ago, and bring it to Alex Grant. Alex would be in charge of passing it along to its new owner—the new champion of the Scots. Although Drew didn't wish to leave Avelina, understandably, he trusted Logan to get her safely to Grant land. Not that anyone would be able to harm her while she carried the sapphire sword.

Logan rode his horse a little closer to the burn, watching as Drew climbed up the rocks, tugged on several boulders and tossed them to the ground. After removing four of them, he smiled and reached behind a small grouping, tugging out a cloth bundle. He climbed down carefully, then carried it back to Avelina, and the two opened it together. Logan didn't have a good enough vantage point to see the sword, but he could tell by Avelina's posture that it was inside, hopefully just as they'd left it. She lifted her face to her husband, and he cupped her cheeks and kissed her. Had to mean they'd found what they were after.

She looked down again, for longer this time, then glanced over her shoulder, her face radiant. Seeing no one else around, she swept the cloth back over the sword and carried it to Logan. "I thought you might like to see how beautiful it was."

She swept aside the old cloth, revealing the sword in all its glory, the blue gemstones shining in the moonlight.

"Hellfire, 'tis more beautiful than I remembered. And the rubies and emeralds on the hilt are quite stunning, are they not? You did a fine job hiding it and protecting it, Lina. I'm sure many have sought it out, only to come up empty."

She smiled as she wrapped it up, then leaned over to kiss Drew. "Husband, *we* did a fine job, and you don't look a bit different than you did the day we hid it."

Logan snorted.

The next morn, Chrissa made her way out to the lists, looking for Drostan so she could tell him what she'd learned about King Robert.

She also wanted to see him. Although her feelings confused her, she knew she was interested in more from him than friendship. She just had no idea what to do about it.

He wasn't at the lists, so she headed to his sire's cottage, hoping to find him there. She passed several people tending to the fields or drawing water from the well, and wished each of them a good morn with a wave. Most everyone was friendly. Although some in their clan believed women belonged at home, others took a great deal of pride in the clan's female archers.

She could only be herself.

His sire was like that, without a doubt. Drostan's mother was rarely seen outside the home, spending her time cooking and cleaning. She wasn't the kind to offer her talents up at the keep, either, one of the reasons Chrissa did not remember her well. Drostan had said his sire wouldn't allow her to leave that often. He wanted her at home caring for her family.

Their donation to the clan came in his warrior skills and vegetables from their garden.

A sudden fear popped into her mind. What if Drostan wanted a nice biddable wife to stay home and take care of their bairns, do nothing outside their home? Would he expect her to change for him?

If the thought hadn't been so horrifying, she might have laughed. Her mother, Kyla, might not be a talented archer like Dyna and Branwen, but she certainly didn't shy away from conflict. She'd always followed Grandsire around, ever since she was a wee lassie, and although Aunt Gracie and Aunt Sela were the laird's wives, it was Mama who ran the keep like the head of an army, always providing for everyone, dividing up tasks in a manner that was fair yet exacting.

Although Chrissa and her mother often argued, it wasn't their differences that set them apart, or so

Grandsire said—he thought they fought because they were too much alike.

She shook the thoughts away. Surely Drostan knew her by now, and if he wanted her, then he couldn't expect her to sit home on her bottom and do cross-stitching.

She knocked on the door, and Drostan's father swung it open. "Good morn to you, Chrissa. Did you bring Drostan with you?" Inan Chisholm had been a handsome man at some point, though Drostan looked like a mix of his mother and father. She recalled his mother, but not that well.

The woman had been ornery, of that much she was certain.

"I thought he might be here. He's not?" she asked, glancing around the messy hut.

A voice called out to her, and she spun around, surprised to see Drostan just arriving. "Did you want something?" he asked, his gaze worrisome.

She wanted to tell him she was not there to cause trouble or confront his father, but only to update him on what she knew.

As he came up behind her, she turned back around to face his sire, Drostan just over her shoulder, close enough for her to feel his heat and pick up his pleasing scent. Both of those things sent her belly into a spiral, as if a thousand butterflies had just set flight inside her.

What the hell was happening to her?

"Are you not well? You're flushed," Drostan said, his lips close to her ears.

She quickly sidestepped so she could face him,

taking the temptation of their closeness. "I'm fine. I ran a bit to get here."

"Come inside, both of you," his sire said with a smile.

Poor Drostan. His father was a conundrum. One never knew how he would be. He could be kind first thing in the morn, but once the ale came out, he changed, bristling like a quill-backed hedgehog. And there was no denying he had some old-fashioned notions.

She followed his father inside, surprised that Drostan's hand moved to the small of her back to usher her in. He moved past her to the table, setting a few things down. "Papa, I brought you a fresh bowl of porridge and bread still warm from the oven. They gave us honey this morn, also."

"My thanks to you," the older man said, sitting down at the table and motioning for them to do the same. He broke off a hunk of bread and took a bite with an eagerness that suggested he was starving. Nodding to Chrissa, he said, "Have some while 'tis still warm. I'll not eat it all. Then tell me what they say about our warriors going to battle."

Chrissa peeked at Drostan and said, "Our men will fight with King Robert on Midsummer's Day. We're waiting on word from the king, but if he's agreeable, the plan is to send out one group to assist in training his troops and another to search out information about the English."

"You mean spy?" Inan said. "My son would do a fine job at that."

"Papa, I can earn my way by working hard,"

Drostan said softly, taking the seat between his father and Chrissa just in case he was in a swinging mood today. "We'll see where they send me."

Inan waved a hand, and Drostan's hand instinctively went to his eye as if he needed to protect himself.

His father noticed and said, "My apologies to you, Drostan. 'Twas an accident. I didn't mean it."

Drostan nodded his head, avoiding Chrissa's gaze. "Eat your bread, Papa."

So much for his taking a branch to his eye, although she'd known better than to believe his story.

"Where's Sky?" she asked, just thinking about the wee pup who was missing.

"I left her with Hendrie. Testing him to be my squire if I'm fortunate enough to be chosen."

"We're awaiting news from the king's messenger, Drostan. I came to let you know. Naught will be decided until we hear from him. He'll likely be back later today or on the morrow."

Drostan nodded and took another bite of bread.

"Chrissa," his father said. "I would have thought you'd be married by now. You are not going to fight are you?"

"Aye, I wish to be there. This could be the largest battle in the history of Scotland. I'll not miss it. I have plenty of time to marry and have bairns, if I choose to." She snuck a quick glance at Drostan, looking away when she discovered he was staring at her.

"'Tis a shame your sire hasn't found a match for

you." Inan shook his head slightly. "If you weren't of noble blood, my son here would make a fine husband. I'd hoped for that one day, but I suppose it won't happen. And you are much like your mother. She's a headstrong woman. I don't know if you'd be happy giving up your archery, your freedom, to stay home and clean for Drostan and me. He needs a hard-working lass who will move in and care for both of us, cook our meals. Do you not agree, Drostan?"

Chrissa glanced at Drostan to see how he would react, and she wasn't surprised that he stared at his father, his jaw slack.

"What's wrong, son?"

Drostan gulped and stared at the table. "I don't see my wife doing those things, Papa. I like that Chrissa is a strong archer. If she were my wife, I wouldn't ask her to change."

His father scowled, though he kept his tongue, something she was grateful for at the moment. She didn't wish to be blamed for any arguments between father and son.

She had to try to diffuse the situation. "My grandsire allows us to choose our own spouses," she said, tilting her head. "Why did you think we'd be a good match?"

From her peripheral vision, she could see Drostan tilting his head, listening.

"You two were inseparable when you were younger. Why, I recall the day you tried to teach Drostan how to nock an arrow. You two giggled and laughed for hours." Glancing at Drostan, he added, "I recall your mother…your mother saying you belonged together." He paused and stared at the table, his features tightening as if freezing over. "She should have stayed." He shoved away from the table, rubbing his arm where he'd taken that fateful slice so many years ago.

"Papa, there's no reason to dredge up the past."

His father sighed and returned, sitting down with a hard plunk. "Not for me, but you two should think on all you've been through together. You made a pledge to each other a long time ago. I think you've both forgotten."

Chrissa had no idea what he referred to, but she thought it a fine note to leave on, so she stood and said to Drostan. "As soon as I've learned of the chieftains' choices, I'll find you. I must go, but my thanks for the bread." She grabbed a small hunk to take with her.

She left, hurrying down the path and through the village, heading to the archery field. Practice would help her sort through her confusing thoughts. Poor Drostan. While his sire had been kind this morn, she knew it had hurt Drostan to see him dwell on his old hurts and pains—wounds that only worsened due to the amount of ale he drank. His memory was apparently fine though—better than hers in some ways. She had no idea what event he'd been speaking of.

"Chrissa," a voice came from behind her. "Wait for me. Please?"

She turned around, crossing her arms so she'd appear stronger than she felt. Willing the slight misting of tears away. When he caught up with her, she started walking toward the field again, Drostan keeping pace beside her. She didn't look at him, because if she did, she felt sure she'd shed more tears.

"Do you remember?" Drostan asked.

"Do you?" She risked a quick glance his way, and fortunately, he wasn't looking at her.

"Until he said that…it was so long ago I'd forgotten, or at least I'd stopped thinking about it, but I remember now. You fell climbing up the tree, and I came to help you. You were crying so hard, and I needed to find help for you."

"But I didn't want any help, probably."

"Nay, you surely did not." She glanced at him briefly again, seeing the ghost of a smile on his lips. "I'd never heard some of the words coming from your mouth. There was quite a bit of cursing after you fell, and I couldn't figure out how to move you."

Then it came back to her. "But you stayed with me until my sire came on his horse. You figured out how to help me. I'm sure you did, though I barely recall it."

"Something else happened that day," he said, stopping them both. He looked into her eyes, putting a finger on her cheek to turn her gaze to his. "We vowed to marry when we were older. The only stipulation was that we had to marry in the summer. You wanted a big festival with all of your cousins present. The Ramsays, too."

Chrissa had completely forgotten this information. Hugging herself, she looked up into his eyes. Had his eyes always been so expressive? "I did?" she asked in a small voice, her gut telling her he was right.

"'Twas what you said. And you said you'd only marry me if I was a good enough swordsman to defeat half the warriors in Scotland. I'd have to be the strongest in all the land to marry you because your mother would accept naught else for her daughter." The volume of his voice had dropped as he spoke, though she had no idea why. "It was as if you wished me away, but I took it as a challenge."

"I said all of that?" But she knew the answer. As he told her about that day, the memories came creeping back, grasping her in their warm, honeyed embrace.

"You don't recall the last thing you said to me, do you?"

She shook her head, unable to speak for the words that stuck in her throat, words that would cause a flood of tears to slide down her face.

"You said that I was the only one you would ever want for a husband, but I'd have to work hard for many years. Then you made me promise to work hard. I had to promise…"

She nodded, tears finally coming and spilling over. They'd been so young, she must have been only six or seven summers. Staring at the ground to gather the gumption to say the words, she finally lifted her chin and said, "I made you promise to be the best swordsman ever. To be in the lists every day." She swiped at the tear, pursing her lips. "Silly words from a bairn."

"They weren't silly," he said. "I promised, and I still do go every day. But until Papa reminded us, I never knew why."

"Drostan, don't be ridiculous. You don't go because of me."

"I'd forgotten it until my sire reminded me." They both stood there silently, considering that long ago day when they'd promised themselves to each other. He finally nodded to her, a small smile on his face. "I have to go. I'll talk to you later."

"Where are you going?"

"To the lists. I have work to do." He smiled at her over his shoulder. "I made a promise to someone."

The following morn, Drostan was still thinking about the promise he'd made—the pledge that had been given and forgotten...but only because he'd internalized it so deeply it had begun to guide his behavior. Now that memories of that day had come back to him, they were crisp and clear. He'd been nine or ten probably. And he'd thought Chrissa was the finest lass in all the land.

True, he had *not* been checking out how her arse looked in her leggings back then. He'd been more intrigued by her skills. She was the shortest person at the archery field, but she was dedicated and could beat many others who were twice her size. He'd never seen another lass shoot like her except for Dyna Grant. And even then she'd made him feel special. Their time together had always been so comfortable, as if they were at home with each other.

Still, none of that changed a crucial fact: she lived in the keep and he didn't. He had no noble blood. Some of the other warriors teased him about that. Once, after he returned to the lists from working with her in the archery field, one warrior had spat on the ground and said, "You'll never be good enough for that one. Her mother was spoiled and so is she. Give up on it before she breaks your heart."

If anyone could break his heart, surely it was her. For he knew what lay beyond her boldness. He knew that when she tugged her braids it was a sign she was feeling vulnerable. And that she thought the setting sun a thing of uncommon beauty. She was a complicated lass, and he loved her more for it.

Loved her more. Aye, he *did* love her. And it appeared he'd done so since he was a laddie.

He made his way toward the lists, pleased to see Hendrie running toward him, Sky tripping over the high grass as she attempted to follow. He made his way over and picked up the dog, who responded with a wee yip as she cuddled close to his warmth. "You love to snuggle, do you not, Sky?"

Hendrie said, "She's smaller than many hound pups. 'Tis why she likes to be close. The air can be cold for her at night."

"How do you know so much about hounds, Hendrie?"

"I raised many on Ramsay land. They have more

wolfhounds than they can handle. 'Tis why the chieftain brought a litter here."

"You left the clan?"

"Aye, a while back. My da wanted to return to the deep Highlands. Mama met Papa at one of the Ramsay festivals, and he moved there for her, but we came to Grant land after her mother passed on."

"And you? Did you wish to move here?"

"I've always dreamed of being a Grant warrior. Papa had the skills, so they accepted him as a warrior and Mama worked in the kitchens. She was a fine cook." A pained look crossed his face. "They're gone now."

"How did you lose them?"

"Both from the same fever. I was sick, but I got better. They never did. My uncle took me in."

"Sorry to hear that, lad. 'Tis hard to lose a parent, and you lost them both at the same time." He looked at the lad, realizing he must have a strength in his core to have gotten this far. "So 'tis your goal to be a Grant warrior still? Is that why you wish to be a squire?"

Hendrie laughed and peeked over his shoulder. "I couldn't go to King Robert's camp any other way. I have to find someone who will be chosen for the cavalry in order to come along. They're the only ones who will wear the armor and need a squire."

"Why me?"

"'Tis like I said, you're the best swordsman of all." He made a face. "Well, other than Connor, Alick, and Derric. After them, you're next. But you're not a member of the lairds's family like they are, so you're my best hope." He shrugged his shoulders and said, "And I like puppies. Will you please take me?" Hendrie's eyes looked huge in his wee face.

"I'll do my best, lad." He tousled Hendrie's hair, then moved over to the lists.

Twice now the lad had told him he was of the best swordsmen. That meant he'd accomplished something.

Would it be good enough to fulfill his end of Chrissa's pledge?

CHAPTER FIVE

DYNA CAME RUSHING TOWARD ALEX from across the hall. He wasn't surprised. He'd been expecting her, and he had an odd feeling that he knew exactly what she was about to say.

"Grandsire, I've been having dreams again."

He pointed to the laird's solar, not far away. "We'll talk inside. I know why you're here." He used the thick, wooden arms of his chair to push himself to a standing position, then grabbed his wooden stick, a new one crafted for him by his grandsons Alick and Broc. The lads had worked on it for hours to ensure it was the perfect height for their grandfather.

She stopped abruptly. "What? How could you know I've been having seer dreams?"

"Inside first, then I'll explain it to you. Just stand next to me and I'll be fine."

He made his way to the large chair behind the desk and indicated for Dyna to close the door behind her.

"How could you know about my dreams?" Dyna

asked, clearly stupefied by his declaration.

"I'll explain to you, if you can tolerate one more story about the olden days."

Dyna broke into a wide grin. Many of his grand-bairns teased him about his habit of telling old stories, though it was all done out of affection. "You know I will always love your stories. But I'm guessing this is not one I've heard retold ten times."

"You are correct." He sat down and leaned back in the chair. "This story is from my childhood, although I'm amazed I can remember back that far."

"'Tis something Great-Grandmama or Great-Grandpapa told you?" she asked, her tone one of excitement. Dyna was an old soul, and she'd always cherished his stories.

"I was about ten summers, if I recall, and Aunt Brenna would have been eight then. Mama told us about the fae..."

Dyna's face brightened. "I love fae stories."

He nodded and then continued, "While some faeries like to taunt and tease people, the fae typically stay hidden. My mother told us they watch over our land to ensure evil never overtakes good. Sometimes they have to step in and offer tools to help guide us along. The fae have what she called chosen ones, people they empower with gifts others don't have."

He paused, watching his great-granddaughter absorb this information. Dyna was more aware of uncanny things than most because she had been given the gift of sight.

"Evil, good, chosen ones... What does it all mean, Grandsire?"

"Mama told Brenna and me to be aware of the cast in the land. 'Tis a feeling, an unnatural aura created by a surge of evil."

A strange look came over Dyna's face. "I've been dreaming about storms and rain and...darkness, Grandsire. Is that what you mean?"

"Aye, it can manifest as storms."

"Is evil here now?" she asked, her expression intent.

"I'm afraid so, and someone must stop it."

"When did you feel it before?"

"When Gregor Ramsay was a wee bairn. It nearly killed him. But the fae came to Avelina Ramsay and granted her a powerful sword to fight off evil."

"The sapphire sword?" Her eyes widened at the mention of the special weapon. Even if she hadn't heard this particular story, all in the Highlands had heard of the sapphire sword.

"Aye. The fae came to Avelina Ramsay and told her what to do. She vanquished the evil force." Alex Grant closed his eyes, saying a quick prayer to bring them through this turbulent time safely. When he opened his eyes again, he looked at his great-granddaughter. "The sword was hidden long ago. The cast is back, though, and Maddie has visited me again in my dreams. She tells me the time has come for the sword to be retrieved from its hiding place. Avelina is on her way, with Logan Ramsay, and we must find the new owner of the sapphire sword."

Shortly after the evening meal the next eve, Chrissa sat and listened to her family discuss the coming battle at Stirling Castle.

She rolled her eyes, something she did a little too much according to her mother, although she'd replied to that accusation by making one of her own. "I roll my eyes as often as you squeeze yours nearly shut to intimidate me."

Her mother had said, "Finlay, she's your daughter, not mine."

But her mother didn't chastise her for the eye rolling tonight, perhaps because she was too distracted to notice.

Chrissa wasn't interested in all the drivel about who would be where and when. And she had difficulty listening to endless conjectures about what might happen. She just wanted to know where and when her skills would be needed. Once she knew that, she'd get back to practicing. Her mind was on something else…or rather someone else.

Her mother had said once that when you kissed the right lad, it made you feel as if you were floating in the sky. That comment had made her roll her eyes, of course, but it had also roused her curiosity. She'd kissed a few lads before, none of the experiences good enough for her to repeat them. Her mother was clearly daft with her talk of clouds.

And yet…after hearing about the pledge she'd made to Drostan all those years ago—and he to her—she couldn't stop thinking about kissing him. Would it be different with him?

The evening meal had been open to the warriors again, probably because of the upcoming battle, and Drostan had come inside, bringing Sky along. At least with the pup there, her mother wouldn't question her interest in the man, thinking her attention was only for the dog. After he finished eating, he set the wee thing near the hearth and started speaking with another warrior.

Chrissa went over to coo and pet the pup, hoping to talk to Sky's owner, too, but by the time she got there, Drostan had already picked up the pup and headed for the door.

She didn't even consider the merits of her decision before she followed him.

"Chrissa? Where are you going?" her sire called out from the table she'd left.

Oh, heavens above, she was nearly twenty years old. Would they never leave her be? "Outside for fresh air, Papa."

She glanced back to see if they would try and stop her, but they didn't, though her mother looked at her with a narrow-eyed gaze that had her rolling her eyes. She headed out the door, ignoring her mother's comment to her sire. "You spoil her so, Finlay. You know she's after trouble."

Being the only lass in her family *did* have its advantages. And Chrissa had never been shy about taking them. Drostan was not far ahead, and he took a quick turn toward the periphery of the bailey, searching out the grassy area near the curtain wall for the pup was her guess.

Sky probably needed to take care of her needs.

And if so, Chrissa couldn't think of a better time for *her* to take care of Drostan's needs.

She wanted to kiss him. Now, if she only knew how to use her wiles to tempt him.

What the hell was a wile, anyway? She'd heard the phrase often enough, but no one had ever said.

She followed him quietly, not wanting to attract attention from anyone else until they were off the common path. They were nearly to the curtain wall when Drostan set Sky down in the grass. The wee pup started sniffing, turning, and sniffing again.

"Drostan," Chrissa called in an undertone, and he flinched and turned back to face her.

"Chrissa?" he asked. "What are you doing out here?" He paused, taking her in, his gaze starting at her boots and traveling up her legs, finally stopping at her face.

The longing she saw in his eyes sent a tingle down her backbone.

He took a step closer, and she felt a sudden rush of heat, some of it from him but most of it from her. It shot from her belly to her core to parts that she didn't wish to think about because she'd never felt anything *there* before.

What was happening to her?

His thumb came up to brush her cheek, the softest of touches. Her cheek felt as if something hot had been laid upon her skin, branding his name across the span of her face.

The edges of his lips quirked up in a slow smile.

He leaned forward.

And…

Oh…

He was going…

Before she could react, his lips melded with hers as his arm swept around her back, pulling her closer. He pulled back for a moment and whispered, "I've always wished to do this, but I never knew if you were interested." He nuzzled her ear and she squeaked as the now-familiar tingling sensation ran across her neck and landed directly on her…

"Are you interested in me, lass?"

Incapable of speaking, she nodded and an involuntary moan came from her lips. Her own lips!

"The hell with it. I want you, Chrissa." His lips found hers in a searing kiss, and she was powerless against him.

Her nipples tingled as his tongue pushed against her lips. This was no regular kiss. He tugged her close to him, so close she could feel the hardness of his chest, his belly, and oh!

Something else was hard against her belly.

She couldn't stop another little moan from erupting so she threw her arms around his neck in the hopes he wouldn't notice. His tongue pushed against the seam of her lips again so she opened for him, his tongue sweeping inside of her mouth until it mated with hers.

And she was lost in Drostan, tasting him, savoring the press of his body against hers. She hoped their kiss would go on forever.

This…was a kiss.

Forever. *Kiss me forever.*

Sky barked, interrupting their sweet interlude, and Drostan pulled away, his breath coming in short pants.

So was hers. What the hell? She could hear herself breathe, something that usually only happened if Dyna made her run four times around the archery field.

Drostan leaned down to pick up the pup, cuddling her close. He reached over and touched Chrissa's chin, closing her mouth with a smile. "You liked it, too. Aye, lass?"

Not knowing how to answer, she nodded and stepped back, hoping he wouldn't notice her labored breathing.

What the hell was she supposed to do now?

"Come, sit down with me. Have they heard from the messenger yet?"

He sat on a bench, taking her hand and tugging her down next to him.

"Nay," she said, smoothing her skirt. She hated that her mother always insisted she wear a gown for the evening meal. "They expect to hear back on the morrow."

"Do you not love to hear the tales of the traveling spy teams?" he said, tracing the lines on her palm. "Wouldn't it be amazing if we were working together? We could be a team just like Logan and Gwyneth Ramsay. Would you not like that? Everyone would know our names."

She stared at his lips, wondering how those two wet pieces of skin could make her tingle everywhere. She smoothed her skirts again just to see if her private parts were still tingling.

Indeed they were.

"Aye, I'd like it just fine." At this point, she didn't give a shite where they sent her so long as she got the chance to kiss this man every night. "They're meeting in the lairds' solar after the messenger returns. I'll request to attend, though I don't know if my mother will allow me."

"Ask your sire," he said, leaning in toward her. "You can convince him of anything."

"'Struth. If they turn me down, I'll ask him."

"Chrissa? Where are you?"

At the sound of her mother's voice carrying over the courtyard, Chrissa bolted up from the bench and took off toward the keep. She knew better than to be found so close to Drostan. He stayed back, but she heard his final plea.

"Tell me on the morrow what you learn. Promise?"

She glanced back over her shoulder, put her finger to her lips to shush him, then said, "Promise."

She ran directly into her mother as she turned the corner to head back to the keep.

"Where were you?" her mother said, pulling back with a scowl.

"Taking a stroll," she said with her most innocent look. Oh, she could look as innocent as a wee lamb just born under a tree in the meadow when the need arose.

"Why did you not answer me?"

"I never heard you. What was your question?"

Her mother's gaze narrowed again. "I asked

where you were." Her jaw clenched, usually the last warning sign before she erupted into a fury.

"I'm here, obviously, Mother. You are getting on in years, are you not?" She stepped around her mother and headed back toward the keep.

"I hate it when you hide things from me, daughter," her mother said. "And asking me a ridiculous question means you're trying to hide something from me."

"Well, I must tell you that you were right about something."

Her mother hurried to keep up with her. "And what was that?"

"It *does* feel like I'm floating in the sky." She smirked and raced inside, knowing her comment would stun her mother.

She loved it.

CHAPTER SIX

THE NEXT MORN, DROSTAN CLIMBED off his pallet in the warrior's sleeping area inside the gates, off to see his sire as early as possible, knowing it was the only time he was likely to see him sober. Afterward, he'd go to the lists to meet Hendrie.

Heading out to the line of cottages outside the gate, he passed the outside stables, surprised to hear a voice call out to him.

"Will you not spar with me, master?"

Drostan coughed, nearly dropping Sky, and spun around to find Hendrie behind him. He hadn't expected to see the lad so early. "I shall return." He paused for a moment, a sudden idea popping into his mind. He moved toward the young lad and said, "Will you watch Sky while I visit my sire? I'll return within the hour and we can spar. Protecting her is an important duty I assign to you. Do not take it lightly."

"I'll do a fine job, you'll see," Hendrie said, his tone quite serious. "I'll feed her something special." He took off toward the stables, a sure place to find a meal for a dog.

Drostan chuckled at the lad's exuberance, then continued on toward his sire's cottage, waving to the people he encountered along the way. He entered his sire's cottage, his heart sinking when he saw his father seated at the table, his head in his hands.

He already knew this man would be completely different than the one they'd seen yesterday.

"Head paining you, Da?"

"Aye, and you know it," he grumbled, his tone already hostile.

"Stop drinking so much ale and you might feel better," he said, pulling up a chair and setting down the day-old loaf of bread and trencher of porridge he'd found for his sire.

"Did you bring me ale?"

"Nay, just food."

"Why not ale?"

"You know why, Da." He pushed the trencher in front of his father.

"Why'd you come?" He pushed his thinning hair back away from his face, the gray becoming more and more prominent. "I've seen more of you these last few days than I have for the past moon."

"Because you're too thin. Eat." He pushed the bread toward his father and took a hunk of his own to chew on.

His father gave him a strange look, then surprised him by saying, "Sorry that I yelled at you." He waved at Drostan's face. "Who hit you?"

Shock slackened Drostan's jaw. "You know who hit me," he finally managed to say.

His sire sat up straighter to glare at him, his hands dropping to the table as he reached for the bread. "How would I know? I never leave this cottage. Ever since your mama abandoned me…"

"She left you because you get drunk and turn into a miserable old goat who no one wants to be around. You hit me, or don't you remember? 'Twas an accident, but you did it, Da." His father often pretended not to remember the things he'd done while in his cups, but Drostan didn't believe him.

"Hit you? I would never hit you…" Tears misted the old man's eyes. "Why would you say such a thing? I need more ale. Be a good son and get me more. 'Tis too hard for me to go out for a pitcher."

"Papa," he said, standing. "'Twas an accident. You were in your cups and your hands were flying about."

"Pay more attention next time!" The old man stood up so quickly he knocked his chair over. "Get out. Get the hell out. My head aches too much to deal with this. Just leave me be." His father ranted and weaved a path around the small hut, tossing things about in his frustration. "I loved your mother. She was everything to me. Why did she leave me? I'd have given up the ale for her."

He knew talking to his father would not help at this point, so he ignored the older man's comments. "Da, I came by to bring you some food and to let you know I'm probably leaving on a patrol. I know not when I'll be returning."

"Go. Just go." His father picked up a pot and tossed it across the small space, the clatter a loud assault on the ears.

"No more, Da. I'm gone."

"I was not trying to hit you. 'Twas not even close," he bellowed after him.

He left, his sire's ranting carrying to him as he walked away, but once the door closed, he heard nothing. The thick stone walls had protected his sire's reputation. Somewhat. Three doors down, one of his neighbors said, "You should come around more often, Drostan. He's turning daft some nights waiting for you. He's verra proud of you."

"He's not waiting for me."

The man looked confused. "If not you, then who?"

"He waits for my mother or death, I'm not sure which one." He snorted at his own comment as he strode away, not needing any more guilt on his shoulders. "Don't think he would know or care which one came along first."

How he wished he could make either of his parents proud, but that was quite impossible.

Chrissa sat in on the meeting of Grants and Ramsays in the solar. The messenger had finally arrived, and she was excited to find out what action would be taken.

Would she be allowed to go or would she be forced to stay at home? Grandsire was present, of course, and so were Uncle Jamie, Uncle Connor and Aunt Sela, plus her mother and father, Dyna and Derric, and Alick. The small Ramsay contingent was also present. It was a lucky thing Grandsire had expanded the solar before passing the lairdship on to his sons.

Uncle Connor started the meeting. "Jamie, now that there are no listening ears, please tell everyone what you learned from the messenger from King Robert."

Uncle Jamie leaned back in his chair, balancing on the back two legs for a few moments before he banged back down with a jolt. "He'll face Edward head on. He's training his forces to fight in groups. Though he hasn't made his strategies known, I'm sure he'll use schiltrons. He'll also have some mailed knights with cavalry, and he's attempting to collect as many archers as possible. You know that has been a weak spot for him in the past."

"Because the English have strong archers," Molly said. "He gave me a formal request to gather as many archers as possible, male or female." Chrissa wished to let out a wee yip of happiness but decided it wasn't quite the right group for that.

Uncle Jamie said, "We've also received a request for foot warriors, horses not necessary. That puzzled me."

Maggie laughed. "Oh, he'll take all your mounted warriors, but he's eager enough to have Highland forces, he'll take them without. The English fear the savage Highlanders so much, he'd take us even if we insisted on fighting nude like in the times of old."

Maggie's comment sent the group into gales of laughter. They'd all heard the stories, although it wasn't a method any of them had ever used.

"Duly noted," Grandsire said. "What does he want from us now? Or does he wish to wait until we are closer to Midsummer's Day?"

"He requested ten of our finest to meet with him. Some may be used to train his people, and others may be sent out on patrol." Uncle Jamie glanced across the solar. "He specifically requested Derric and Dyna be among the group. Said he could use your special skills."

"How soon?"

"As soon as possible."

Grandsire said, "Since we're all here, I'll add that he has asked for the Highland Swords group to gather. Alasdair, Emmalin, Els, and Joya are on their way."

"Has he told you how he plans to use us?" Dyna asked. She was a member of the group.

How Chrissa wished she could be part of that group, but it was mostly chosen and managed by Grandsire. He believed it had something to do with the three cousins being born on the same night. And even though Dyna was younger, she was an active part of the group. It was what happened whenever the group fought together that truly determined who was involved.

That and Grandsire's dreams.

"Nay, I've heard naught on this," Uncle Jamie said.

Derric said, "The messenger said Robert believes

he can be successful without it, but he'd like to have them available in case the Scots start to lose the battle. If so, King Robert wants us to be the final act, the grand show of lightning celebrating our win."

"I'd like to bear witness to that myself," Uncle Jamie said. "We can only hope he's right." He nodded to Derric and Dyna. "Stay, and we'll decide who to send to King Robert with you. The others can leave, if you like."

Maggie stood up and headed to the door. "I don't think you'll need Molly and me for anything else. We'll stay one more night to help train before we take our leave back to Ramsay Castle to ready our group for Midsummer's Day. Torrian, does this suit you?"

"Aye, I need to ensure our land is properly protected. We're not far from Berwick Castle, so we should find out quickly if the English are on the move."

Molly and Maggie left, and Chrissa had to hold back not to chase after them, just for the pleasure of training with them one more time, but she needed confirmation that she and Drostan would be allowed to travel to the king's camp.

She had to know.

She needed to know for herself and for Drostan.

Her mother surprised her by getting right to the point. "So Dyna, you and Derric will head out, leave your two bairns here with your mother and Claray?"

"Aye," Dyna said, glancing at her husband to see

if he had anything to add.

"We'll leave on the morrow," Derric said. Glancing at Dyna, he added, "Your mama has already said she'll watch the bairns. He turned to the lairds then. "Who shall we take with us? I leave it to you to choose."

Chrissa's heart beat so hard in her chest that she feared they could all hear it.

Uncle Connor named off several warriors, and the very last one he named was Drostan. That came as a relief, because she wouldn't have to use any of the half-formed arguments she'd thought of to convince them to take him. Now, she only had to convince them to take *her*. She tried hard to act disinterested, but that was a lie to everyone. They all knew how badly she wished to go, although she doubted they knew of her interest in Drostan.

Or perhaps they did. He *had* tried to punch Torrian.

Uncle Connor glanced at her mother and father, the silent question as obvious as if it had been spoken. Chrissa held her breath as she waited, saying a quick prayer that her mother would finally relent and allow her to do something meaningful.

It was time for her to make her own legacy.

Her father looked at her mother, who gave him a small nod before turning to face her. "Chrissa, we'll allow you to go, but I'll be giving Derric and Dyna strict instructions about watching you, and you're not to cause any trouble. None. Do you agree? In fact, I'll send extra warriors just in case you need to be sent home for not following orders, understood?"

"Hell, aye," she blurted out, then turning a deep shade of red. She cleared her throat, doing her best to look sheepish over her outburst.

Her mother's gaze narrowed again—a thinly veiled threat for all to see.

Grandsire remarked, "Kyla, I do think your daughter is mature enough to recognize that her part in this is to follow directions. She'll act differently than she does on Grant land. If not, she'll pay the price. Being captured or injured by the enemy is not something she wishes to risk. Is that not true, Chrissa?"

Chrissa blushed. She'd thought to say something more, to convince them she was serious, but Grandsire had said it all. They'd given her what she wanted—and she understood the dangers that lay ahead.

Then Grandsire surprised her with his last comment. "I'm sure you'll keep King Robert entertained, Chrissa. But please do not embarrass us too much."

She had no idea what he meant with that remark.

CHAPTER SEVEN

THAT AFTERNOON, CHRISSA FIRED ANOTHER volley of arrows at the target, still filled with exhilaration that she would be going on the journey to see King Robert.

With Drostan.

She hadn't seen him yet to tell him, but she supposed he'd already learned from Derric. Part of her had wanted to run right to him so she could see the smile on his face when he learned he had been chosen. But she wasn't ready to let on to her family that their friendship had changed.

"Stop thinking about lads and shoot," Dyna yelled at her. "You missed one."

"But the rest hit the center," she called out.

"Are you whining?" Dyna called out.

"Nay," she said, wide-eyed. "Not at all. I'm sorry, I was a bit distracted thinking about this journey."

"The question is who on this journey has you rattled?" Dyna was pacing the clearing behind her, her hands on her hips. Fortunately, they were the only ones left with Maggie and Molly. The others had abandoned the practice after the first hour.

Maggie snorted. "I think we know. Do we not, Chrissa?"

Chrissa blushed but fired off another five arrows, hitting dead center on all five of the targets she'd chosen. "Nay, you don't." She wished to pout but didn't dare act the part of a bairn in front of three of the women she admired more than anyone.

Molly must have felt sorry for her because she said to Dyna. "Chrissa's admirer has her unsettled. Drostan is going along. Can you not remember what it was like to have your mind on a man when you're on the practice field?"

Dyna glanced at Molly with a smirk and asked, "Do you? 'Twas a while ago, was it not?"

Molly said, "Be careful. I am still capable of some trickery, my dear." She waggled her brow at Dyna. "I had to fire an arrow to save my cousin while Tormod watched. I hate to admit how difficult it was to focus. If not for our sire and all his evil training, I surely would have failed."

Maggie huffed a laugh. "I recall having my own issues. Will distracted me more than I care to admit. My daggers often went wild whenever he was around. 'Tisn't every day a lass gets wooed by the Wild Falconer." Maggie's husband had earned a reputation as an outlaw for a time, bolstered by his trained falcons.

"Aye," Molly said, glancing at Maggie. "Coping with distractions is an important part of training, especially before going into battle. When our sire arrives, I'll have you two practice with him. He paces and yells at you while you're trying to aim. I used to get furious with him over it, but he told me 'twould make me stronger, and he was right. 'Tis why I was able to hit Ranulf MacNiven the way I did."

Chrissa had heard plenty of stories about Ranulf MacNiven, of course. He'd caused a lot of trouble for her clan and the Ramsays back in her mama's day.

Dyna nodded to Chrissa. "You should take the time to ask an expert how they did it. Molly killed the man whom many had tried to take down. The time she referred to, she shot him while he held her cousin in front of him and Tormod was off to the side. That kind of focus only comes from training."

Chrissa cocked her head. "You shoot when the enemy is in front of you. I don't care if someone is yelling near me. 'Tis not difficult."

Molly sat on the soft grass. "But what if the man you love is off to the side, within range of the enemy, and the villain has his dagger at the throat of your wee cousin? What if your sister is behind you crying and your father is in front of the villain ranting like a daft man, trying to distract the fool so you can get a better shot?"

Well, when she phrased it that way…

"How did you do it?"

"'Tis as Molly said. Our father trained us brilliantly."

Molly added, "Ask our mother how hard it was to fire at the man who killed her father and brother.

She couldn't do it. Not until she practiced for days with Papa yelling at her while she tried to aim."

Chrissa had shot arrows at men before, but the circumstances they were describing…she hadn't considered facing something like that. "I don't know what to say. I don't know if I could ignore all those things. I've worked so hard, but…"

Was it foolish of her to wish to go? Perhaps it had been a naïve wish. The goal of a child. Her mind was so woven up with Drostan of late, she wasn't sure she'd be able to shoot straight if he stood anywhere within eyesight.

Dyna sat down and motioned for Chrissa to sit. "I know what you're going through. You just need to learn to tune out whatever's going on with you while you're fighting. Believe me, Derric Corbett does *not* like being forgotten, but I had to learn how to do it."

"Mayhap I don't belong with you. Mayhap I'm too inexperienced," she muttered, yanking on the grass as if it had offended her.

"Look, you've accomplished the difficult part," Maggie said. "You're a hell of an archer, and we'd be proud to have you along on any of our jaunts. But you don't stop challenging yourself just because you can hit dead center of a target. Can you hit the target while you're moving? While someone is taunting you? When the one you love is standing two feet from you? Or the worst—when a family member you love is being held by the enemy? Don't settle and think you have naught more to learn, because there's always more to learn. As Papa often told us, our enemies like to dance in our minds, making us question everything we thought we knew."

Dyna asked, "Will Drostan distract you on this journey? I don't need to know anything but that."

She shook her head, knowing that her voice would betray her if she spoke. Then she stood up, anxious to fire a few more arrows to help exorcise her emotions. A thought popped into her mind that helped her gain control of her emotions, something of merit. "'Tis not as if we'd just met. Drostan and I have known each other forever. And we've trained together for years. He won't upset me if he's nearby. I'm used to him."

Maggie gave Chrissa an assessing look. "There's good news, too. If two people know each other verra well, they might also do well as spies."

"Really?" Chrissa had never heard that before, but she wished to hear more. "How do you know?"

"You need look no further than our mother and father," Molly said. "Or my husband and me." She tipped her head toward her sister. "Maggie and Will. And do not forget Dyna and Derric. They've gone on many missions together for the clan and King Robert." Her expression turned sly. "A man and a woman can infiltrate different parts of an operation. If you have strong feelings for Drostan, you should consider spying with him. In fact, we could make the recommendation to King Robert. *If* you see a future with him. Couples are the best spies."

The Ramsays' words sent her thoughts into a

confusing spiral. Drostan had mentioned the possibility of them spying together. Could it happen? What would it be like if they married? Would they stay in love, like Dyna and Derric and the Ramsays and their husbands, or would they suffer the fate of his parents?

She shot off several more arrows, almost in a daze, and only realized how much time had passed when she noticed Dyna and Maggie were moving around the field, collecting arrows and cleaning up the practice area. The sun was going down. Mayhap she should return to the keep. Moving her shoulders around a bit, she felt a familiar soreness that told her the practice had indeed gone on for too long.

As they headed back toward the gates, the three married women slipped into conversations about their family, so Chrissa thought some more about Drostan. The guards who'd accompanied them followed on horseback. Although it was a goodly distance, Chrissa preferred to walk some days, enjoying the fresh air. Her mind was so preoccupied she didn't notice her cousin Astra until she was nearly upon her. "Drostan is looking for you everywhere. He's taking a squire with him. May I go along as your squire?"

"What?" she said, incredulous that her cousin would suggest such a thing. "I don't need a squire." She also doubted that Drostan would be taking a squire to see King Robert. Mayhap for the battle, but that wasn't for a while yet. He'd have no need of armor for training or spying.

"You might. How do you know? When you get to camp, I could be useful." Astra fell in behind her like one of Torrian's pups, not at all put off. "I could pick up all the arrows that miss your target. You'll have to have an endless supply."

Chrissa stopped in her tracks. "Astra, squires are there to help their masters don and remove their armor, their helm, even their boots. I don't wear any of that, so you would fulfill no purpose. And think you that your mother would allow you to go? I doubt it."

"My mother allowed Dyna to go wherever she wished. Mayhap you don't wear armor, but you could use my skills. I've verra good at eavesdropping."

"We all know that. You never stop." She waved her hands up over her head for effect.

"So you admit I'm good at it. I can listen to the English and tell King Robert exactly how they'll attack."

Chrissa spun on her heel with a growl and headed toward the keep. "Nay, you'll not be my squire. Ask your parents if they'll allow you to go. I think not. But if you're allowed, you'll not travel with me." She put as much emphasis on the last word as possible before she yanked on the door and hurried into the keep.

She ran right into Drostan's chest, and she felt as if she'd been scorched. It was as if her body knew him before her eyes did. Hellfire, she had to stop acting like she was in love with Drostan just because of one kiss. Of course, it wasn't just one kiss. It had started long, long before that, as his father had reminded them. There had been other moments, too, when their friendship had felt like something more. She recalled a time a few moons ago when they'd gotten too close, Drostan standing behind her to show her how to fling her dagger, and it had sent strange sensations tumbling through her body. Unfamiliar sensations.

She'd dismissed it back then, not realizing it was the start of something that would continue to grow inside her. Was the same happening to him?

"Chrissa," Drostan said, stepping back from her after they collided. He reached for her as if she needed steadying. Or mayhap he simply wished to touch her? "I'm sure you've already heard, but I'm going to King Robert's camp. I'm verra pleased. My thanks for your assistance."

"I didn't have to say anything. You've earned it on your own, Drostan, and I doubt they would take someone just because I asked, so remove that thought from your mind. You deserve it for all your hard work." She found herself thinking of the pledge he'd made to her all those years ago, when he was no more than a laddie. He had worked hard, and although she knew he'd done it for himself, she couldn't help but feel a little pleased by the thought that he'd also wanted to impress her.

"Are you coming?" he asked.

"Of course I am." She tugged on her braids. "Now and on Midsummer's Day. King Robert wants a large group of archers because the English will have so many. But we can best them."

He glanced back. No one else was about, but he gave her a small push out the door and down the steps to the keep before taking her hand and guiding her to a bench in the garden. Once there, he pivoted to stare at her. He didn't sit, however, and he looked strangely agitated. "If it were Midsummer's Day, and you were traveling with all the guards and a group of three score archers, I wouldn't worry. But this is a small group. We may be attacked by marauders or English. Are you prepared for that? Would it not be better to wait for the battle?"

It was as if he'd read her mind. After the conversation she'd shared with Molly, Maggie, and Dyna, she was having second thoughts about joining the small group. And yet…she and Drostan had always talked about traveling together, fighting together. Hadn't he just told her he wanted them to spy together? How *dare* he suggest that she stay home, especially since he was going.

She crossed her arms and pursed her lips. "I'm not afraid. I can do this, and I will. I've been training for just as long as you have."

"Do your parents approve? They cannot possibly think 'twould be safe for you out there with all the English crawling around."

"Aye, they gave their approval. So did my grandsire, my uncles, and my cousins. I'm nearly twenty years old. Dyna was chasing around at the age of six and ten on her own. She did fine, and so will I." She leaned forward, poking a finger at him for emphasis, but it landed on his chest. His chiseled, perfect chest.

It was then she realized her mistake. He was too close. So close she could see the fire in his brown eyes, flecks of red dancing with shades of gold and brown. His jaw was clenched tight, and she had the strange desire to run her fingers over the stubble on it.

She did, eyes on him, and his agitation turned to heat. He panted, staring at her, leaning so close she could inhale his scent of horse and pine and mint, of the wind across the Highlands.

"God's bones, must you lean so close to me?" He reached for her shoulders and tugged her behind a tree, and within moments their bodies were pressed together. His lips ravaged hers, his tongue darting inside with a savage need that she matched as she lifted her hands to his cheeks, cupping them as if to bring him closer yet.

He pulled back long enough to whisper, "If you come, I'll go mad with worry."

"Why?"

He kissed her again, this time softly, sucking her lower lip. "What if you're hurt? I'll not be able to watch you, I'll pounce on any man near you, I'll…" He kissed her again, devouring her so thoroughly that need radiated up to the top of her head and down to her toes, welling in her core. "Did you forget about the Ramsay chieftain so soon?"

She stopped the kiss, her fingers coming up to tap on his bottom lip. He didn't smile as she'd hope, a hiss sliding out between his teeth instead. "I cannot watch…you don't understand…when another man nears you…"

She whispered, "Then don't watch." Their foreheads touched and his hands settled on her hips.

He closed his eyes, his resignation obvious. He knew her too well to doubt she would do just as she pleased. She was going.

"Can you not stay back, Chrissa?" he said, more as a statement than a question. "Just this once?"

"Nay," she whispered, then finally took a step back. "You know how hard I've worked for this. We've worked for it *together*. You'll have to manage."

He pulled her close again, nuzzling her neck. Kissing it. "I wish I could sleep with you every night. In our clothing…in the forest…under the stars. You in my arms. But I suppose that won't be allowed."

"Nay, though it sounds heavenly."

He pulled back slightly and ran his hand through his thick hair. "I suppose it will be safe enough with all the others along."

She reached up to fix the lock of hair that had fallen forward in his ministrations. "Drostan, do you not recall the way we used to chase each other through the woods, watching for reivers and marauders? Even when we were young, we used to spy on people in the courtyard and pretend we were saving people from villains." She ran her finger across his eyebrow, lightly touching his bruise from where his father had hit him. Then she kissed it lightly. "He shouldn't hit his own son, even by accident."

"'Twas just a door," he said, pushing her hand away lightly, the acquiescence audible in his voice.

"You forget that I was there when he apologized," she said, her fingers trailing back down his strong jaw. Why did she feel the need to touch him everywhere? It was like she'd felt it without realizing it all these years, and now the repressed well of wanting was rising up and drowning her.

He changed the subject, something he often did when they discussed his father. "I recall pretending to be the knight in armor who came to the castle to rescue his princess. Do you remember screaming from the parapets for help? Your uncle thought you were in trouble and raced up the steps so fast he was breathless."

She giggled. "There was a time when I wished to be rescued by a fierce Highlander, but when I grew older, I wanted to be the fierce rescuer."

"But I wasn't willing to shout from the parapets for you to save me. I couldn't agree to that one, lassie." He chuckled as he nuzzled her neck, then pulled back with a sigh. "You never were like the other lasses, were you?"

"Don't you like it that I'm different than most lasses?" she asked, intertwining their fingers as they stood at arm's length.

"Aye, I do. I'm not interested in a simpering lass who wishes to sit and sew all day. I love that you ride through the forest with me, practice in the fields."

"Do you know what Molly said?"

"What?"

"The best spies are couples."

"Truly?"

"Think on it. Logan and Gwyneth, Maggie and Will, Dyna and Derric, Molly and Tormod. We could add two names to that, if we prove ourselves."

"Drostan and Chrissa?"

"Nay," she scoffed. "Chrissa and Drostan." And because she intended to have the last word on the matter, she dropped his hand and sprang away from him, rushing toward the keep. Giggling all the way.

She needed to drench herself in cold water in the bathing chamber.

When she opened the door, she held on to it and whirled around, knowing she would see him. She'd heard the thunder of his footsteps following her, but he'd never once tried to overtake or stop her. Which hopefully meant he understood what she was about to say. "I'm going, Drostan."

The corner of his mouth quirked up, telling her he'd relented a bit. "I knew there'd be no convincing you otherwise. I look forward to our journey together."

CHAPTER EIGHT

THE TIME HAD FINALLY COME for their trip. Maggie, Molly and the rest of the Ramsay group would travel with them down the mountain until they split ways. The Grant contingency consisted of Magnus, Ashlyn, Derric, Dyna, Drostan, Chrissa, Alick and his brothers—Broc and Paden—and Dyna's brother Hagen, along with several guards.

A large group had filtered out of the castle to send them off, including Astra and Hendrie, who stood next to Drostan with Sky tucked under his arm. The horses awaited the travelers, saddlebags packed and ready.

"Now you take good care of her, Hendrie. I trust you."

"I'll do a fine job," Hendrie said, "and I'll keep practicing with the others to get better with the armor." The armorer had been producing armor in preparation for Midsummer's Day, giving the warriors time to find the best fit. The next step was to practice donning the armor and removing it. Hendrie struggled a bit because it was so heavy. "'Tis easier every day, Master Drostan."

"Drostan is fine, Hendrie," he said. "I'm not your master." He took Sky from the lad for one last snuggle and then set her down on the grass, where she promptly ran over to Drostan's stallion, barking as loudly as she could manage. They all had a chuckle at it until the stallion began to prance a bit. Hendrie quickly picked up the pup and said, "Godspeed with you all. I'll take her to the lists now."

"You'll be with me next time, Hendrie. Keep practicing." The lad hurried off, and Drostan's attention was captured by Astra, who was arguing with her sire.

"But Papa, I could help if I went along. I could be a spy and learn what the English are planning. I could find their camps, and we could take them out in the middle of the night. Then there would be no battle on Midsummer's Day."

Chrissa strolled out of the keep, taking a few sips of water from a skin. She moved next to Drostan and said, "Please tell me he has not given in to her begging."

Drostan shook his head. "He won't, do not worry. But I do think she would be a fine helper for you." He waggled his brow at her, grinning, and she promptly swung out and slapped his arm playfully.

"Nay, she'd be a burden, not a help."

"Please, Papa. I'll be good for a whole year if you let me go," she begged.

Connor turned to his daughter and said, "This is

the last time I'll tell you. You're not going, Astra."

"But Hagen is going," she whined. "I'll prove to you I can be helpful."

"Hagen is three years older than you. Stop whining, or I'll have the guards tie you to that tree until the entire contingency is gone."

Astra stomped her foot and ran back to the keep.

Drostan opened his mouth to speak, but Chrissa held her hand up. "I'll stop you before you say anything. I was not like her at all."

Magnus, the lead in the group, whistled, their sign to mount up, so Drostan lifted Chrissa onto her horse. "And the journey begins."

She glanced over at him with such excitement, he couldn't help but feel the same way. Mayhap he had no cause to worry. They had planned this for years, as she'd reminded him, and there was no reason to expect they wouldn't be back within the sennight.

They arrived at King Robert's camp shortly after dusk two nights later.

Drostan dismounted and reached for Chrissa, setting her down gently. Surrounded by her family as they were, he didn't allow his hands to linger, but it was difficult to touch her chastely when all he wanted to do was touch her, run his hands over her soft skin and nuzzle her neck while she leaned into him.

He had to stop allowing such visions to dominate his thoughts.

At least he could speak with her openly.

"Behave yourself, lass," he whispered. Her long dark hair was arranged in multiple braids that hung almost to her hips, some tied together, others waving in the wind. She and Dyna liked to try different ways to plait their hair, sometimes odd, but this one he liked. Chrissa claimed it was from Dyna's Norse heritage.

Ever since he'd watched Derric unplait Dyna's hair as he massaged her scalp, Drostan had thought about unplaiting Chrissa's hair. He'd love to see it loose. His mind kept dancing back to her. He chided himself that it was a dangerous preoccupation for a warrior headed off to dangerous lands, but nothing seemed to help.

She glared at him and he couldn't help but smirk. It was reassuring to know that for all that had changed between them—for all Chrissa herself had changed—some things were still predictable.

Derric waved to one of the king's men, who hurried off to retrieve Robert. Drostan's heart raced in his chest. He wished to be near the man, to feel his power. Robert the Bruce was a living legend, much like Alexander Grant. He could hardly believe his luck. They'd all heard stories of the king from Els and Joya, from Derric and Dyna, and meeting him had long been one of Drostan's life goals. King Robert had stood strong against all of his enemies: King Edward I and II, the English, countless earls and barons intent on burying him. His brothers had been killed, his wife kidnapped and placed in a cage for all to see by King Edward.

Even though she was no longer in a cage, his wife was still held captive by Edward.

Robert the Bruce had much riding on this battle. Freedom. Of his wife, his family, for all of Scotland. The freedom of his wife from the chains of English bindings was one of the main reasons he still fought. He was so dedicated to the cause of freedom for the Scots that seven years ago, he'd insisted on being carried to battle on a litter despite being gravely ill. Through all of that he had persisted, slowly but surely defeating his enemies, both Scottish and English, with careful and thoughtful stealth, using whatever means available to him.

Derric's gaze landed on a Drostan. His thoughts must have been written on his face, because the older man smiled softly and said, "He may not be what you're expected, lad. He's no courtly man. He's lived many of his years in the forest of Torwood."

But when the king's man exited a tent with another man, one who was shorter than many of the Grants, Drostan knew him at once. There was something regal about him, an indefinable quality that had nothing to do with the state of his dress, his height, or the length of his hair. King Robert headed straight toward Derric. "Corbett, good to see you again. And you've brought your lovely wife with you. Greetings, Dyna." His keen eyes took in the rest of the group. "Please, if some of your warriors will see to your horses, my men will bring them ale. The rest of you may come into my tent. We have much to discuss." His gaze traveled over the group. "If my eyes don't deceive me, I believe I see a couple more excellent archers with you. Aye?"

Derric nodded. "Aye, we have Ashlyn and Chrissa, who are Dyna's cousins. We accept your kind offer."

The group followed him into his tent, guarded by several rough looking men. King Robert waved to two other men to join them. Once they arranged themselves within the large space, he said, "Thank you for coming so quickly. As you know, Midsummer's Day will be here in less than a fortnight. I could use your assistance in training. The Grant warriors are known for their skills."

Derric said, "What are your weak spots? Our lairds are prepared to help you."

"Chief Ramsay has promised you many archers," Dyna added.

"That pleases me. We need all the archers we can find. How many solid archers from Clan Ramsay?"

"Probably two score and another two score from Clan Grant, though you should know many of them are female."

"We welcome them. I'm requesting all able-bodied Scots to join in this battle, however, so do not allow the women to stray far from your warriors. Some have been raised rough and might not recognize your plaid and its meaning. As you well know, there are many in Scotland who still believe they can steal their bride and be within the law. I've also need for mounted swordsmen. My schiltrons will only get us so far."

"Schiltrons?" Chrissa whispered. "I've heard the word before, but I've no idea what it means."

Magnus tried to shush her, but King Robert laughed. "I'm glad to answer. 'Tis my favorite way to fight the English. We'll never have their numbers, but we're smarter and stronger. Whenever possible, I prefer to take the enemy by surprise. Attack from three sides with small groups of men bearing spears, axes, and spikes. The schiltron moves as a unit. They never see us until 'tis too late. I'll need men for that force. Then I'll have archers, followed by a cavalry led by one of my best men. Behind that force I'll be leading the Highlanders myself on horseback, and a large force of Scots on foot. They will be one of my last defenses but not my weakest. I'm counting on our Highlanders to fight strong. We're facing the end of this war, my friends, but I cannot be in charge of all. And the Highland Swords. I've heard much about their power. Will you be able to summon that power against the English? Does it happen when you will it to happen? I've heard conflicting tales of their power."

Dyna answered, "We must travel together, and when we do, the result can be quite incredible. Our force together seems to weaken our opponent, but not for long."

"Then we'll save them for one of the last forces. Allow the others to bring the English onto our land, into our fighting landscape that we are so familiar with and they are not. We'll beat them. We just need to know exactly what kind of troops he will bring. The number, the weapons, the armor.

What is the bastard doing to ready for this battle?"

"Aye, King Robert. That plan is sound," Derric replied, though Chrissa would have liked to see the Highland Swords lead, apparently she was one of the few who thought that way.

"Which brings me to my next question. I'll post it to you, Corbett. Think you and your wife would be willing to go to Berwick and travel as spies? Uncover information about that bastard Edward's plans?"

Derric glanced at Dyna, who nodded. "It would be our pleasure, my king. The Ramsay chieftain said he would send a messenger if he found out anything that would help our cause, but I believe we could uncover more information if we were directly in Berwick. We can leave shortly. We'll take two others with us—two new ones in case we're recognized."

Drostan glanced at Chrissa, wondering if he'd heard correctly. Could they be the two Derric referred to?

Did he dare hope? While he worried about Chrissa on the battlefield, he had to believe spying would be safer. He'd trained her well on how to use a dagger. This could bring all his dreams to fruition—to spy, to fight for Robert the Bruce, to work as a Grant warrior.

And to do all of those things with Chrissa by his side. What more could he wish for?

Could he willingly spy with Chrissa and not worry about her?

Aye, he could. True, he'd worry, but who better

to protect her than him? The clench of his jaw was so strong while he waited that he forced himself to stop.

"Four should be enough to accomplish your objectives, and the timing is good. I wish to know everything. What they're doing to feed their men, how many they have, and where they're from. Stay a sennight. Give him time to gather his forces." Turning to Magnus, he asked, "And how many warriors will Clan Grant send along?"

"We're prepared to send close to one thousand men, if that suits you, King Robert."

"That will work perfectly. How many on horseback?"

"Half."

"Stay, tell me of your training methods, Magnus." His gaze shot back to Derric. "Do you have any questions? Spend the night, familiarize yourselves with my new group. Have an ale. We've received many foodstuffs as support from the neighboring clans so we'll not go hungry."

"Nay. We're ready to do our part," Derric said. Then he motioned to Dyna, Chrissa, and Drostan, and the four left the tent together.

As soon as the flap closed behind him, Drostan hurried forward to talk to Derric. "Who…I mean…your group…"

"You're wondering if we're bringing you on the spying mission," Derric said, preempting him. His smile was hard to read. "Think you we would bring you when we could bring Alick and Broc or Magnus and Ashlyn?"

His face fell, and he didn't even try to hide it. Hell, but he'd hoped for a chance to prove his worth.

And if he caught some bastard, perhaps he'd make his sire proud.

Derric shrugged his shoulders playfully. "Dyna and I had already discussed this possibility. We're bringing you and Chrissa. Can you pretend to be a couple?"

He peeked over at Chrissa, her face alight with excitement, just like the day she'd brought down her first pheasant. She'd always outdone him on those hunting trips, a much better archer than he was by far. Would the same be true when it came to spying?

He looked forward to finding out. They'd be learning from two of the best, too. Perhaps this could lead to other assignments, to the two of them going out on missions together, alone, spying as a couple like they'd discussed.

A familiar pang of worry caught him, but if they were always together, he'd always be around to protect her.

"I think we'll start by teaching you how to hide your feelings," Dyna said. "You cannot be that obvious or you'll get us all caught."

"We can control ourselves," he said at once.

Derric cocked his head. "This will only work if you both agree to do exactly as we instruct."

"Understood." Drostan wished to shout to the moon above, but he had to keep quiet. They were going to travel as spies. Drostan and Chrissa—

together.

His luck had finally changed.

Logan Ramsay found his way out of the cave in the morn. His sister was still asleep. Avelina was softer than his wife or his daughters. Although she used to ride often as a young woman, those days were behind her, and this journey had already gone on past the point of comfort for her. He could tell she'd be aching later today, though he doubted she'd admit it.

They were all growing too damn old.

He took care of his needs and moved to the burn to wash his hands, his memory taking him back many, many years to the kidnapping of Brenna Grant. That one decision had turned his life upside down. Actually, set it to rights.

He'd stolen Brenna from her bed to tend his brother, who'd been gored by a boar, but her talent had been such that he'd convinced her to come to Clan Ramsay to help others who were ill, primarily his niece and nephew. The two bairns had been struck down by a mysterious illness that had plagued them both since birth. Only Brenna had discovered the true cause: they couldn't eat anything with wheat without vomiting. She had saved his niece and nephew, and his brother had fallen in love with her. Their marriage had brought Clan Ramsay close to Clan Grant, the beginning of an alliance that now ran deeper than a river.

He laughed, still remembering the way she'd

yelled at him out in the forest. That wee lass had screamed at him to wash his hands before he touched his injured brother. And she'd made the same demand of everyone who cared for his niece and nephew.

It had left a lasting impression on him, if only because his brother had lived, and his niece and nephew had flourished. The first time he'd seen his nephew walk with his faithful wolfhound Growley at his side, trained to catch him whenever he fell? It was one of the few times in his life when his eyes had misted.

Most of the others were directly related to his wife, the only woman who'd bested him in an archery contest in full view of the entire clan.

"Just luck, Gwynie," he mumbled to himself, thinking back on that day. He knew it hadn't been luck—it had been pure skill…and one other thing.

How her arse looked in those leggings.

Avelina came out of the cave and yelled, "Please bring water so I may wash up."

Cailean called out, "I'll check the perimeter."

Even though he really didn't need anyone to help him travel with Avelina, he'd asked Cailean and Sorcha to travel with them. They'd met up with them last eve shortly after they'd left Drew heading toward his land. He liked having the two around, it was that simple.

"You do that, MacAdam. Finally, you've found a way to be useful," he retorted, smirking. He loved the boy as if he were his own, but he'd never let him know. He and Sorcha had gifted them with three grandbairns, and one was a wee golden-haired lass just like her mother. Gwynie was home watching over the castle and the grandbairns. While Avelina insisted that she didn't need protection since she carried the sapphire sword, he had a difficult time believing that. Erena had said it was his job to protect and escort her, so he did that the best way he knew. Though he'd never tell him so, MacAdam was their best warrior.

"And don't forget to wash your hands after you pish, MacAdam."

Every single person in Clan Ramsay had learned to wash their hands before eating or preparing food. Never mind if they looked clean. And the only reason was because Mistress Brenna had said so.

He grabbed a small basin from the saddlebag Lina always carried and filled it with fresh water, taking his time to climb across the rocks. He couldn't afford to risk a fall at his old age. Hellfire, what he wouldn't give to be young again. He'd be unstoppable if he could fight like he had at twenty summers but keep all the wisdom he'd gained over the years.

When he returned, he posed a question to Avelina. "So do you think I'm a dead man once I deliver you to Alex Grant and you give him the sapphire sword?"

Lina nearly choked on the piece of oatcake she'd just taken a bite of. "What made you ask that?"

"Do you think 'tis possible the two of us have been granted long lives so we could get the sapphire sword to Alex Grant when the time was right? You know I'm much older than most, and so is Gwynie. So will we both fall off a cliff once this is done?"

He looked at his sister, still lovely after all these years, though her hips had widened a bit and her hair had turned nearly white. "Oh, Logan. You've always been a man who loved life. Don't shy away now. Besides, Gwyneth wouldn't know what to do without you."

"Gwynie's younger than me," he said, pacing a bit. "Never mind. The sword will help you sense the evil coming for the Scots, aye? Tell me what you feel."

"I don't feel anything yet."

"But you will?"

"Aye, I expect so. I did before. And you may feel it, too, once we are closer."

"'Tis probably the English. Do you not agree? They've been bothering us for years. They've finally gotten out of control, so Erena has sent someone to save the Scots. 'Tis the reason we're here, I'm certain of it." He didn't give her the chance to answer because he didn't wish to consider any other possibility.

"Except it may not be the English. When I had it before, I was called upon to stop one person. Mayhap 'twill be the same this time."

The two stared at each other for a moment, considering all that had transpired, then Logan shook his head.

"I better awaken Sorcha." His daughter liked to

sleep later whenever she could. "Do you have any other suggestions before I head back into the cave and risk the mouth of the beast?" He chuckled at his own joke.

"Your daughter is far from a beast. She's one of the most beautiful women I know."

"Hmmph. You haven't seen her in the morn lately, have you?"

He headed into the cave, then returned a few moments later after awakening his daughter.

"I tell you what, Lina. I may not be a seer, nor do I have a special connection with the fae, but we are nearing the evil. I can feel it." His voice dropped and he stared out over the landscape, acting as if the evil person were lurking somewhere watching them.

"You see, Logan," she said with a smile. "I thought you might sense it. Or mayhap you're just practicing a new method of scaring the bairns."

"True," he said, sitting down and slapping his knee. "But it does delight me to hear their screams."

He stared up at the gray skies, a bit of mist visible. "This will be a grand story to tell. You'll see."

CHAPTER NINE

CHRISSA WAS EXCITED FOR THE journey ahead, especially since it promised to bring her even closer to Drostan, but a strange feeling of foreboding preyed on her. It had set in as she and the others rode away from Torwood Forest, the woods where Robert was hiding from English forces.

She wasn't upset to leave King Robert, but it had unsettled her to watch the men in the red Grant plaids ride away, back to Grant land, and know she wasn't going with them. It had felt as if she'd swallowed a large stone and it planned to stay deep in her belly.

She was doing exactly what she'd hoped, yet part of her felt she should be riding toward Grant land, not away.

But Chrissa did her best to ignore her misgivings. She had no reason for feeling the way she did, after all. They stopped in a clearing for a short break—Chrissa and Drostan, Dyna and Derric, and two Grant guards Magnus had insisted on sending.

Dyna motioned for the guards to watch the area while Drostan and Chrissa sat on a log. She threw a quick glance at him, wondering if he felt the same sense of warning.

"You all right?" he asked, giving her a strange look.

"I'm fine, just had an odd feeling when we didn't head back to Grant land. I haven't been away often enough if I were to guess."

"I had the same inkling, like we should have gone with them," he said in a low voice since Derric and Dyna were still fussing with their saddlebags. When they finished, the two sat on a log facing Drostan and Chrissa.

"Where exactly are we going?" Chrissa asked.

Dyna chewed on a hunk of cheese, sharing it with the others. "We're searching for any camps of Englishmen. We need to keep a count of the number we see, look for any larger garrisons, and you and I will do our best to talk sweetly to any men in their cups to get them to tell us what they know."

Derric said, "And you'll need to dress your parts."

Dyna groaned and said, "So be it. Why must you always remember that, husband?"

"What do you mean?" Chrissa asked.

"Derric always reminds me that if I wish to act like a simpering fool, I must dress the part. I have a couple of thin gowns in my saddle bag that we can wear over our leggings so we can pretend we're proper Lowland wives." She tilted her head at Derric. "'Tis equally imperative that you and Drostan wear no colors to define yourselves as Highlanders."

Derric waved his hand at his outfit, black on black. From the stories Chrissa had heard, he'd been dressing in this fashion since he'd started with Robert. "I never had clan colors to wear, so no problem here. Drostan, you must stuff your plaid in your saddlebag."

"You wish for me to wear a gown, too?" Chrissa asked, a little shocked. Of course, it wasn't unusual for a woman to wear a gown—the only women who wore leggings were those who'd been taught archery by Gwyneth Ramsay or one of her bairns—but it wasn't Chrissa's preference.

"Aye, men go after women in gowns. They look more helpless, and 'tis what we want. We seek to be underestimated and thought simple." Dyna gave a quick snort.

The word "simple" would never fit Dyna. Nay, it wouldn't fit either of them, for that matter. "And you just talk with men, and they tell you all?"

Derric tipped his head one way and then the other. "'Tis usually not quite so easy, but if they're deep in their cups, it can be. Edward hasn't left Berwick yet, so the Englishmen we encounter won't be his best men. They will join him when the time comes, but they likely don't have the training to keep their mouths closed. Hopefully, they'll know enough information to be useful. Chances are they spent much of their lives marauding or stealing from the English and have gotten bold and excited about the prospect of moving into Scotland."

"'Tis nearly dusk, so we'll spread out a bit and

start searching," Dyna said. "Though we haven't seen any English yet, they have to be roaming about, looking for information just as we are. Make sure your dagger is handy. Hide your bow under a blanket on your horse, but keep it close at hand. You may need it."

They mounted their horses and rode for about half the hour. Just when Chrissa was starting to think they'd find nothing, they found fresh tracks. The tracks separated, and Dyna declared she and Chrissa would head one way with the guards while Derric and Drostan went the other direction.

As they shimmied into their gowns behind a tree, Chrissa heard Drostan ask, "Shouldn't one of us go with each woman? To protect them?"

Chrissa waited for Derric's answer, curious.

"Nay," Derric said. "They can handle themselves. 'Twill be to our benefit if they're the ones who come across the English. The confrontation will be less bloody."

Drostan didn't say anything, but he cast a worried look her way as she emerged from the trees. A worried look that soon took on a lustful, covetous edge. She smiled in encouragement, wishing she could kiss him instead. Then they left, riding away from Drostan and Derric.

They hadn't gone far before Dyna held her hand up, directing the two guards to stay back, and motioned for Chrissa to dismount. Men's voices had filtered to them, loud and inebriated. English. They crept closer to the gathering, moving slowly and strategically.

They adjusted their gowns before leaving the clearing, and Dyna moved over to the burn, leaving Chrissa to follow her. Dyna splashed her hands in the water and giggled, prompting her to do the same.

Sure enough, four men surrounded them in quick order.

"Greetings to you," one of them said. "What are you two sweet plums doing out here alone?"

"My grandsire is behind us. We raced ahead because we were overheated." She waved a leaf in front of her face, then mopped her brow, wiping away the water that she'd just splashed on her face.

One of the men poked the other in the ribs and whispered, "Their grandsire. We've got ourselves a couple of treats for this eve."

A third man shrugged. "You wish for a Scot? I don't." He strode away. "I need more wine." His crooked path clearly illustrated he'd had more than enough wine already.

Dyna headed toward them and deftly tripped, falling forward, one of the men catching her before she hit the ground. "Oh my. Many thanks to you. Are you not headed for the big battle we've heard about?"

"Aye, we are. We'll kill all the savage Scots before they even see us coming."

She stopped to stare up at him, wide-eyed, her lips parting in surprise. "It would take many men to kill all the Scots, and there's only four of you."

The look of fright she gave them, lips forming a perfect round circle, was so convincing Chrissa almost laughed. Then Dyna slid her tongue out, licking her lips, and one of the men coughed and tripped. "Give her to me."

"Nay, I'll have her."

The first said, "I'll tell you all you wish to know, pretty lass."

She stepped back and feigned another trip, falling toward the third man. He barely caught her, but she said, "How many…you are all so big and strong…"

He smiled, puffing his chest out a bit, and said, "I've never seen eyes the color of yours, and with hair that light, I wonder where you come from, lass. Are you a Scot?"

"Norse. My mama is a Norsewoman."

"Then you're safe. But I can't say the same for your friends. Our king is bringing twenty thousand men to fight the Scots. We'll pummel them until there's nothing left of them."

"I don't see that many behind you."

Chrissa repressed another urge to laugh. They were falling for every trick Dyna tossed out. She'd have never guessed spying could be so easy.

"They're going to Edinburgh in a sennight, then on to Stirling Castle."

Dyna rubbed the talkative man's arm and said, "I hear King Edward is verra strong."

Derric and Drostan stepped out of the trees with a whistle, heading straight for the English. The remaining two men spun around, though one of them tripped, the talkative man instantly dropping his hands from Dyna.

"Grandsire," Dyna said, smiling.

The first man returned to see what was happening, and stopped to gape at the two new arrivals.

It was all Chrissa could do not to burst out laughing. And one look at Drostan told her he was having the same struggle.

"You aren't old enough to be her grandsire," one named Edwin said, his tone accusatory.

Derric grabbed him by the collar and tossed him into the air. "I'm her grandsire, now keep your hands off of her."

"You're one of those savage Scots they told us about," the first one said.

Derric grabbed him and punched him in the belly before tossing him aside and going for the second man. He grabbed him by the neck and said, "Did you touch her, too?"

"Nay, only Edwin. I'd never touch a young lass like that."

Derric punched him in the face and he dropped to the ground. The man squirmed up to all fours and crawled away from Derric like a whipped dog. "Why'd you hit me? I said I didn't touch her."

"Because I wanted to. Now get the hell out of here. All four of you." Derric had a fury on his face the likes of which Chrissa had never seen. Nay, she *had* seen it before. Drostan's expression had been similar when he'd attacked the Ramsay chieftain on the archery field.

The four Englishmen found their mounts and hurried away, never looking back.

Drostan finally burst into laughter. "Funniest

fight I've ever seen."

"Easiest fight," Derric drawled. "Hedge-born lymers. Wife, you promised not to let them touch you. You know I don't like that."

She shrugged. "They were so drunk Chrissa and I could have felled the four of them in two minutes. Why'd you send them away? They were giving me good information."

Derric strode over and wrapped his arm around Dyna and hauled her up against his side. "Why waste such a nice clearing? There's a burn, a small outcropping if it rains, and a cover of pines right next to the cave. What more could we want?" He leaned down and kissed her hard on the mouth. "Sorry, but 'tis hard for me to watch another man touch you."

"He barely touched me, Derric. He caught my fall. And are you sure you wish to stay here? They could find reinforcements and return."

"Don't care. He still had to pay. And we're not leaving this place. Those fools were too deep in their cups to lead anyone back here. They'll go a short distance and pass out, and if they tried to find their way back, they'd fail. Now what did he tell you that you're so proud of?"

"Edward has twenty thousand men, and he's moving to Edinburgh in a sennight."

Drostan stared at her in shock. "Twenty thousand? Can we beat that many?" His gaze shifted to Chrissa, and she saw the worry in it. "I know people talked about the possibility, but I didn't think it was truly possible."

"How many Scots do we have?" Chrissa blurted. "Not even half, do we?"

"We'll be lucky if we have five thousand," Dyna said. "This will be a tough fight."

Derric's expression tightened with anger. "Did you not see the one yellow-bellied bastard crawl away from me on his hands and knees rather than throw one punch at me? Bloody hell, we'll take them down easily. One Scot can handle three Englishmen easily."

Chrissa kneaded her hands together and said, "I can't take on three men."

"And don't forget we can use the spectral swords against them," Dyna said. "My cousins will all be there to fight, although we have to hope Branwen doesn't deliver early. We can handle that many if we use the power. The lightning alone will scare half of them away."

"But how long has it been since you've fought together?" Chrissa asked.

Dyna sighed. "It has been a while, but I believe we still carry the same power. Grandsire says little about it these days, but I believe if we're all together, and Derric allows me to climb on his back again, we can do it." She gave him a saucy look and a wink. Everyone in the clan knew the tale of how Dyna had unleashed incredible power by climbing onto Derric's back during a battle. It had been the first sign they were meant for each other.

Derric waved his hand at her. "And you'll be safely hidden in the trees with the other archers.

You'll take down many English, and they'll never see you."

But Chrissa's mind was still stuck on that number. Twenty thousand. When had she ever seen that many men?

CHAPTER TEN

ALEX GRANT WAS AN OLD man. Beyond old. He knew his time was coming, but he didn't fear death. Perhaps because he believed all of the dreams he shared with his dear wife were true. Some believed they were just creations of his mind, but he knew them for what they were—visions from heaven.

His dear Maddie was in heaven, but she came back to give him important advice when necessary. Whatever others chose to believe, no one could deny that whatever Madeline Grant told him came to fruition.

Alex moved around his chamber slowly as he prepared for bed, appreciative of all the tools his sons and daughters had crafted to make his life easier. At last, he climbed into bed and lay back, resting his head on the pillow and staring up at the beams overhead. He hadn't seen Maddie in a while, so he wondered if she would visit him this night. Things in Scotland were heating up as they prepared for the onslaught of the English and King

Edward II.

Suddenly, as if his mind really had conjured her—a talent he wished he had—there she was, standing in front of him in a white, translucent gown. She looked exactly as she had the day they married. "Was that not the gown you wore the night of our wedding?" He arched his brows at her, surprised to see her teasing him with such skin, her voluptuous curves glorious beneath the fabric.

Maddie glanced at her gown and waved a hand at him. "Oh, Alex, whatever I wear is a product of your memory. This must have been a favorite of yours, but you know it has naught to do with this visit."

"Aye. I always did love you in that night rail." He smirked. "Go on. I know that look. Who's at risk this time? I'm certain someone is in grave danger, so I'll wait for you to tell me who the trouble-maker is this time."

Maddie sighed and leaned toward him, taking his hand. "I'm not sure. You must keep an eye on Chrissa. Something is going on, and I know not what. She looks so much like you and her mother. Do you not think so? And she's headstrong like Kyla. They have your blood in them, for certes."

"And yours," he reminded her. "The English are after her, or is it the other force? The one that wants to take over our castle."

She lifted a hand to her lips, thinking. "Would that I knew. There is evil lurking, that much I can see clearly. I've heard it will rival the evil we faced many, many years ago. It pleases me that Logan is coming. Perhaps he'll help you figure out who seeks to cause trouble between our clans."

"Do Logan and Lina have the sword in their possession yet?"

"Aye, Lina will bring it to you, and you must help her decide on the proper protector. I cannot say anything else about it, nor do I know who should take ownership. But I do know this. Chrissa is in trouble, and the battle on Midsummer's Day will be pivotal. The lads must send as many guards as they can to Stirling."

"But?" he whispered in her ear, taking advantage of their closeness.

"The other force, the one that seeks to sow discord between the Grants and the Ramsays, will come as a surprise. You must assist them in rooting it out."

"Will you take me home with you when this is over?" he asked, his heart racing as he awaited his answer. He was so ready to be with her again.

"Alex," she said, leaning into him so their bodies melded together. "Much as I would love to, you know I cannot tell you. Oh, drat." She looked at her hand, the vision disappearing. "I love you, Alexander Grant. Thank you for taking such good care of our bairns, grandbairns, and great-grandbairns. We have some feisty new lassies."

He opened his mouth to tell her how right she was, but he didn't get the chance.

She was gone.

Drostan awoke in the middle of the night, rubbing the sleep from his eyes because he'd lost something for sure. It took him a moment to realize what had happened: Chrissa had left his arms.

She caught his gaze at the edge of their camp, creeping off into the darkness by the light of the half-moon. He supposed she had to relieve herself so he stayed put.

They'd set up camp shortly after the fools had left them, leaving the guards to alternate duty while they slept. That left one decision. Where were the two of them to sleep?

Dyna had made the decision easy. "Chrissa, you'd be a fool not to sleep in Drostan's arms because men are like the largest hearths loaded with wood. And Drostan, if I see your hands roving and touching where they shouldn't be, I'll cut your bollocks in two."

He'd turned a bit green at the thought of his bollocks being ripped in two, but Derric had clapped him on the back. "The image in your head is more useful than you'd think. It guarantees any erection will be quickly lost. Serves its purpose quite well. I've even used the imagery myself a time or two." He grinned, casting a sideways look at his wife, who promptly slapped his arm.

"And who were you thinking on when you needed it?"

"You, of course."

They shared the ale they'd brought along and settled down in the clearing. Chrissa had been uncharacteristically quiet, but she'd insisted nothing was wrong. She'd lain down first, wrapping herself in a plaid, and he'd lowered himself down next to her, tugging his plaid over her shoulders.

A smile had crossed his face, simply because it felt good to be close to her. She'd glanced back in warning, but she'd fallen asleep faster than he did, giving him time to appreciate her finely formed arse.

He didn't touch, just looked. He wanted his bollocks to remain intact in the morn.

When she didn't return to the clearing after a few moments, he got up and made his way into the woods, careful not to sneak up on her. He found her leaning against a tree, wide awake.

"Something wrong, lass?"

The expression on her face guaranteed it. He'd never seen Chrissa look like that.

"I can't sleep. 'Tis too different being out here with you, with marauders not far away. And boars, snakes, bats… Something is wrong. I can feel it. We're going the wrong way, or something bad is about to happen. I can't figure it out."

"Don't think on it."

She held her hand up to him to silence him as she pushed against a tree. "I heard something. Did you?"

He moved in front of her, and though her hand went to his shoulder to try to push him out of the way, he wouldn't allow it. Listening, he thought he heard horses in the distance. Still a ways off, but the sound left little room for interpretation.

"Mayhap they'll pass us," he whispered over his

shoulder.

"I doubt that," Derric said, rubbing his hand down his face as he walked up to them. "Hell, why could you not have let us sleep?"

"We did not awaken you," Chrissa said.

"Drostan's noise did."

The two guards and Dyna joined them. "What should we do, Derric?" she asked. "Are they stopping?"

"I'll be right back," Drostan said, touching her arm lightly. He hurried off to a better vantage point, looked down at the ravine below them, and cursed. "At least there are no drunken reivers coming this way," he mumbled to himself as he turned around to head back.

Once he was close enough to be heard, he explained, "Scottish sheriffs. Two, and they're coming this way with a few more guards. Look to be Lowlanders, although it's impossible to say in the dark."

The sheriffs were upon them several minutes later. One of them called out, "Corbett? Is that you?"

The sheriffs dismounted while their guards remained on horseback, staying back a distance and checking the periphery.

Derric said, "DeFry, what brings you to this area?"

"We're looking for any roaming English. Some came rushing ahead of the king, thinking they'll be able to steal before the king's forces arrive. Have you seen any?"

"One group of four Englishmen," Dyna said. "They were in their cups, so they're no threat to anyone. I'm surprised you didn't pass them. They left a couple of hours ago."

"They should be heading north."

"They went south."

It was the other one who answered, not the man Derric had addressed as DeFry. Drostan only knew he was a sheriff from his clothing. "Who knows what they're doing. I'm more interested in finding out why you have lasses out here during these tumultuous times. You know not who you'll run into and your numbers are too low for you to protect yourselves."

"Who the hell are you?" Derric asked.

DeFry said, "This is Sheriff Henry Percy, a Scot. You don't know him?"

They all shook their heads, so DeFry added, "He's a reputable sheriff, one you can trust. And Percy, this is a group of Grant warriors. Their women are some of the finest archers in Scotland."

The man didn't act impressed, but he took the time to carefully study each person, as if committing them all to memory. "Why are you here? You shouldn't be about."

Dyna snorted. "I'll do whatever the hell I want. You aren't stopping me."

"You dare to speak to a Scottish sheriff like that? I'll have you tied to a whipping post for disrespecting the law."

DeFry coughed and said, "Allow me to introduce you to two of Alexander Grant's granddaughters, both trained by Gwyneth Ramsay."

Percy paled, but he didn't flinch, nor did he attempt to apologize. "Be on your way when dawn arrives." Then he tugged on the reins of his horse and sent it back toward the path.

DeFry said, "Pay him no mind. He's always had a certain jealousy over Alex's reputation in the Highlands."

With that, he rode off too, following Percy into the night.

No one spoke for a long time, until Drostan couldn't take the silence anymore and said, "I wouldn't trust either one of them."

CHAPTER ELEVEN

"YOU TIRE, LINA," LOGAN SAID as he watched her walk slowly back to her horse after taking care of her needs.

"Logan, I haven't ridden this far in a long time. Drew did not want me to leave, certain I'd have trouble, but I'll survive."

He turned to Sorcha and Cailean. "I know of a small kirk about an hour up ahead. 'Tis nearly dusk. The priest was a friend of Father Rab's, God rest his soul. I'm sure he'll take us in for the night. I don't know that I ever met the man, but his name is Father Dowall."

"Don't do this for me, Logan," Avelina said. "I'll manage. We'll be on Grant land in another day."

"Aunt Lina, please," Sorcha said with a groan. "I'd be pleased to sleep in the church, anything for a little padding between my arse and stone. Besides, 'tis too cool for my bones, too. Papa, I say aye, we go to the kirk."

"MacAdam, you and I will sleep outside. It's a small one, but there should be plenty of room for the two lasses."

"Suits me fine," Cailean said as he lifted Sorcha onto her horse.

A little over an hour passed before they came to the small church, its spire pointing proudly to the heavens. Logan said, "Before we all dismount, let me check to see if Father Dowall is still here."

He knocked on the door, then stepped inside, a candle lighting up the interior. A priest came from near the altar, heading directly toward him.

"Father Dowall?"

"Aye," he said, a bit timidly if he were to guess. "Who is visiting Our Lord's house this eve?"

"'Tis Logan Ramsay, Father. I'm looking for a place to rest our weary bones for one night. I have two women in my group. If you can offer them shelter, the rest of us will sleep outside."

Father Dowall clasped his hands together, his eyes dancing with delight. He looked younger than Logan had thought he'd be, but then they'd all gotten older quickly, hadn't they? The man had a slight build, but his smile made him seem like a larger presence. "My dear friend Rab mentioned you, Logan. You are married to his sister, correct? You are welcome here. Please, come around back to my quarters. I have room for you I believe, though some of your guards might be able to fit in the aisles."

"Our guards will sleep outside, but if you can offer sleeping arrangements for my daughter and sister, I'd be deeply appreciative. My son-in-law and I will sleep in the aisles of the chapel. I'll help with the horses and come inside. Many thanks to you."

"The meal will be meager, but I eagerly share with you all. I have a vegetable stew cooking over the hearth, and there's plenty for all of us. I always hope that visitors will stop by, and God has blessed me this day with you. I'll meet you in the entrance at the rear of the building. I'm pleased to see Father Rab is sending me blessings from his place inside the gates of Heaven."

"Blessings?"

"Aye, he must have learned of my weakness over this upcoming battle."

"Weakness? I see no weakness in any Scot who dreads the consequences of any battle brought on by the gluttonous, self-serving, conniving Englishman who calls himself the King of England. Everyone should fear what will happen. Before we leave, we'll help you with anything at all that will ease your worried mind."

"Actually, I was hoping for a different favor now that you're here."

"Name it. Anything for a friend of Rab's."

"Good, I'm pleased you feel that way. I feared you'd reject my request."

An odd feeling washed over Logan. Why would they not wish to help a priest? He got his answer sooner than he expected.

"Since you're heading north, I'd like to go with you."

Dumbstruck, Logan searched for a good answer, but he couldn't come up with one, so he simply asked, "Where are you headed, Father?"

"North. Take me straight to Stirling. I can't miss any part of this battle."

Logan nearly fell over.

Chrissa and the others had spent the day searching for Englishmen, but they'd found nothing. They were nearing dusk, so they gathered as a group before deciding where to spend the night.

"I'm starving," she said. "We need something more than oatcakes and berries. I want a duck or a pheasant." Pheasant was her favorite, though a single bird would be more than the four of them could eat.

"Get that pheasant and I'll see 'tis eaten in full," Drostan said. "I'll try for a rabbit or two."

She couldn't help but sigh at the thought of roasted meat. "Even that would please me."

"Consider it done, lass," he said with a confidence she admired…even if it made her want to laugh.

"Shall we make a contest of it?" Dyna said.

Derric was usually easygoing, but he didn't seem as pleased with the idea as the rest of them. "This is an area where ambush is easy. We need to be careful. Drostan and Chrissa, take that path." He pointed ahead of them. "'Tis a short one, and most of the ambushes take place on the longer paths."

"How long are they?" Chrissa asked.

"We'll send the guards with you. The paths separate for at most five hundred paces. If it takes longer for you to emerge, we'll come after you." A smile finally crossed his face. "We'll see who the best archer is. Will it be duck or pheasant? I don't know about you, Chisholm, but I'm just going along to protect my wife. I'll lead the way, but she has a much better chance of downing some dinner than I do."

"I'll lead, Chrissa. You follow and the guards can stay close to you."

"Don't take any other paths," Dyna warned.

Off they went, each with a preemptive smile of victory. Chrissa was so hungry that her desire alone might be powerful enough to bring down a duck. She followed Derric down the meandering path, listening for any sound of birds, searching for a clearing where she'd have a better view of game overhead.

She saw nothing until they came near the end of their path. It branched off to the right and then opened into a clearing. She heard the rustling of pheasants in the trees. "This way, Drostan." She headed down the path with glee, surprised by his furious response.

"We're not to go off the path, Chrissa! Turn around."

Then she saw it. A plump pheasant sat inside a tall hawthorn hedge, its head visible to her. Unable to tear her eyes from her quarry, she slowed her horse and pulled out an arrow, aiming carefully before she shot. Her reward was the satisfying thump of the bird landing on the ground.

"I got it, Drostan!" She glanced over her shoulder, looking for him. What she saw instead made her heart jump into her throat.

An empty horse.

"Drostan!" she called out, then whistled, hoping Dyna or Derric would hear her. She headed back toward his horse, but a sound sent her gaze back toward the clearing. Two men were leaving the area on horseback, and one of them had a prone man slung over the back of his saddle, his dark hair covering his face.

"Drostan, nay!" She followed the horses, praying he wasn't dead, praying Dyna or Derric might come along and help her. Where the hell were the guards? She passed one with an arrow in his sword arm, writhing on the ground.

"Go," he said, "two men have him."

She pursued the horses down a different path, the area they were in a maze of paths that she hated. The second guard lay on the ground, blood running down his forehead, his eyes closed. She wanted to check on him, but she didn't dare lose Drostan.

Fool, a voice in her head accused. *What will you do if you catch him?*

But she couldn't stop, not now. Not with Drostan as their prisoner.

Five men came out of nowhere, one grabbing for her horse while another snaked an arm around her waist and lifted her onto his lap. She fought with all her might, kicking, biting, and scratching while she screamed for Derric and Dyna.

She should have gone back.

A blow to the back of her head nearly knocked her unconscious, but she fought to stay awake. Someone tossed her through the air, and she landed face down on another horse, two arms catching her and tying her hands behind her back.

Just like Drostan, she found herself face down over a horse, but with a bag over her head and her hands tied behind her back. She hadn't gotten a good look at her attackers, so finding her way would be difficult once she managed to escape—because she *would* escape. But she did recognize the voice of one of their attackers.

She knew the bastard.

CHAPTER TWELVE

DROSTAN WOKE UP AND NEARLY moaned, but he kept his mouth shut because he found himself in a dark, windowless stone chamber. No one else was present, so he pushed himself to a sitting position and leaned back against the cold stone wall.

The chamber was empty but for a pitcher of water that sat nearby and a basin to pish in against the opposite wall. A tiny window embedded in the door gave him a dim view of a torch in the passageway.

He'd actually been thrown in a dungeon. Over the years, he'd heard many tales of Grants who'd suffered just such a fate. Loki's adventures had always been his favorite. But Chrissa's mother and Branwen had been locked up too. He would have to be strong.

Chrissa. He stood, bracing himself because his head pained him so badly, then crept over to the window to look out. There was one other chamber across from him and down a bit, so he whispered.

"Chrissa? Dyna?"

He hoped no one else had been caught, but he highly doubted anyone was after *him*. If they had targeted their group, it had to be for one of the Grant lasses. But which one?

"Chrissa?"

Dead silence.

He didn't like that either.

Chrissa had a problem. She had to pee furiously, and though she'd asked to stop so she could take care of her needs, they'd ignored her. The need only became worse with every bounce of the horse, especially when the bastard she rode with forced her to a sitting position, settling her on his lap so he could fondle her. She didn't like that one bit, and she had a sudden inspiration on how to make him stop.

So she did it. She pished her leggings, soaking his hand before the liquid spread from her clothing to his trews.

When he stopped his horse and roared in a fury, tossing her off the side, she guessed he was a wee bit wet.

He took the bag off her head and slapped her. "You no-good whore."

"Try touching me again, you hedge-born bastard."

He yanked her forward by her bound hands, making sure to wipe his hands on her tunic.

When one of his peers noticed the wetness on

the two of them, he burst into laughter. She didn't know either of them, so she focused on memorizing her surroundings. They'd come upon a dilapidated, deserted castle, its curtain wall incomplete but the keep in decent shape.

Unfortunately, she didn't recognize it.

They yanked her across the hall and all but shoved her down a narrow, dank staircase before giving her a push down one of four passageways. When they reached the last door before it dead-ended, one captor opened it and pushed her inside. The second one tossed her saddlebag in behind her.

His friend asked, "Why the hell did you do that? We're not an inn."

"Because she pished herself."

"So let her sit in it." He locked the door behind her and peeked at her through the small window embedded in it. "I'd make you sit in it."

She caught the saddlebag since he'd untied her hands but said nothing.

"Why did you even grab it off the horse?" He asked his friend as they left down the hall.

"Wanted to make sure there was a Grant plaid inside."

"Is there?"

"Aye."

"I told you she was a Grant. Consider her protection. Our last resort." Their voices disappeared as they moved up the steps.

It occurred to her that her mother had once been left in a dungeon too, a thought that made her feel braver. Glancing around in the dark, she picked out a pitcher full of water plus a basin. She assumed it had been left out so she could take care of her needs.

When she had the chance, she'd wash her leggings, but until then, she smelled, so she changed and cleaned herself up to the best of her ability, still smirking over what she'd done.

She didn't know if she could ever admit it.

But that thought brought her back to Drostan, the one person she'd definitely never tell.

Where the hell was he?

Alex made his way through the great hall, stopping at the trestle table halfway across. His old bones had aged enough that he struggled to make it across without stopping. He'd never expected to live this long—almost eight decades—but he had a purpose.

At least, that was what his wife had told him in his dreams. There were things he had to do before he could leave and join her in heaven. Each day he grew more weary, more ready. There were many people he'd love to see again besides Maddie—his parents, his brother, his son and his wife, and the bairn he and Maddie had never gotten to know. And so many more. Too many.

He sat in the large chair at the hearth, setting his wooden support down, and gave himself the chance to look over the group in the hall. How proud he was of his family, his clan.

Jamie and Connor were situated around the

hearth, their wives and bairns not far. He suspected they were still debating the numbers to send to King Robert. Midsummer's Day was less than a fortnight away. They were all dedicated to contribute whatever they could to the battle. It was time to end the tyranny of King Edward II.

A noise caught his attention by the door. Visitors. Something he loved more than anything simply because his kin were spread far and wide. To his surprise, it was his brother Brodie and the clan from Muir Castle. Brodie's son Braden was there, along with his wife, Cairstine. Robbie's son Roddy and his wife, Rose, had also come, and both families had their bairns.

Cairstine's son Steenie rushed over to his side first. "Greetings to you, Uncle Alex."

"Steenie, will you ever stop growing? I think you may be taller than Connor."

Steenie threw his shoulders back a bit to enhance his height. "Aye, I'm tall, but my goal is to develop sword skills as strong as yours were."

Alex peered around him at the rest of the group. "Is your wife carrying again?"

"Aye, she is. Still wants a laddie, although I'm loving my lassies."

"Steenie, sit with me for a wee bit. I have a question for you." He waved his brother and nephews away, wishing to speak with Steenie alone.

"Aye?" Steenie pulled a chair up.

"It's about your pony. The one who everyone thought had an old spirit inside him. I remember the stories about him verra well, about how he came to you, protected you, and then he showed up at Muir Castle on his own. I heard he even helped you find a lass who'd been buried in the snow. He led Braden to a cave where she'd been living with her younger brother. Is this all true?"

"Paddy? Aye. He was an amazing pet and a true friend to me. How he knew some things, I'll never know. We lost him several years ago. Oddly enough, sometimes I feel he's still around watching over our daughters. What do you wish to know about him?"

"Humor this old man who's trying to learn about this world I've lived in for so long. How did you find Paddy?"

Steenie rubbed his chin, staring up at the beams on the ceiling. "Give me a moment to think on it, Uncle Alex. The memory is slow to come, and I was only around five summers."

"Take your time, son. I'd like to hear the full story."

He had his reasons for asking. As he approached the end of his long life, he found himself wondering if perhaps he was wrong. What if he wasn't going to meet up with his dear Maddie when he passed on? He'd always had a strong belief in the hereafter, but part of him longed for proof.

Was there a heaven? Would he see the others who'd passed before him?

Steenie tapped his finger against his chin, then dropped his hand down, leaning back in the chair with a smile. "I remember leaving Muir Castle in the middle of the night. My true sire, the bastard, had forced me to sleep alone in the hall, which I hated, and my mother was in the dungeon."

Alex only arched a brow at this travesty, not wishing to interrupt the lad's thoughts.

"I went outside to relieve myself, then ended up outside the gates because I had brought my play sword. I wasn't paying much attention to what I was doing, to be honest, and suddenly there was Paddy, nudging me with his muzzle."

"He found you, not the other way around?"

"Aye. I recall that I was staring at the stars when he nudged my elbow. I never heard or saw him approach. I tried to direct him back to Muir Castle, but all he did was shake his mane at me and snort. He led me to Grant land. I had naught to do with the direction he headed. It was a long trip, and I do believe I slept on him for part of it. Otherwise I don't think I could have made it this far on my own. I have to believe 'twas some sort of divine intervention."

"Interesting." He paused, then added, "Didn't Brodie tell me that at one time you thought he could communicate with you?"

"Aye, the more time I spent with him, the more I believed I could hear his thoughts. Whether it was true or just the fancy of a young lad longing for a friend, I know not, but it was as if whatever he wished me to know would just pop into my head. Like how many swords to make for Christmas the year he found the bairns sheltering in the cave. I only wished to make two, but he gave me a nudge and this voice in my head said, 'You need to make more. And get some ribbons.' Some people thought I was daft, but I swear he could send his thoughts to me."

"Did he do it with anyone else?"

"Not to my knowledge," he said, sweeping his brownish-red locks back from his face. "He was a beloved pet to me. Our stableman used to tell everyone he was an old spirit. He was afraid of him." That made Steenie chuckle.

Alex laughed with him.

"What do you think?" He wasn't sure he would like Steenie's answer, but he had to ask.

"That I'll see him again someday. He told me so right before he died. His head rested on my lap…" He stopped to take a few breaths, the memory clearly painful for him. "He rested against me for two hours before he passed on. That wee pony treated me better than my true sire. He protected our first wee lassie after she was born, always acted as a guard whenever we set her in the basket."

"He told you he would see you again?" Alex pressed, his heart beating fast in his chest as he thought of Maddie in her white night rail.

"Aye. I fell asleep in the stables, and in my dream, I stood there as a bairn again, waving to him as trotted away. He said we'd meet again. 'Tis how I'll always remember him. When my mother woke me up, he'd already passed."

Alex crossed his arms in front of his chest. "Any of your lassies have a pony as a pet?"

"Nay, dogs. No more ponies. Paddy was too stubborn and unpredictable. Why do you ask about him, Uncle Alex?"

"My mind turns toward the hereafter as I grow older, and I found myself wondering about your relationship with the wee beast. Sometimes the veil between our world and the one beyond is thinner than others."

"Aye," Steenie said. "Do you recall Rose's owl? She believed her sire's spirit was in that bird. And what about the woman in white and the thunderstorm at Sona Abbey?"

"Have I heard that one?"

"Connor and Roddy saw a spirit in the middle of a thunderstorm."

"Send Connor over, please," Alex said, deep in thought. But there was no need. His son glanced over sharply, hearing his name, and a small gesture got him moving. "Many thanks to you, Steenie. Enjoy your stay with us. You're welcome anytime."

Connor sat at Alex's side. "What is it, Papa? You are hale?"

"I'm fine. I'm not going anywhere yet, but Steenie mentioned something that I never heard about. Or perhaps I'm so old I've forgotten. Did you witness a ghost at Sona Abbey?"

Connor shrugged after glancing over his shoulder.

Alex caught his movement and quickly asked, "Why did you do that?"

"Do what?"

"Look over your shoulder. Who are you checking for?"

"No one…it's just, she was…I haven't thought about her in a long time. She made me look over my shoulder for many moons. And you're not forgetting. We never said anything because we thought we were losing our minds."

"We?"

"Roddy and me the first time. Daniel saw her another time. Then Sela."

"All of you and you never told me?" Alex was shocked something so unusual had transpired in his clan and he knew nothing about it.

"Because it didn't happen on Grant land. Papa, you were a busy man." His father narrowed his gaze at him, waiting for his explanation. Connor continued, "The first time was at Sona Abbey in the middle of a thunderstorm. We were the only ones in their guest house. At the time, I had trouble believing it was happening."

"Go on."

"A female ghost appeared in front of Roddy and me. She had blonde hair and a white gown with a blue band around the waist. We could see through her. I know it sounds odd, but her looks changed. One time she had red hair."

"Who saw her then?"

Connor thought for a moment. "Daniel and I. We were in Inverness, I believe."

"So the red hair was because of Constance."

"Aye. How'd you know? Each time we had to save someone. First Rose, then Constance, then Sela."

"Did she speak?"

"Verra little. All I remember her saying is, 'You must save her.' 'Tis what sticks in my mind. 'Twas a verra long time ago." Connor watched his father, waiting for his response, but he never got one.

"What's bothering you, Papa? What brought this up?"

Alex shrugged his shoulder. "Curiosity. I've been thinking about otherworldly events. Things that cannot be explained. I asked Steenie about Paddy, and he mentioned your ghost and Rose's owl."

Connor crossed his arms. "You'll have to ask Rose about the owl. All I know is that it watched over her." He waved to her from across the chamber, calling her name. She and Roddy walked over together and offered their greetings.

"Papa was asking me about anything otherworldly we'd ever experienced or heard about," Connor said. With a slight smirk, he turned to Roddy. "I told him what I recalled about our abbey ghost. I figured you wouldn't mind anymore after all these years. Besides, Steenie knew about it, and *I* certainly didn't tell him."

"I've heard all I need to about that," Alex said. "I'd love to hear more about this owl, Rose."

She sighed. "I believed Papa's spirit lived inside the owl to watch over me. He knew Mama was evil, and he couldn't rest until I escaped from her. Once my mother's deeds were uncovered, I rarely saw him again."

"Did he communicate with you in any way?"

"Not directly. I wish he had."

"He sure made me uncomfortable," Roddy offered. "I was trying to sneak a kiss once in the courtyard, and the owl persisted in staring at me.

Even squawked once. I didn't dare do it again."

Roddy and Rose left to join the others, and Connor said, "I can't believe you're asking all these questions after what you've observed with the spectral swords. If that isn't evidence of otherworldly elements, I don't know what is. The lightning, the thunder. The lads swear they can swing their swords much easier when they're all together, and we both know my Dyna knows things she cannot. What exactly is driving your curiosity, Papa?"

Their conversation was cut short when the door leading outside burst open. Alasdair, Emmalin, Els, and Joya had arrived, he observed with satisfaction, along with their bairns. He'd been waiting for this moment.

Connor jumped out of his chair. "I'll welcome them."

"Send Alasdair and John here, please."

His son acknowledged his request with a nod before heading toward the door. As he approached the newcomers, however, a couple burst in after Alasdair's group.

Derric and Dyna, and Dyna was inconsolable. She looked straight at her father and shouted, "They've taken Chrissa and Drostan."

Alex muttered to himself, "Here we go again."

CHAPTER THIRTEEN

DROSTAN HEARD THE KEY IN the lock before the door opened, surprised to see two people he knew step inside: Sheriffs Percy and DeFry. The latter tossed him a chunk of stale bread. His hands had been bound, so an attack would be difficult, but he could figure out another way to fight back if need be. First he needed to find out more about the situation, including whether Derric and Dyna had been captured too.

"This is my meal for the day?" he muttered. "You feed me well. Where's my partner?" He wasn't sure they would remember Chrissa's name, so he decided to play it safe. It would be best if they didn't know she was a Grant.

"Chrissa is in another cell in the tower room. You're in the dungeon of the keep. You're far away from each other, so don't bother trying to call out to her. I heard you the last night. Don't waste your time and strength," DeFry said.

"A couple of proud and loyal Scots standing in front of me," Drostan said flatly. "Wouldn't your clans be proud? Although I swear I heard DeFry mentioned as a trustworthy sheriff. I'll try my best to remember the name of the fool who told me that."

"I'm sure it was Chrissa's cousin Alasdair, or possibly Dyna," DeFry said. "The matter is a simple one: coin ranks above all else, and Edward pays more than Robert. Someday you'll understand, but you're young and naïve. Going to conquer the world, are you not?"

"Nay," Drostan drawled. "Just England."

Percy crossed his arms and leaned against the wall. "Now what will we do with you? 'Tis too early to use you as a bargaining chip. Though once we are closer to Midsummer's Day, your pretty wee lassie will be an advantage for sure."

"Is that what we are to you? You think you can bargain with the Grants? I doubt it."

"Aye, because we won't ask for much. All we need to know is when the Grants are set to leave for Stirling, and how many men they're sending."

"I'm a Grant warrior. I don't sit in on their solar meetings, nor am I in charge of anything. They won't bargain for me." He spat coarsely off to the side, a small way to let them know what he thought of them.

"Yet you travel with their spies, Corbett and his wife, so you must be worth something," DeFry said. "I'm sure we can convince the Ramsays not to stand for the Bruce if they know we have both of you…whether we still have you or not."

Percy said, "You think this is just about a battle

between kings, don't you? How foolish the young are. King Edward is wealthy, and he plans to distribute his wealth to those he deems worthy. I'm not the only man who wants a piece of it. When and where are the Grants meeting the Ramsays?"

"I have no idea."

Percy stormed over to Drostan and kicked him in the ribs. "I think you do. With or without your help, we *will* put an end to the alliance between the Ramsays and the Grants. If we eliminate those two groups from the fight, Robert's numbers will drop by thousands."

"I surely don't know how you think you'll accomplish such an impossible task, but it does not matter. Whatever you try will not succeed. The chieftain of Clan Ramsay just left Grant land, and the two clans as close as ever."

He decided not to share the fact that he'd tried to punch said chief.

"Where are they meeting?" Percy ground out, his jaw clenched tightly.

"I don't know."

Percy swung out to kick him again, but Drostan was faster. He caught the bastard's leg with his bound hands and flipped him onto his back. He was about to pin him to the ground, but a dagger found its way to his throat so he stopped.

"Get back," DeFry said. "Back against the wall."

Drostan did as he was told. They still held Chrissa, so he needed to be patient and learn where exactly she was being held…and where the hell they'd been brought.

Percy got back on his feet and brushed the dirt off his hands in an aggrieved manner. "You will help us. The two groups plan to meet before they travel to Stirling. We need the exact location. We have other things to attend to at present, but we'll be back and we will have our answer from you."

"You can't get information from someone who doesn't know the answer."

"You have it. We'll bring your sweet lass with us, and we'll play with her—" Percy paused to smirk and lick his lips, "—until one of you tells us what we want to know."

"What the hell does that mean?" The thought of them hurting Chrissa or touching her inappropriately made him want to rage. To break the bonds on his hand and strangle both of them. Chrissa was hale. She was a fighter, but he didn't like the thought of her sitting alone in a cell. Injured. "You didn't hurt her, did you?"

"Only a little bump on her head. It won't bother her for long."

"Bastards beat up on lasses. Does it make you feel strong?"

"Here's what we're going to do with you two," De Fry said, ignoring him. He crossed his arms and leaned against the stone wall. "We'll do as he says. Keep the two of you in a chamber, torture you alternately until one of you speaks. We need the location of the meeting point between the Grants and the Ramsays. Not sure where it is? Then you better think on it. We'll be back."

Drostan had only one thought in his head.

If they dared to hurt Chrissa, he'd kill them both.

Alex watched as the group descended into chaos. Finlay had rushed to Kyla's side and wrapped an arm around her shoulders, and she leaned into him, letting him support her weight.

"Oh, my God, please save my daughter. And Drostan," she said, her words barely audible. He could tell his daughter prayed over and over, her lips moving frantically as if the more prayers she said, the better her chance of seeing her daughter again.

Once Kyla was steady on her feet, Finlay stepped away. "She's as strong as you are," he said. "She'll be fine."

Kyla just sobbed as Finlay started pacing, his hands on his hips. Alex knew he was already thinking of the best way to patrol for Chrissa's captors.

Alex used his wooden stick to make his way over to the hearth, where he could sit in the large cushioned chair Gracie had made for him. "Tell us exactly how it happened, Corbett. Dyna, you will add your thoughts at the end."

Dyna crossed to her aunt, giving Kyla a big hug while she murmured something in her ear. Then she moved to her sire, hugging him with her head to his chest while Derric talked and paced.

"We were hunting, in the area with several paths just past the caves an hour south of here. We were nearly on Grant land, for God's sake." He threw his hands up in the air for emphasis.

"You mean the area where we've been ambushed many times before?" Jamie asked, lifting his brows.

"Aye, but we sent our guards off with Chrissa and Drostan. We were only separated for less than five minutes. We heard a scream from Chrissa, but by the time we got to her location, she was on another horse. Both their horses were taken, the two guards were hurt and on the ground. We tried to follow, of course, but we quickly lost the trail."

Kyla said, "How could you leave them alone?"

"We are not looking to place blame, daughter," Alex said. "'Twill not help us find them. And the blame falls on their captors, not our clanmates."

"As you wish, Papa." Her words were accommodating, but they were accompanied by a seething glare. Then she shifted her attention back to Derric and Dyna. "What direction did they go? Connor and Jamie, get four patrols ready to go while we wait for the ransom offer I think we'll get soon."

"I doubt they'll ask for ransom. 'Tis too close to Midsummer's Day," Alex said, steepling his fingers in front of him, his elbows on the arms of the chair. "'Tis less than a fortnight now."

"Then what, Papa? What could they possibly want? They've tried to make our warriors fight for England twice in the past. They tried to kill you before. Is that what they wish to do with Chrissa? Kill her? What the hell do they want?"

"I think they're hoping to convince us to stay home, or…"

"Or what?" Kyla responded, her tone carrying plenty of heat.

"Keep us busy elsewhere. If we have to send contingencies of warriors after Chrissa, then we cannot help King Robert, can we?"

"Just tell me where you think she is, Papa. I'll go get her myself." Tears drenched her face. Kyla was a strong, powerful woman, but she'd never been afraid to show her emotion. It was one of the many things he appreciated about her.

"We need you here, Kyla. In case she returns. Or in case they bring her here."

"We'll find her, Mama," Alick said, glancing around at his cousins. "If we go together, we can use the spectral swords. We're all here now. Just give us an hour to plan. As Grandsire always says, 'tis much better to go in with a plan."

"We don't have an hour. She'll never survive being in a dungeon."

"Kyla." Alex's voice was so quiet everyone stopped to listen, which was exactly what he'd wanted. They would not win this if they made emotional decisions. "She'll survive just fine. She's her mother's daughter. Or do you not recall your worst moment?"

"I know I was held in a dungeon at Thane Castle, but I'm an adult. She's too young."

"How old is Chrissa?" Alex prompted.

"Nine and ten." Kyla's sobs had slowed, just as he'd hoped.

"And how old were you when you were locked in a dungeon, lass?" Kyla would always be a wee lassie to him, his memory of her strapped to his chest as a babe still firm in his old mind. "How old were you when you left on your own to visit an enemy's castle because you wished to save another lass?"

Her breath hitched as she thought, her gaze now locked on his as if he'd stirred a memory she wished to forget.

"Do you not recall being in a dungeon with Simon de La Porte?" he whispered, the hall silent as the forest before a hunter loosed the first arrow.

"I was seven and ten." She stared at the floor, but her countenance changed. "But I was…"

"Daughter, could you fire a bow like Chrissa? Could you use a dagger as well as Dyna?"

She shook her head, a small smile on her lips. "Thank you, Papa. You and Finlay are right. She'll be just fine. But we still must hurry."

"'Struth is, she's probably been hoping something like this would happen. Was she not thrilled when those men held her at knifepoint so they could kidnap you? If I recall, she was quite proud of her involvement in that episode. And Drostan is with her. Just like you had Finlay with you."

Her scowl indicated she'd only then realized there might be something between Chrissa and Drostan. She hated it when someone picked up on something faster than she did.

"Is it truly a surprise to you? I was fully aware of the attraction between you and Finlay," Alex said, looking from Kyla to her husband.

"Good for you, Papa, because I didn't know of the attraction between us then."

Alex smirked, glad to see evidence of his daughter's fire.

"I think we've all seen something between Chrissa and Drostan, Kyla," Connor said. "She is stronger than you think and she has a solid helper with her, someone she trusts. Let's make our plan, using our minds instead of our emotions."

Kyla leaned over and kissed her father. "Thank you, Papa. I don't know what I'd ever do without you."

Alex hated to tell her the truth. She'd have to learn how to do without him soon.

He'd also have to thank Maddie for telling him he had to stay.

He *was* still needed.

CHAPTER FOURTEEN

CHRISSA WAS ABOUT TO LOSE control. She hadn't seen or heard anything since she'd been locked inside her cell. She'd had no food, only water from a pitcher that was now nearly empty. She'd searched through her saddlebag for anything she could eat or use to help her escape, but her captors had already gone through it and removed her dagger.

She was hungry, tired, and eager to go home. She'd slept on and off overnight, exhaustion taking over, but then fits of fear broke into her consciousness, forcing her awake. Visions of bad men, spiders, and odd creatures made their way through her head, probably from bad dreams.

Her thoughts went to her cousin, Dyna. What would she do?

About an hour after she awakened, she heard steps coming her way. She heard the lock turn over, and the two sheriffs from the other day stepped inside. Percy and DeFry.

Surprised, she reacted the only way she could.

"And here are the traitors. What do you want with me, and where is Drostan?"

Percy said, "Your friend is far away. He'd never hear you, so don't bother attempting to call out to him. You'll fail."

DeFry stood in front of her, hands on his hips. "Your words do not hurt me. As for your friend, he did a fine job fooling all of you."

Chrissa had no idea what he was implying, but she remembered what her grandsire had always said about interrogations. *They'll try to get into your mind and play with you. To convince you of things you'd never believe on the outside. Don't let them.*

"I don't know what you're referring to."

"Drostan has been working for us for a long time."

Rather than comment on his lie, she said, "Who are you? The English? Scots who turn on their own are the lowest of the low."

Percy came forward, too close. "Why, you wee bitch. How dare you speak to us as if we aren't worthy to be near you. We control you. Can't you see that? We could hand you over to our guards as a treat if we wished to do so. We could beat you until your own kin wouldn't recognize you. You should be a bit more respectful."

She spat on his boots.

Percy grabbed her plait and yanked her onto her feet. "You'll pay for that."

"Leave her be," DeFry said.

He did as he was told, something that surprised Chrissa. She stepped back, hoping they would elaborate on what they'd said about Drostan. If nothing else, she wanted confirmation he was alive.

DeFry leaned back against the wall and crossed his arms in front. "Drostan is a spy for the English. He's been spying on Clan Grant for us for a long time."

"You are such a bad liar. Drostan loves Clan Grant and he's extremely loyal to my uncles and my grandsire. He would never risk their fury. Never." This she knew to be a lie. Completely, unfathomably a total fabrication.

DeFry paced a wee bit, limited by the small space. "Did you not wonder how we managed to locate you in the middle of the Highlands?"

"Nay, 'tis not the first time we've come upon marauders in the Highlands." She crossed her arms, refusing to believe anything he said about Drostan.

"He was given instructions to meet us there. And then we instructed him on where to lead you. We kidnapped the two of you easily, though 'twas just for show with Drostan."

She almost laughed. A good show, indeed. They'd knocked him out cold.

"Lies. All lies. I don't believe any of it."

"Mayhap you'll believe this person." DeFry moved over to the door and opened it, calling out to someone.

"I won't believe anyone," she said hotly. He was a fool if he thought anything could convince her of his guilt.

A beautiful woman with dark hair entered the cell. She stared down her nose at Chrissa and said the only thing anyone could have said to make her question everything she thought she knew.

"I'm Drostan's mother. And I've been spying for England for years now."

Astra ran outside, her hands over her ears, tears falling down her face. "Nay, nay, nay."

She didn't go far before she nearly stepped on a wee gray pup. Stopping short, she bent over to pick up the small dog. "What are you doing here?"

Someone shouted behind her, so she spun around, not surprised to see a lad racing toward her. Hendrie. She knew his name for the same reason she knew everything: because she listened. Other people didn't pay attention to half of what was going on around them, but Astra took in everything. The lad ran as hard as he could, fear written across his face. "She's mine. Please give her to me. She's confused."

"Why is she confused?" she asked, handing the pup back. She was a cute pup, but her eyes were sad.

"Because Drostan hasn't returned." Hendrie picked the pup up and petted her, cooing softly.

"He won't be returning anytime soon, so don't get her hopes up." Was she imagining it or did the pup widen its eyes at her statement?

"What? Why? What are you talking about?" Hendrie stepped closer to her. This close, she was struck by the green of his eyes, like pines in winter. His long red hair was neatly tethered in back.

"He's been kidnapped by the English. He and Chrissa. Have you not heard?"

"Nay. I'm not of noble blood, so I'm not included in those conversations. But I am his squire. I'm supposed to travel with him to the battle at Stirling Castle."

She cocked her head. "Why didn't he take you with the four of them if you're his squire?"

"He's not wearing any armor. They rode out from King Robert's land to patrol and gather information."

"You mean they were sent to spy on the English."

Confronted with his innocent surprise, she felt a slight pulse of guilt. Maybe she shouldn't have spoken so bluntly. She studied him, almost wishing her eyes were green instead of the blue of her family.

"And your sister? Was she not with them?" Hendrie cuddled the pup up close to his face. Something told her he needed the comfort of the soft, sweet animal.

"Dyna and Derric returned. Chrissa and Drostan were stolen away. They know not where they were taken."

"Will you help me?" Hendrie asked, his tone beseeching. "Find out where they were last seen, then come and tell me. I'll wait right here for you."

"Not unless you tell me why you wish to know," Astra said. It was her duty to know everything that happened on Grant land. "And how old are you?"

"I'm one and ten. How old are you?"

"Three and ten. You didn't answer my question." She waited, tapping her foot in the dirt.

"You're taller than I am," he said.

"I'm older and my parents are both tall. Or haven't you noticed? You still haven't answered my question."

He sighed and leaned toward her. "Promise not to tell?"

Astra nearly snorted. Everyone knew she told everything she could to anyone who would listen. "Of course."

"I'm going after him. I'll not wait to be invited. I have no parents who care since they're both dead. I live with my uncle, and he won't even notice I'm gone since I sleep with the warriors most of the time. I just need a horse. Sky will sniff Drostan out. She's a hound, as you know."

"I'll help," she said, deciding on the spot, "but I'm going with you." She'd always admired Chrissa more than any other of her cousins. If she got really good at archery, mayhap someday she'd be allowed to travel with Chrissa. They wouldn't need to take any lads along.

Well, perhaps this one time she could use Hendrie's help, but only because of the wolfhound. And Sky was a girl, so it would be two lasses to one lad. If she could convince him to let her come without tattling.

"Like hell. I don't need a lass slowing me down. I'll be moving fast."

"Can you use a bow like I can? Or a dagger?" She placed her hands on her hips for emphasis. And because he was pishing her off. Mayhap she should impress him with her language. "Don't pish me off."

"You have a foul mouth for a lass." He paused, considering, then said, "If you find out where they were last seen, you can come. And steal us some cheese and dried meat. You have easier access than I do."

"I'll do it," she said, practically bouncing with excitement. When had anything like *this* happened? "Meet me outside the stables in two hours. We can leave right away."

"Agreed. And tell no one." Hendrie nodded and took off toward the stables.

"I promise." Astra had to chuckle at that promise. For once, she was being honest.

There was no way she'd tell anyone what she intended.

CHAPTER FIFTEEN

THE LATEST PATROL TO GO off in search of Chrissa and Drostan wasn't due to meet for another hour, but someone started banging on the keep door, loud enough to wake half the castle. Alex was quite sure he already knew who'd made the racket. Turning as the door flew open, he said, "Ramsay, you're an old man and losing your touch."

His old friend stepped through the door with a smirk. "Am I not the one you've been waiting for?" he asked, lifting his brows.

"Not exactly, Uncle Logan," Jamie said. "But we're pleased to see you. We could use your help if you're not overtired from your journey."

"I'm always available to help. What has happened now? I can tell from the look of you, 'tis more than this battle on Midsummer's Day that has everyone in Scotland unsettled."

Logan held the door open and ushered his sister inside, Sorcha behind them. "You all remember my sister, Avelina, and my daughter Sorcha, do you not? Cailean's settling the horses." A man Alex didn't recognize came in behind Logan. He was dressed like a priest. Guards piled in behind him, seeing to their small bags and outerwear while Connor stepped in to explain the situation with the lost couple.

"Chrissa and one of our warriors, Drostan, are missing," he said. "Kidnapped off their horses. Robert the Bruce sent them on a mission with Dyna and Derric. They were on their way to Berwick."

Kyla, ashen-faced, greeted Avelina and Sorcha, then went to the kitchens to arrange for food for the travelers.

"Suspects?" Logan asked, seemingly unfazed by the news.

"Other than the English? None, at the moment."

"And what are you doing about it?"

"We have sent patrols out over half the Highlands," Jamie said. "But we've found no sign of them yet."

"No ransom demands? Edward is a greedy bastard, you know."

"Naught," Alex said. "It makes the waiting difficult. But I wish to hear more about you. I was expecting you, Ramsay. How was your journey?" He found himself smiling, because Maddie had been right, again. Aye, Torrian had told them about Logan, too, but Maddie had brought the news to him first.

Logan ushered his group inside and got Avelina settled near the hearth as the others exchanged greetings and well wishes. One older man, a stranger, waited by the door.

"Here now, Father," Logan said to him. "Come inside and warm your bones. This is Father Dowall, a friend of Father Rab's. We stopped at his kirk along the way, and he asked to ride with us."

"Welcome, Father. Come sit by the fire and we'll find a trencher of stew for you," Connor said. The man nodded and removed his mantle, leaving it by the door.

Logan turned when the door opened again. "And you all remember Sorcha's husband, MacAdam, do you not? You may not recognize him with all the gray in his hair, but he's the one just coming inside."

"I remember him as Cailean," Alex said with a grin. He'd missed Logan's antics. "At least, 'tis what the rest of us call him. Have you not accepted him as your son-in-law yet? I think the man's done more than enough to earn your respect, Ramsay."

Logan screwed up his face. "You have my respect, do you not, MacAdam?"

Cailean looked as if he would have preferred to run in the opposite direction. "Aye, I suppose so." He glanced from father to daughter to see if either one was going to argue with him. Neither did.

"What can I do to help?" Logan asked once they'd exchanged hugs. "I assume I must have missed the others from my clan? My daughters and Torrian have moved on?"

Connor said, "Aye, they've gone home to prepare for the journey to Stirling."

"Tell us what you learned along the way," Alex said. "Many English out there yet?"

Dyna added, "We learned that Edward is sending his troops to Edinburgh a sennight before the battle is to take place. Twenty thousand is the number I heard."

Logan snorted. "Edward thinks he'll get that many, but he won't. He forgets more and more Scots have come forward to support our rightful king. He may get ten thousand, but twice that is naught but a dream. Don't believe all the rumors. And every Scot can take on three Englishman, so he can have fifteen thousand and our five thousand will still beat them. But I'm starving. Can we eat and strategize afterward?"

Once food was brought out and everyone got settled, Alex made his way into the solar and motioned for Logan to follow him.

"You're an old man, Grant," Logan said, taking a seat across from the one Alex took behind the desk.

"'Tis true, but only a couple of years older than you, old man."

The two chuckled, Alex giving Logan the chance to get comfortable. Then he posed his question. "Why are you really here, Ramsay? I've a feeling you brought something with you. A cherished piece of Scottish history." The smiles were gone from both of their faces. The two men had been in charge of running two of the most important clans in all of Scotland. Though Logan had never served as chieftain, everyone knew he'd had a major impact on the decisions made in the clan, especially since he and his wife had been spies for the Scottish Crown.

Logan leaned back in his chair, running his hands through his long wavy hair, half light brown, half white. "Your intuition is still good, Grant. I brought Avelina here. She was instructed by the Queen of the Fae to bring the sapphire sword to you."

"You've seen this fae?"

"Aye, she appeared in front of me this time. Surrounded by butterflies, but she only stayed for a few moments. She disappeared after giving Lina her instructions." He planted his elbows on his knees, leaning forward this time. "I know how it sounds, Grant, but I saw it with my own eyes."

"If they're anything like my old eyes, you're lucky you can see anything at all."

Logan snorted and said, "True. I couldn't make her face out clearly, but I'd have to be totally blind to miss the mass of butterflies that surrounded her one moment and disappeared the next. And her voice was as clear as a hooting owl in the quiet of dawn."

"Mayhap you blinked?" Alex suggested, a smirk on his face.

"You always were a wise arse." Humor creased his face but faded quickly. "It actually gave me a little faith in the hereafter. There's more to this existence than we know."

"Say I believe you. What were her exact instructions?"

"Lina was told to bring the sapphire sword to

you. You're the one who must decide who is to receive it next."

"And how am I to know?" Alex flashed to what Maddie had told him in the vision. She'd told him the choice was his alone. This was the kind of decision he hadn't made since he was laird of the clan—it had the ability to save or ruin lives.

Logan shrugged his shoulders. "She said you just would."

Alex looked across the desk at his old friend, still fine looking and fitter than he had any right to be at his age. Nothing had slowed him down other than a few fists in his younger years. His mind was as keen as ever, and he pitied the man foolish enough to underestimate Logan Ramsay, at any age.

"Such is my challenge."

A knock sounded at the door, so Alex bid the person to enter. Avelina peeked around the corner. "I think I belong in this meeting, do I not, Logan?"

He pursed his lips and nodded, waving her inside. Once the door closed behind her, he said, "The Queen of the Fae apparently only trusts *you*, Lina."

His sister's eyes twinkled. "You're upset that a woman has control of something you don't, are you not?"

Alex chuckled. "The queen chose a strong-minded, intelligent Ramsay. The only way she could have chosen better is if she'd given the sword to a Grant."

Logan cast him a glare, accompanied by a harrumph that could likely be heard in the hall. "It clearly belonged with a Ramsay, and I'll admit she did a fine job. She held on to it without any fuss, and we've had many years of peace. Still, it could have been me."

"Logan, you've always ridden your horse around Scotland with a target firmly square on your back. I don't think you would qualify for what they needed."

Another glare, although there was an edge of humor to it. Shaking her head slightly, Avelina pulled a package swathed in a plaid out of her bag. She carefully unwrapped it and presented it to Alex, handing it to him across the desk. "Erena, Queen of the Fae, said you will know who to give it to."

They all stared at the small sword, which was a thing of beauty with its inset gemstones and the strange sheen that could be seen in any lighting. It looked as if it belonged in a case somewhere.

"'Tis not the least bit dull after all the years," Alex remarked.

"Nay, it looks the same to me," Lina said, leaning over to run her hand down the hilt. "I expect its power to vanquish evil remains unchanged too."

"Can it be used against a king?" Alex asked.

"I would say if it's a king with a truly evil heart, then aye. 'Tis Scottish, so the meaning of it is to save the people of its land from whatever evil befalls us."

"Have you any advice as the previous guardian of the sword?"

"There must be someone in your clan who is

special. I think I was chosen for my restraint. I suspect it should go to someone in the younger generation, under four decades. Someone you would trust to guard it well and use it for the good of the people of Scotland."

Alex said, "That thought is helpful. It eliminates all my bairns."

"Aye, they're too old."

He held it out to look at it. "My mother would have loved to see this. She believed in it whole-heartedly, although I'm not sure my sire did. Did Erena offer any other advice?"

"Nay, not a word," Logan blurted out.

Avelina shook her head slightly again, her lips tipping up at her brother's hasty reply. "The person who finds it must marry within two moons in order to keep it. Otherwise their family or clan will suffer."

"So it must be someone unmarried."

"Aye. I asked her if I was to tell you about the legend, and she said the one who is to receive the sword is too young to marry but has already chosen his or her mate. So the rule does not apply this time."

Logan snapped his fingers. "How could I forget that?"

"I told you, you're getting old," Alex said. "And this is yet another reason Erena chose the right protector for the sword." He fidgeted at the desk, thinking. "Too young to marry. Already chosen their mate."

Logan grumbled a bit, but he ignored his friend,

lost in thought. The answer came to him in a flash, so obvious he wondered why it had taken him so long.

Because you're getting old too, a voice supplied.

No matter. He knew who the new guardian of the sapphire sword would be.

Drostan went over everything in his mind one last time. He and Chrissa had been kidnapped. The Grants and Ramsays were meeting somewhere before they traveled to Stirling Castle, but he had no idea where it would be. Even if he did, he'd never tell. The sheriffs' scheming could mean death for hundreds in his clan.

But then he thought of Chrissa. If they tortured her in front of him while he was bound with no weapons, he'd lose his mind. He had to come up with a plan.

It was easy enough. He could lie. Just make up some place between Ramsay and Grant land where they could meet. They'd have no way of knowing if he was right or wrong. Lie and be let go.

Would they let him go?

Nay, fool. They'll never let either of you leave with your lives.

But he had to believe patrols were out searching for them. The sheriffs had said nothing about Dyna or Derric, so they had to be free. They knew exactly where Chrissa and Drostan had gone missing, and after searching the area, they must have gone back to Grant Castle. The Grants wouldn't rest until they were found.

That gave him his second strategy. Be patient. Waste time because the Grants would come for them. Chrissa had a family who adored her. Her mother would be sick with worry and her father would overturn every rock in the Highlands to find her.

Not that he expected the same effort from his father. In all likelihood, he was so deep in his cups he hadn't even processed that Drostan had been taken prisoner. Still, Drostan was with Chrissa, and he was a Grant warrior. They were both worth saving.

If they waited too long, though, the sheriffs might hurt them. They might even kill one of them. Could Drostan escape and free both of them? Wouldn't that be the best way?

He paced and paced, but nothing better came to mind. He'd save Chrissa.

Somehow.

CHAPTER SIXTEEN

ASTRA AND HENDRIE FOLLOWED THE tracks into the heavy brush down the side of the ravine.

"Astra, I don't like this."

"I know you don't. Stop being a wee bairn. I saw Chrissa's hair tie, her favorite one. It must have come off after they took her away. You know what that means, do you not?"

"That her hair is untied?" Hendrie asked, reaching into the pocket sewn in the front of his warm tunic to feel for Sky. He and Astra had worked hard on it so the dear pup would be able to join them. With that and the other preparations required for their journey, it had been impossible to leave as quickly as they'd hoped. So they'd decided to leave the next morning instead. Then they'd packed their clothes, asked Dyna exactly how to get to the spot where the two had last been seen, then snuck out to the stables the next morning before dawn. Hendrie had told her Dyna would figure out what they intended, but Astra knew that Dyna never took her seriously. She was so much younger Dyna still saw her as her wee sister.

"That's the best thought you came up with? Her hair is untied?" Astra rolled her eyes, thinking this was going to be a difficult journey if Hendrie persisted in being so literal. He lacked the ability to read situations, something her sire said she could do too well for one her age. Another skill she possessed, luckily for them, was an uncommonly good sense of direction. She could picture an area as clearly as if she were looking down at it from the clouds. Her father had already had her draw various maps for him. She'd actually started working on a map of all the Highlands, but she hadn't traveled far enough yet to fill it in much.

Her goal was to travel through all of Scotland and make a complete map for her clan. One they would use forever. When she'd given her last map to Grandsire, he'd frowned, staring at the fine details she'd made for bridges and ravines, making her own symbols for meadows and glens. She'd even indicated where the best caves were located.

Grandsire had stared at it for a long time and said, "Why, Astra, this is the finest map I've ever seen, lass. You have an unusual talent." Grandsire didn't hand out compliments lightly. Her mother had patted her shoulder, another rare demonstration, and she'd puffed up with pride in her special skill.

She brought herself back to Hendrie's facile answer. "Nay, it means she was fighting her captors. We'll have to look for more clues, like pieces of torn clothing, or… Wait! There! Do you not see it?" She tugged on the reins of her horse and led him over to a tree that had something hanging from it. Hendrie beat her to it and pulled the piece of fabric from the branch, peering at it closely.

"'Tis definitely a piece of a Grant plaid, but it could be anyone's." Just then, Sky stuck her head out of his pocket, sniffed the fabric, and yipped excitedly. Hendrie and Astra exchanged a look, and he said, "And there's a fork in the path ahead. Which way should we go?"

"Let's see if you were right about her abilities as a hound," Astra said, a wide smile on her face. They'd just gotten the help they needed. She dismounted, reaching up for Sky and the piece of fabric. He seemed dubious, but he handed them both down to her.

The fabric was about half the size of a man's palm, but she hoped it was large enough. If the pup had picked up his master's scent, she might be able to guide them to the prisoners.

She set the pup down on the ground, held the cloth in front of her face, and waited. Sky sniffed the plaid again, then barked up at Astra, her tail wagging so hard it must hurt.

Sky took off toward the two paths ahead. She started down one, sniffing along the way, but her tail didn't wag. She went far enough that Astra began to worry. If that was the right way, the scent couldn't be strong. She whistled for the dog, who ran back right away, then gave her the fabric again. She promptly rolled on it, tail wagging furiously again, and yipped two times.

"Find him, Sky. You know where he is." She pointed the dog toward the other path and waited as she padded over to it, nose to the ground. Nothing unusual happened until she sniffed in one area, her tail wagging furiously again.

Hendrie, who'd dismounted and now stood beside her, gawked at the pup. "I told you she would pick up Drostan's scent. Good lassie!"

Sky took off down the path at a frantic pace, following the scent, her tail wagging. Stopping once, she turned around and barked at them as if to say, "Come on!"

"You heard her," Astra said, "Mount up. We have a dog's nose to follow."

"Are they that good?" Hendrie asked.

"She's a wolfhound. Of course she's that good. Now pick her up, grab the fabric, and we'll set her down when we get to the next fork in the path."

The Grant solar was practically overflowing two days later. Everyone was eager for their voices to be heard. Midsummer's Day was about a sennight away, and King Robert wanted all of the warriors and archers in place a few days before that in case the English resorted to trickery.

Clan Grant also had a larger problem. Astra and one of the young lads were both missing. Connor said he knew exactly what she was doing, that she'd gone after her cousin, and Dyna had agreed.

"Aye, she'd asked me exactly where Chrissa had gone missing," Dyna muttered.

"And you didn't tell me or your mother?" her sire had asked, his hands on his hips and the glare in his gaze.

"But Astra always says things she's going to do and then never does it."

Alex had been listening to the conversation and had to take a stand. "She's right, Connor. Astra talks much, but Dyna? Due to the seriousness of this, you should have mentioned it to someone."

Dyna's hands had gone up in the air. "But we know exactly where she is."

Her father said, "And I guess we know where you're going."

Alex didn't like that they'd heard nothing about Chrissa yet. No ransom request had arrived, and none of the patrols had found any evidence of Chrissa or Drostan. Kyla was sick with worry, and Alex feared she'd go out on her own to find her daughter. The two were more alike than they cared to admit.

Alex cleared his throat to silence everyone in the solar. Jamie and Connor were there in their capacity as co-lairds of Clan Grant, and Logan represented the Ramsay clan. The cousins were also there: Alasdair, Alick, Els, and Dyna, along with their spouses. Alex had invited John to join them, and the lad sat quietly next to his sire. He wasn't usually involved in these kinds of meetings, but Alex knew it was time, even though the lad was only a decade old.

Finlay and Kyla were also there, of course, along with Avelina.

"We have two serious tasks ahead of us," Alex

said. "My sons have asked me to speak today as the issues we face are of such grave importance. First, we have a group of warriors we wish to send to King Robert. This group will leave in two days. Magnus and Jamie will lead them, while Ashlyn and Isbeil will lead our archers. Torrian will be leading the Ramsay warriors, who will be joining King Robert. The Ramsay and Grant warriors will meet at Gallow Hill and camp together. Maggie will be leading the Ramsay archers with Gavin, Merewen, and Gregor. Do you not agree, Logan?"

"Aye, Molly will not fight. She trains. Torrian will lead with his son, Lachlan. Kyle Maule will be with them."

Connor nodded, then continued, "The force King Robert has gathered is so large, possibly between six and eight thousand, that we wish to be able to keep track of our men and women. Godspeed to this group.

"The second group will go off in search of Chrissa and Drostan, Astra and Hendrie. We still do not know their location, but I think this group, working together with their special strengths, will be able to determine where they are being held. Hopefully, they'll find Astra looking for Chrissa. The group of cousins—Alasdair, Emmalin, Els, Alick, Dyna, and Derric—will travel together."

"What do you think it means that you've heard naught?" Alasdair asked. "The other times the English kidnapped Grants, it was for a purpose. What is there purpose this time?"

Alex shook his head, uncertain of the answer to

this question. "My guess is they are looking for information and they think they can get it from one of them. Although I have no idea what information they seek. The English know when the battle will be, where, they know who they're fighting. What else could they be looking for? And I think their numbers are such that they're underestimating our ability to defeat them, but I could be wrong about that."

"Neither of them would know the answer to that question either," Alasdair said. Then, as if noticing Alex's disquiet, he added, "Don't worry, Grandsire. We'll find them."

"What about me, *Seanair*?" John asked. Already a tall lad, he looked much like his father and grandsire. Long dark locks surrounded a strong jawline, though he showed no signs of a beard yet. His blue eyes took in everything they could, and he had a memory unlike anyone else Alex had ever met.

"I have not decided that yet, lad. I'm waiting for more patrols to return. Once I receive this information, I'll decide where you are to go, John. Probably with your sire."

Chrissa paced in her small cell, still furious. Drostan's mother had confirmed the sheriff's story: he was a spy for England. To hear her tell it, he'd spied for them for the past two years.

Chrissa had a hard time believing it, and yet the woman had been so convincing. She'd known about Drostan's father's abuse of ale, and she fit the memory she had of Drostan's mother, right down to the ring she wore on one finger. It was a sapphire with a pearl on either side of it, quite a beautiful design. Drostan had hoped to give it to his betrothed one day, but his mother had taken it with her when she left.

"If he was working as a spy as you say, he would not be concerned with making his sire proud, but that still drives him," Chrissa had challenged her. "Admit it, you left your own son without looking back, and the guilt is now eating at you. Because if you'd taken him with you, he'd be forsaking his father for you rather than the other way around."

His mother had scoffed, sending her a look of derision that hit her deep in her belly. "He doesn't give a shite about that drunken fool. He's trying to make *me* proud. And DeFry. He doesn't care about Clan Grant, about his father, or about you. If you foolishly thought there was something romantic between the two of you, you were wrong. He is in love with a beautiful, blonde-haired girl who has a large dowry. He does not need a bossy, whiny lass who acts like a man."

With that, the bitch had whirled on her heels and pranced out the door without a backward glance. Percy had laughed, but DeFry had pretended to be a bit more understanding.

"Sorry, lass. That had to hurt." But she'd seen the grin on his face as he walked out and then locked her inside with her thoughts.

So Drostan was a spy.

Nay, remember what Grandsire told you. They're play-

ing games with you!

Was it possible it was all a ruse to undermine her loyalty to Drostan? To confuse her and get her to do whatever insidious thing they wanted?

Still, a small part of her feared the worst. Was it possible Drostan, who'd always spoken so excitedly about being a spy for the Scots, had turned on them and tattled to the enemy? Lying on the cold stone for hours had made her question everything she believed in.

Just as they want you to do, lass.

It was as if her grandsire were in her head talking to her, admonishing her for not trusting those closest to her, those she loved the most.

A key turned in the lock, catching her attention, and she stopped her fretting and waited for the door to open. She no longer had any perception of whether it was day or night, or of how long she'd been held captive.

DeFry stepped inside and said, "I'm bringing you to see your friend. You'll keep your mouth closed when we travel through the passageway. We need information from you two, and one of you will spill all you know. Turn around. You'll not be allowed out unless your hands are bound."

She did as instructed, eager to see Drostan and confront him with what she'd learned. His reaction to the news would tell her whether he was innocent.

DeFry pushed her ahead of him, guiding her down three different passageways before he shoved her into a small chamber where Drostan stood against the wall, his hands bound. No one else was in the cell.

Drostan rushed to her side and asked, "Did they hurt you?"

Sheriff DeFry followed her in, his expression inscrutable, but his name was called by a man farther down the passageway. Something flickered in his eyes, and he left the chamber, saying to both of them, "I'll be back for the answer to my question, Chisholm. Don't think I won't get it."

The door clicked shut behind him as he yelled, "I'll be there shortly" to whomever was calling his name.

As soon as they were alone, Drostan repeated his question. "Did they hurt you?"

"Nay, but I'm so confused I don't know what to believe."

"About what?" he whispered. "They wish to know where the Ramsays and Grants are meeting before the battle. They say they'll set us free if we tell them, but I suspect 'tis bollocks. By the way," he said, dropping his tone even more, "I have no idea where the clans are meeting, do you?"

"What are you talking about?" Chrissa's eyes widened as she stared at Drostan. No one had said anything about the meeting place to her.

He held his hands out. "Untie me." They stood back to back, maneuvering against each other, touching and rubbing in ways Chrissa had never imagined, but they finally managed to free each other. Even in captivity, his touch ignited her.

Chrissa took in Drostan's appearance—hair in disarray, a light stubble on his cheeks—then launched herself at him. He must have had the same thought because he grabbed her shoulders and pulled her close, his lips finding hers, their tongues dueling as if they thought to consume each other. His hands roamed down her sides, finding her breasts, and she tugged him closer yet. She wanted his hardness against her, reminding her of how absolutely fantastic they were together. Moaning as his thumbs found her nipples through the fabric, she ended their kiss and tipped her head back, inviting him to kiss her neck. He obliged, trailing hot kisses all over her neck and down the front of her tunic.

"Wait," Drostan said, holding her at arm's length. "Much as I'm enjoying this, we're both untied. Mayhap we can find a way out before DeFry returns."

"You're right," she muttered, doing her best to straighten her clothing. "I don't have any idea what you're referring to about the clans' meeting place. He said nothing to me about that."

"So what did he say?" he asked, looking out into the passageway to make sure no one was coming.

"He brought your mother in to me…"

"My mother?" He grabbed her and turned her around.

The look on his face was one she'd never seen before. He looked…stricken. But all of the anger and confusion she'd felt in that meeting came roaring back. "Aye, your mother. She said you've turned traitor to Clan Grant and you're both spies for England."

"What?" He stepped back, his hands lifting to his hair, tugging it. "My mother? She's here?" But as soon as he said it, he started shaking his head. "I can't believe 'tis truly her. I've not seen my mother since she deserted us. They're using trickery to fool us."

"I've met her often enough, Drostan. Plus, she told me things only a mother could know. About your father and how mean he turned whenever he started drinking ale."

"That's no special thought. What does she look like?"

"I remember your mother. It was her. She changed a bit, but there's no doubt 'tis her, I'm telling you."

"And I'm telling you it cannot be her."

Chrissa's voice dropped so no one would hear her comment. "Drostan, if you don't trust my ability to recognize someone I've met several times, then perhaps you'll trust this. She wore your family ring. The heirloom!"

"What did it look like?"

"It was a large blue stone with a pearl on either side of it. Is that not what it looked like?

"Aye. But it could still be someone pretending to be my mother." He tugged his hair again, this time hard enough she was surprised he didn't come away with a handful. "Or it could be her. I guess it could be her. But all she said about me was a lie. A blatant lie."

"So you swear you're not a spy?"

"Aye." His expression hardened. "And if you

believed anything that woman told you, you're not much of a friend to me, are you?"

Something bubbled over inside of her. Whether it was due to the captivity, the hunger, the fear, or her confusion and uncertainty about Drostan's mother, her emotions finally took over. In a sudden fit of rage, she shoved at his chest, sending him back hard. He lost his footing and fell against the door, which was when it happened.

The door opened and no one was in the passageway.

DeFry had forgotten to lock it.

CHAPTER SEVENTEEN

ASTRA AND HENDRIE CONTINUED ON that way for an hour, using Sky's skills whenever they were stuck. The pup started yipping softly as they crested a hill, smoke filtering through the bushes ahead.

"Hendrie, if we find Chrissa and Drostan, mayhap we'll get a big reward."

"I'd rather have an award than a reward."

"What difference does it make?"

"Because 'twould be more special." Hendrie pointed to a well-hidden area and said, "Sky needs a rest. We should sit for a wee bit so I can feed her. She's tiring and we may still need her."

"I don't see how an award would be better." She sat back inside the bushes, pondering their situation. What she really wanted was for someone to tell her she was going to be as strong or stronger than Dyna. Her sister was part of the Highland Swords group, and everyone thought she was special. Maybe even magical. And now Dyna's wee daughter Tora acted like she was Thor himself.

Why did no one pay any attention to Astra? She was as smart as any of them. Why did no one else see her for who she was, instead viewing her as a wee lass who needed to grow up?

She was tired of that image.

Hendrie sat down, grabbing Sky and feeding her an apple and some oats he'd stolen from the stables. "All I know is my parents are dead. At least you still have yours. My uncle doesn't care much about me. You are blessed to have been born with the parents you have."

She couldn't deny he was right. What would she do without her sire or her mother? Her father did often give in to her, and while her mother was busy handling all the grandbairns, she knew she was loved. "You're right. I'm sorry you lost yours."

"And I have no siblings or cousins or anyone to care about me. Look at all the people you have in your life. I've always been quite jealous of anyone in the keep. If you get mad at one cousin, you have many more. But you should stop tattling on people. I've heard all about that. 'Tis not the kind of thing you wish to be known for."

She frowned, hating that he was calling her out on her behavior. "If you're so smart, what do you wish to be known for?"

He thought for a moment and pursed his lips before answering. "You'll laugh at me, but there's someone I wish to impress...someone I wish to be like."

"Nay, I won't laugh. I promise." She had no idea what he was thinking about. Was it one of her relatives—could it be her father? Her grandfather? Or perhaps one of the cousins in the Highland Swords group.

"I wish to be like Loki Grant."

"Loki? Why?" She loved Uncle Loki, as did everyone, but she didn't recall what he'd done other than be adopted by Brodie Grant.

"You don't recall all the old tales? He was only a lad, an orphan like I am, but he protected Celestina for Brodie Grant. He followed the bad men who meant her harm and even put stones in one's shoes, making him yell. Then he used his slinger at the Battle of Largs to kill the Norse, and he got Brodie to a healer after he was injured. Your grandsire called him up in front of the whole clan and told everyone about his accomplishments, then he gave him his own sword and had all the warriors encircle him and lay their swords down for him too." Hendrie stared up at the sky and sighed. "They vowed to protect him with their lives."

"Because he became a Grant."

"Nay, because of his deeds. 'Tis what I wish for. To do something noble enough to be recognized for. Come, we must move forward. No sense in dreaming."

Astra nodded, considering Hendrie's words. Perhaps he was right about the whole award versus reward thing.

Hendrie put his finger to his lips and said, "Hush. I hear something."

They crept forward as quietly as possible.

When they were closer, Astra peaked through

the branches and saw an old, ramshackle castle in the distance, dark and dreary, with crumbling walls. This had to be where Drostan and Chrissa were being held. Then she spotted exactly what she'd hoped for.

Chrissa's horse was tethered to a tree off to the side, along with another beast she didn't recognize.

They'd found them. Now what would they do?

"We have to go inside, Hendrie," Astra whispered.

"Nay, not me. And your arrows are no good inside a castle. We need to go back and get help."

"What if they leave?"

"We aren't that far. Less than a half day's ride. We'll get help, and the others will come for them. You can bring them straight here now that Sky's showed us the way."

The sound of thundering hooves interrupted them so they found a grove of trees to hide in, off the regular path. They watched as nearly two score Englishman arrived at the castle, all carrying battle axes or swords, dressed in armor and helms.

Hendrie paled and turned to look at Astra.

"All right," she said, because she might be brave but she wasn't stupid. "We go for help."

Sky yipped.

"Get her," Astra hissed. "And get on your horse. We have to get the hell out of here and fast. If they hear her, we're in trouble."

Hendrie said, "Aye, we go now. I'll be right behind you."

They took off in the opposite direction, pushing

their horses to travel as fast as possible, but they weren't riding large stallions. In fact, Hendrie had taken one of the smallest horses in the stables. With the upcoming battle, they hadn't dared to take any of the mounts that would be missed.

A pounding of hooves caught Astra's ears, and she whirled her head around and let out another squeal. "Hendrie, they're coming for us! Hurry! Faster!"

They tugged on the reins, but their horses didn't move any quicker. Worse, they started to slow in fear as big horses came up alongside them, armored men shouting at them. But Astra was so terrified, she couldn't hear a word they said.

"Are you stopping, Astra?" Hendrie shouted.

"Hell, nay!" she squealed, continuing on her way. One of the Englishmen pointed for her to slow down.

"I'm not stopping for you, you ugly bastard!"

"Don't make them any madder, Astra. Close your mouth," Hendrie yelled, though she could barely hear him either. The racket of the hooves was deafening, and the pounding of her heart seemed to drone out all other sounds.

The Englishman next to her reached over and grabbed her, lifting her off her horse as easily as if she were a saddlebag and settling her onto his horse with a thump.

A bolt of lightning shot out of the sky, followed by another and another. The man holding her lifted his helm off and tossed it aside, staring up at the wild sky, the thunder booming and crashing, the ear-splitting noise causing the horses to buck as the ground shook with fury beneath them.

She punched her captor and he laughed. Then she spat in his face and scratched him, something that put a quick stop to his laughter but earned her a painful slap.

"Stupid whoreson," she yelled, holding her cheek where he'd hit her. Then, to her relief, the sound of several Grant war whoops caught her ears. The thunder from the storm was nearly deafening now, but when she glanced away from the fool who'd captured her, she finally saw the source of the noise. Coming toward them was the best sight she'd ever seen.

Dyna rode behind Derric, her knees locked on the horse, her bow lifted overhead. Els, Alick, and Alasdair fought several men with their swords, knocking the heavily armored Englishmen off their mounts. The lightning continued to zip down, tossing some Englishmen off their horses. Ashlyn and Dyna fired their arrows in a fluid succession that was something to watch, though they could only do damage to the riders behind them, who wore no armor.

Then Alasdair came at her captor, whose iron grip on her leg would bruise her for sure.

"Down, Astra!" Alasdair yelled as he galloped toward them.

She did her best to throw herself off the horse, but the bastard dug his fingers into her flesh so hard that she bled. Her head banged against the side of the animal as she flipped over, upside-down.

She was surely about to die, if not from a fall then from the constant battering of her body against a moving beast.

Upside down on the horse, the tears began, but she refused to give up. She clawed at the Englishman's relentless grip on her leg, wishing she had a knife to cut her leggings off. Alasdair hit the big bastard with the flat of his sword, and the man swayed in his saddle. Still he hung on, until Derric charged toward them. Derric stabbed at the man's bicep with a dagger, and Dyna grabbed Astra by the arms, tugging her hard. Astra finally gained enough purchase to kick at the man, managing to catch him between the legs, and he released her—freeing Alasdair to finish him off.

Derric slowed his horse and Astra was finally able to sit up and grasp onto her sister, hugging her as if she'd never let go, tears flooding her face. "Hendrie?"

"He's fine. Els has him."

Once the battle ended, they gathered into a small group in an empty clearing. All was silent for a moment, then Dyna finally looked at her, her expression dark, and said, "Oh, you wee fool. What were you thinking, Astra?"

Sobbing, she stopped long enough to say, "We found Chrissa. She's back in a deserted castle. I saw her horse."

Alick said, "On second thought, well done, lass. Lead the way."

Drostan held his fingers to his lips as he righted himself and stood up, not even caring that Chrissa had shoved him against the door.

Because if she hadn't, they never would have realized it was open.

He glanced one way, then the other, but no one was about. Chrissa peeked into the passageway, whispering, "Sorry, Drostan."

"I'm not." He reached for her hand. "This way. This could be our only chance to escape."

Something flashed in her eyes as she looked at his hand. "I know you're not a liar. I'm sorry. Please forgive me."

He stopped and pivoted, facing her. "Look, we can't discuss this right now. We have to work together to escape. Can you do that? Even if you're tempted to believe my mother, please don't turn against me now," he said, his jaw clenched so tightly it hurt. He was so close to her that he picked up her flowery scent.

No one else smelled as sweet as she did. Didn't matter that she'd doubted him.

"Are you sure you don't wish to leave me behind?" she whispered.

They stood nose to nose, nearly touching, and he had the sudden urge to kiss her. To remind her—and himself—they belonged together and these people around them had been playing with their minds.

She tried to pull away, but he held her hand in a firm grip.

"Nay," he answered. "Even if we cannot work

this out, you are still my lairds' niece, so I'll at least see you back to Grant land. Can you agree? Please, Chrissa. We have to get out of here carefully and quickly."

"Aye."

He didn't suffer any illusions—she was still fired up—but she followed him down the passage. A slight breeze wafted from the end of a different pathway, and Chrissa pointed in that direction. They turned, surprised to find every chamber empty along the way. When they passed the last chamber before the door leading outside, he caught a glint of something out of the corner of his eye.

His sword was propped against a wall, and her bow and quiver of arrows sat on the shelf next to it. There was no one around and the chamber was otherwise empty.

Almost as if the weapons had been left out for them.

He wasn't going to think on that possibility, knowing their best chance was to get the hell out. And now they were armed with their own weapons, something that gave them another boost.

He sheathed his sword, waiting for her to arrange her bow and quiver, and they left the chamber and headed out the door, pausing to listen before they climbed up the stairs.

It all felt impossibly lucky. Their only disadvantage was physical weakness—they'd been held in cells for the past two days, fed nothing but stale bread. Chrissa's eyes had dark circles under them, her skin sallow and drawn, something he hated to see. When they got to the top step, he peeked out above ground level, looking for any guards in the area.

The area was quiet and empty. Eerily quiet. There was no curtain wall, another gift. Their surroundings were unfamiliar to him. The castle looked abandoned, but he asked, "Know you this place?"

She shook her head, snuggling against him for warmth. They searched the area for the best way out, only to notice two horses tethered off to the side, one of them Chrissa's.

Another gift. What was going on? Were they being set up?

No time to think on it. They led the horses away on foot, not wanting to draw any attention with sudden movements, but they didn't get very far before they heard the sounds of pursuit. A group of horses was heading toward them. Hiding in a copse of trees, they caught a glimpse of a small cavalry of Englishmen.

But most of them flew past them in the opposite direction.

Perfect timing because the arrival of the English distracted the guards at the front of the castle. Since they were at the back, away from the rest, they mounted and rode off, no sounds of pursuit.

In fact, it was nearly half an hour before they heard horses behind them. Four men chased them, one of them Sheriff Percy. "Stop, I say!"

Drostan glanced at Chrissa and smiled.

They set their horses to a full gallop across the meadow.

They were free. If they could get past this group of four Englishmen, none of whom could ride like he and Chrissa, he was sure they'd be safe.

Wouldn't they?

CHAPTER EIGHTEEN

ALEX LEANED OVER THE PARAPETS, smiling at the glorious day. The door banged open, disturbing his peace.

"Ramsay," he greeted. He didn't need to look to know who'd joined him.

"How'd you know 'twas me?"

Alex arched a brow at his friend and said, "'Truly you ask that question? No one else has taken so many doors off their hinges over the years."

Logan laughed heartily. "I hear you've received word that Astra and her friend have been found."

"Aye, and the wee troublemaker managed to find the castle where Chrissa and Drostan were being held. The Highland Sword team found them, but by the time they moved into the castle where they were being held, Chrissa and Drostan were gone. But there's every indication they're still alive."

"Good news. I hope your grandbairns can locate them."

"Astra and Hendrie should return soon. Connor will have a few things to say to the two of them."

"I would wager he will," Logan said. He leaned over the parapets next to him and said, "Recall you the day I stole your dear sister away to tend my sickly brother? I find myself thinking about it of late."

Alex chortled, staring at him. "You mean the day I allowed you to *think* you stole her away? My men had come back to tell me you were looking for her. I knew you needed her quickly so I allowed it."

"Hellfire, you hand me such bullshite after all these years? You didn't know it until after we snuck away. You would never have allowed me or anyone to steal one of your sisters away. I'm not daft yet, Grant."

"I cannot argue with that fact. You got by our defenses, but it didn't happen again. And look what good she did for your brother. I did find out about the situation in the morn, and once I knew the circumstances, I decided to allow it. But ten men were following you through the woods." He cast a serious look at him. "And I don't regret it."

Logan nodded. "Brenna healed more than Quade in our clan." He stared out over the trees, ignoring all that took place in the bustling courtyard beneath them.

"Aye, she helped Lily and Torrian, too."

"She healed more than those three, but you know that, old man."

Alex looked at Logan and nodded. "I do." Logan had struggled to handle the sickness of his beloved niece and nephew. "I was there when you took a knee to vow you'd trade your life for hers. Others didn't understand the implications, but I did. That same day we made the best alliance ever for Clan Grant."

Logan glanced over at him, a small smile on his face. "I agree. Too bad we always bested you at the annual Ramsay festival." The gleam in his eye told Alex exactly what he was after, but he ignored his friend's plea for competitiveness.

"Do you think the festivals will continue after we're gone?"

Logan nodded. "I believe Mama and Papa, and Quade are there every year. They'll go on for centuries."

They said nothing for a while, just enjoying the view and the company. Then Logan said, "Do you still dream about Maddie?"

"Aye. About twice a moon. She comes from heaven to deliver messages. She's never able to linger, but I cherish every moment. Every memory. Why do you ask?"

"My Gwynie weakens. She's not what she used to be."

"None of us are, you old goat. She's still better looking than you."

"Aye," he said, grinning. "I cannot argue that point." He looked down at the view for a moment, collecting himself, then said, "But I think her time is near…"

He reached over and clasped Logan's shoulder. "Fear not. When it happens, you'll see her again." Logan looked like he had something to say, but the moment was interrupted by shouts from the gates. "Come," Alex said, "we must see what this is about."

The two made their way down the staircase, Alex behind Logan, grasping his shoulder for the support he needed. Their progress was slow, but they made their way to the balcony.

"What is it?" Alex yelled down.

The door to the great hall opened and closed, Claray shouting, "Astra and Hendrie have returned."

Upon discovering Astra and Hendrie were missing, Connor had been intent on sending out five hundred guards to find her. Alex had argued with him over it, convincing him the two wouldn't be far from wherever Drostan and Chrissa would be found. There was no need for two patrols.

After they'd left, his son had come to him to explain his reasoning. "I'll not have my daughter running about on her own, especially at her age," Connor had said.

"You need to think on how old Dyna was when she wandered. And Astra has an uncanny ability to understand the world and where everything is in it. I say allow her to think she's on her own. Let her lead and see where she ends up. Our patrols have turned up naught, and we've received no ransom message. Mayhap she'll notice something the others haven't. She may be the one who finds Chrissa."

"Papa, with all due respect, you're not thinking clearly. Are you showing a favorite?"

"Connor, one granddaughter is as important

as another. I don't value Astra any less than I do Chrissa, but when you give someone freedom to use their mind, they may surprise you with what they can do. Once our guards perceive any danger, we'll give instructions to end the journey and bring them back."

"It wouldn't have been wise to send out five hundred. They are in training for Midsummer's Day." The clench in Connor's jaw told Alex just how upset his youngest son was.

"The Highland Swords will find Astra and see what she's found. Remember that the two weren't kidnapped. I'm sure Dyna will be able to find her."

Connor had cursed under his breath, but in the end, he'd agreed. "Only if the Highland Swords will do it."

"I'm sure they would be honored to do you the favor."

Indeed, they had.

"Tell me more about Astra," Logan said, bringing Alex back to the present. "I know you wished to give her the chance to prove herself, Grant, but she's mighty young, even for a Grant warrior. Why?"

"Astra is Connor's youngest. The lass understands the land better than anyone I know. The maps she draws are beyond belief. I'd hoped she might see something the others have missed."

The door opened again, and Connor entered the great hall, his hand on Astra's arm. The lass fought him all the way inside.

"But Papa. Listen to me! We found them."

"Why the hell would you go off on your own with only Hendrie to help you? How many times have you been told not to leave the gates without guards?"

Logan looked at Alex and nodded to him. "If you don't, I will."

Alex let out his loudest Grant war whoop. Logan covered his ears and muttered, "You did that apurpose, you old fool."

Alex smirked but followed it up with a bellow. "Silence!" When everyone quieted, he said, "I'll hear everything she has to offer, Connor. You can deal with her transgressions later."

Kyla emerged from her chamber, her gaze intent on the hall. "What is it? What have you found?"

Astra turned from her father and raced up the stairs to stand next to her grandsire, shoving Logan out of the way. "I saw her horse. But when we went back with Dyna, they'd already gone. But they were there. Both Drostan and Chrissa."

Alex patted her back and said, "Good job. Mayhap someday you'll lead a patrol out. Now where is that Hendrie? I'd like to thank him, too."

"He's in the stables."

Kyla reached for the wall to steady herself. "Praise the Lord." Then she looked at her niece and said, "Well done, Astra."

Astra beamed.

CHAPTER NINETEEN

CHRISSA PUSHED HER HORSE, BUT the beast couldn't keep up with Drostan's. He slowed down, yelling at her, "Get her moving. They're gaining on us."

"I know, but I can't make her go any faster. Think you they didn't feed our horses any better than they fed us? 'Twould be my guess." They rode on a for another few moments, her mare slowing further, before she blurted out, "Go on without me. At least you could go for help because you know where they'll keep me if they catch me. Go, please."

"Nay, I'll not leave you."

"Or your mother?" She didn't want to believe that he'd conspired with his mother, but every time something interfered with their ability to get home safely that bitch of a woman popped into her mind.

Then again, she couldn't imagine the man she was falling in love with would want anything to do with a woman like that. He might share her blood, but he was nothing like her at all.

There. The thought had burst through her remaining doubts. She loved him. And love was the kind of emotion that made you believe in someone's innate goodness—and that belief was far more powerful than any doubt an enemy could sow.

But she didn't have a chance to say so, because Drostan responded, "Hellfire, Grant. If the woman you saw is my mother, I haven't seen her in over three years, and I'm not interested in seeing her now." He stayed abreast of her, but they were reaching a small glen, which would force them to slow while the others were still at full gallop.

Glancing over her shoulder, Chrissa noticed two guards were in the lead, with Percy just behind them. The fourth horse had fallen back quite a distance.

She believed him—she truly did—so she set the thought far from her mind. "Drostan, they're catching us. We should stop so I can set up in a tree. You take on one while I take the others down with my bow."

"Can't you turn around and shoot at them?"

"I'm too weak to shoot a moving target from a moving target. I'd have a better chance if we stopped."

He looked ahead of him and pointed to a spot with a large boulder. "We'll stop there. You can put the horses behind the boulder to get them out of the way. We can't risk losing them."

She agreed and they dismounted as fast as they could, Drostan lifting her down and grabbing her bow for her. Once they were both in position, Chrissa in a tree and Drostan concealed by the other side of the boulder, they could do naught else but wait.

She'd always listened to stories of battle with avid interest. With jealousy, even, especially when it was her older cousins doing the talking. Dyna and the lads had always had such adventures. Once she'd said as much to Els's wife, Joya, and her sister-in-law, Branwen. Joya, who'd been a spy, something she'd always considered the most exciting vocation of all, had shaken her head. "Sweetling, I know it sounds exciting, but it wasn't. When you're in the thick of it, it's more frightening than you can comprehend."

"But Joya, were you not thrilled to be such a major part of King Robert's quest for freedom? Had you not pretended to be an English spy at Glen Trool, the battle might not have gone nearly so well for our side. Were you not excited?"

Joya shook her head slowly and said, "Oh, nay. I was so afraid to be struck down by an arrow that I nearly pished myself."

"Someday you'll understand," Branwen had added. "And then you'll wish you never had to."

The time Branwen had spoken of had come. She had a sudden clear understanding of everything they'd said.

Her knees knocked together as she waited, her arrow nocked and ready to fly.

Finally, they were within range. She let the first arrow fly, hitting the lead man on horseback. He kept coming, the arrow protruding from his shoulder, but she had to keep moving.

She nocked another and fired at the second man, missing him. She nocked a third and aimed, only to be interrupted by Drostan's shout.

"Chrissa, you have to take them out or they'll kill both of us!"

"Stop yelling at me! You're not helping."

"You're about to see our blood spilled all over this ground. You wanted to go to battle? You have it."

"Mayhap I've changed my mind about wishing to be a spy." She fired another arrow and caught the second horseman in his thigh. "The thought of it has taken an ugly turn."

"Shoot! And I'm not a spy. My mother might be or mayhap she's not even my mother. Get it out of your mind. We're more important. *You're* more important. Shoot! They're nearly upon us."

Nocking another with shaking hands, she fired at the first man, hitting him straight in his midsection, knocking him off his horse. She fired again at the second and hit his flank, but he didn't fall. She tried to shoot at Percy, the third horseman, but he rode to the side in a wide curve, jumping off his horse and running straight at Drostan, his sword lifted overhead.

Trying to watch them both, she prepared another shot. She fired at the second horseman, hitting him in the throat, blood spurting everywhere as he fell to the ground, dead if she were to guess. So she turned to Percy next. Drostan and the sheriff were now facing off, Drostan blocking the man's parries.

She glanced back to see if any others were coming, but the fourth man had gone back and was nowhere to be seen. Bringing her gaze back to Percy, she nocked her arrow and aimed, watching the men parry, waiting for an opportunity.

When it came, she fired an arrow into Percy's arm. The injury wouldn't stop him—it hadn't incapacitated the arm—but the sight of the arrow had thrown off his concentration. He jumped, staring at her and cursing, and Drostan scored a direct blow to his sword arm.

Chrissa watched what happened next as if in slow motion. Percy's sword flew out of his hands and sliced across Drostan's leg, instantly spilling blood down the front of his trews. Chrissa fired another arrow and struck the sheriff square in the chest, killing him instantly.

But Drostan looked terrible.

She couldn't lose him, not when she'd just figured out that she loved him.

"Drostan!"

Alex sat near the hearth, surrounded by more clanmates than he could identify. He was tiring from all the decisions they had been forced to make, so he nodded to Jamie and Connor. It was their job to see this through to the end. Jamie held his arms up to silence the group, which consisted mostly of men.

"We're going after Dyna's and Alasdair's group

to see if we can assist them," Connor said. "We know not how many we'll be handling. Astra drew a map showing us exactly where Chrissa was held, so we're going there first. Jamie, you take the other group to meet the Ramsay warriors at Gallow Hill. 'Tis time to take a group to Stirling. The archers will travel with you. We'll leave a third group here to protect our land. Uncle Logan, will you be traveling ahead?"

"Aye, I'll meet with the Ramsays before they join up with the Grant group, but I'm leaving Lina behind."

"If anything changes, please send a messenger," Jamie said.

"You have my word that I'll update you with travel instructions. Godspeed to all groups, especially the group going after their own."

Alex hated to see so many of their warriors headed out to battle, but there was little to be done but fight. Watching his sons, his clan, his allies all convene to work together also gave him a deep sense of pride. He and Maddie had raised them well, and they'd built a powerful, meaningful alliance with the Ramsays and their other close allies. They were strong enough to take on their enemies, England included. They had to protect their people, their country, their land.

Father Dowall stood up and said, "May I? I'd like to pray for blessings in this difficult time."

Alex looked at Logan, who nodded his agreement, so he gave his assent to the priest.

Father Dowall said a simple but eloquent prayer,

something that gave them all a quick boost of confidence. When he finished, he glanced at Logan, then approached him while the others mulled about.

"I was wondering if I could travel with the group following the special swords," the priest said. "I'd like to see their swords in action, if you don't mind."

The priest's words surprised Alex, but when Logan looked to him for his opinion, he waved to indicate he didn't mind if the man followed the spectral swords.

"I'm going with the other group," Logan reminded the priest. "I can't promise they'll return you to your chapel, but you'll not be far away if Astra's directions are correct."

Alex had little doubt of that—the lass could find her way if blindfolded.

"Many thanks to you, my lord. I'll be able to find my way, I'm sure. Godspeed to your group." He nodded and left, grabbing a hunk of bread from the trestle table still loaded with various foodstuffs.

"Godspeed to all of us," Alex said, praying his granddaughter would be found quickly. Maybe he should have given the sword to Dyna or Alasdair. A loan to help them find Chrissa.

Only he knew who was supposed to wield the sword, and it was neither of them.

CHAPTER TWENTY

DROSTAN CURSED UNDER HIS BREATH, wanting to scream at Chrissa, at his horse, even at the dead men around him. Forcing himself to stand, he managed to get on his horse without much trouble.

"Drostan, I have to stitch you up. What are you doing?"

"Chrissa, get on your horse. We have to move far away from here." He clutched his thigh, trying to stanch the bleeding.

"Allow me to stitch you first."

"Nay, there are three dead men or nearly dead men. The wolves and other creatures will smell the blood and be here soon. I can't move them, nor do I want to. And if we stay out in the open, others may come along. I know you have to stitch me up before we can head home, but we cannot stay here. Let's move ahead and see what we can find on the other side of the ravine. I can hear moving water up ahead. If we're lucky, there's a burn. We should be able to find an outcropping or a grove of pines as protection. I need to wash the blood off me, too."

"All right." She didn't say much, though she kept staring at his injury. Before they left, she quickly retrieved all of the arrows that were salvageable. She probably would need all of them.

Once they made it through the ravine, he led her off the main path to the right to a place well hidden by a grove of pines. There was a large outcropping that would keep them dry if it rained. He bustled around the area dragging pine boughs behind him.

"How did you know this was here?" she asked, simply because it was perfect.

"I just had this odd feeling, and I could hear the water." He busied himself with the branches, ignoring her. He knew his strength was waning, so he needed to do what he could to conceal their position. After she sewed him up, he'd be of no use to anyone.

"What are you doing, Drostan?"

"Simple. Do you see those trees? I can weave these among the branches, blocking anyone's view of us, plus it will offer protection against the elements of whatever weather Scotland chooses to throw at us." He continued until he'd finished his task, and he had to admit, he'd done a fine job with the branches. It was a good thing, because he was depleting his strength rapidly, though he'd never tell her so.

She grabbed her saddlebag and took it over to a small rock under the outcropping, sitting down to sort out her necessary items. "Come, I must sew up your wound or you'll never survive." Grabbing a small basin, she moved to the burn and filled it with fresh water.

He limped over to her and pulled off his trews, using his plaid to maintain his dignity. At this point, he didn't care. He was in a great deal of pain, and he was more frightened than he'd ever been, simply because he knew he wouldn't be able to protect her anymore. The thought of sending her off alone worried him more than any wound could.

He wiped the sweat from his brow and sat down in front of her.

"I have nothing to give you to help with the pain. Sorry."

"Have you any of your aunt's salve to protect against the fever?"

"Aye, I have a small jar that should be enough."

"'Tis all I'll need. Do not worry about my pain. Just get it done as quickly as possible." He'd only been stitched once, a couple of years ago, and his sire had forced him to drink enough ale to make him nearly pass out.

There was no ale to help him this time. He watched her press on the wound, pushing down hard.

"Why are you delaying?" he asked, surprised by a sudden bout of dizziness.

"Because you're bleeding is heavy enough that I can't see the edges of your wound. I have to slow it before I can stitch it together. Too much pressure from the blood will just pop my stitches as soon as you get on a horse."

He could see the misting in her eyes, so he cupped her cheek and lifted her gaze to his. "We'll get through this. We have each other, and we're both too stubborn to let those bastards who took us captive win in any way." He leaned over and gave her a chaste kiss on the lips, and he was pleased she didn't turn away from him.

A sudden stab of pain jolted him, so he pulled back, nodding for her to continue. Too addled to do anything else at this point, he closed his eyes while she prepared to start stitching.

He must have dozed off because the next thing he knew, it felt like a knife had been plunged into his open wound. His eyes flew open and he nearly roared, but he stopped, transfixed by the sheer beauty of Chrissa hard at work.

She was the most beautiful lass he'd ever seen. Her concentration was such that her tongue stuck out slightly between her teeth as she worked. Watching her truly dulled the pain that shot through him with each precise placement of her needle. He found a rock beneath him and gripped it as tightly as he could, helping him conquer the pain. Crying out might distract her, and he would never, ever strike her out of his own discomfort.

"Lass, I'm not a spy," he whispered, sweat still beading across his forehead so he wiped it down with the sleeve of one arm. "I've always been interested in you, ever since we made our pledge, but this past year it got so you were almost the only thing I noticed. You're my world."

Chrissa nodded, casting an appreciative glance at him before she continued her work. "I believe you. My feelings have been changing for a while now, I realize. It's been…confusing. It was a perfect time for someone to make a fool of me. They wanted us to argue, and they arranged for it to happen."

"I agree." He paused, thinking about their escape from their castle. Other than the confrontation that had ended in his wound, everything had been too easy. "And I found one other thing odd. It shouldn't have been so simple for us to escape. The door was left unlocked, our weapons were just down the passageway, and two horses were tied up in the perfect spot. Who was the last person in the chamber with us?"

"DeFry," she whispered. "He didn't follow Percy."

"True, and your cousins seemed to believe he was loyal to the Scots. He's not on your grandsire's list of traitors either. Mayhap he's a spy for the Scots. Would he do that? Pretend that he supports King Edward?"

"'Tis possible. At this point, it seems anything is possible."

Drostan knew she had several more stitches to place, and he leaned his head back against the stone outcropping because he was so tired. He could take a nap and sleep through this pain.

"Drostan!" she said, nudging him. "You have to stay awake."

"Why?" He kept his eyes open to please her but didn't move his head.

"Because my aunt Jennie, the healer, always says

so. I must get you home quickly."

"Lass, I don't know how to tell you this, but I'm not going home. I'll never make it. You won't be able to get me on my horse and I can't get on myself. You'll have to go for help. Even if I managed to climb on, I wouldn't be able to stay upright." His eyes fluttered shut again. "Keep talking. I'm listening."

He didn't hear another word she said.

The man finished writing his missive, tying it carefully with twine. He handed it to the waiting messenger and sent him on his way.

He worked on the second missive laboriously, phrasing his words just right, then put the mark of the clan at the bottom before tying it carefully with twine, just like the other one. They looked exactly alike.

A second lad arrived and he passed along both the missive and the coin he'd promised for delivery of the message to the right person. The lad asked, "This is to go to the chieftain of the Ramsay group headed toward Stirling Castle?"

"Aye, now Godspeed with you."

The second messenger left and the man leaned back, a huge smile on his face. He'd planned this so intricately that he had to smile. It was a brilliant plan.

He'd sent a message to the leader of the Ramsay warriors explaining that there was a group of Englishmen disguised as Grant warriors out to kill them. It was suggested they kill them all.

Then he'd sent a message to the leader of the Grant warriors explaining that a group of Englishmen disguised as Ramsay warriors had been sent out with instructions to kill the Grant warriors.

The result should be the Grant warriors killing the Ramsays and the Ramsays killing the Grants. He'd signed both as though they were sent by Robert the Bruce. True, he'd only seen the man's signature a couple of times, but since most men did not have the ability to read, whoever read it would not know the Bruce's signature.

He wished to be on the next field to watch.

CHAPTER TWENTY-ONE

CHRISSA SETTLED DROSTAN AS BEST she could. He was built of solid muscle, so moving him was not easy, but she'd managed to lay him down across the fur she'd retrieved from her horse. She rinsed his blood stained trews in the burn, then left them out to dry, hanging them on the pine branches.

He hadn't awakened from the last time he'd fallen asleep. She'd finished the last few stitches, though it had been difficult to see through the tears misting her eyes, and then applied the salve and bandaged it.

She tucked a plaid over him, then leaned down and kissed his cheek. "I love you, Drostan. I'll hurry. I need to get someone here quickly, I know."

After filling the skin with fresh water and drinking deeply, she set it down next to him in case he awakened. Then she climbed on her horse and rode out, a sick feeling in her gut. She found the path she had to take back to Grant land without a problem, but the farther she traveled, the more a small voice niggled at her in the back of her mind.

He's going to die.

He's going to die.

He's going to die.

You don't need to leave. The Grant patrol will find you now that you're out of the cellar.

He never left you.

Her mind returned to that day all those years ago, when she was around six summers. Her leg had hurt so badly she couldn't walk. She'd known her parents would find her, but waiting alone was horrible.

But Drostan had found her and stayed. He'd done it for her—and her response had been to make demands of him. To tell him he needed to be the strongest soldier in the lists if he wished to marry her. A tear slid down her cheek.

And he did it, or as good as. He did it for you.

You cannot leave him.

The more she traveled, the more the last comment made sense. A sudden urge gripped her that she couldn't ignore.

Turning her horse around, she tugged on the reins and flew back toward him. No more running from how she felt. She and Drostan belonged together.

If he lived, she didn't care if she ever fought another battle.

She would fight, of course, if called upon to do so, but life wasn't about reaching for glory—it was about doing the right thing because it was right. Maybe glory would come from it, maybe not. All she knew was she wanted to be with Drostan.

When she made it back, she filled the water skin again, said a quick prayer, then tucked herself up against Drostan, pulling the plaid over both of them. To her surprise, he awakened.

"Chrissa?"

"What? I'm here."

"Did I ever tell you I love you?"

"Nay. Say it again." She smiled, her heart blossoming.

"I was so angry when I thought you believed my mother over me. But you were held captive. They tried to twist our minds and turn us against each other. I understand why you doubted me. I shouldn't have reacted the way I did. I love you, Chrissa." He had to stop to gather strength to speak. "Every part of my being loves you. I'm glad you came back."

"I love you, too, Drostan. I'm sorry I doubted you." Tears ran down her face because she could hear the weakness in his voice.

His eyes closed again. "I'm so tired."

"You must drink some water," she urged.

"What?"

"Mama always made everyone drink water when they had a big wound."

"I am thirsty."

She sat him up, leaning his head back against her chest. He drank several long sips, then closed his eyes again.

"A little more. Please, love?"

He opened his eyes and drank more, then sighed,

but he had a tight grip on her hand. She managed to slide the two of them down to a prone position again, and she fell asleep against him, their hands entwined.

The many groups of warriors moved out of the hall, preparing for their journeys. There were only a few left, among them Father Dowall, who was reading his Bible by the hearth. Logan searched out Alex, Avelina behind him.

Alex could see them making their way across the hall. When Logan reached him, he said in an undertone, as if he didn't wish anyone else to overhear them. "Lina and I must speak with you."

Alex knew exactly what they wanted. He looked across the hall and called out, "John, help me to the solar, please."

John hurried across the hall, eager to help his grandsire as he always was. "I wish I could travel with them, Grandsire. How old must I be? Papa asked me to stay here while they search for Chrissa, but he said I could go to Stirling with him after they return."

Alex wouldn't tell the lad that it was his fault he was still here.

Once they were settled in the solar, Logan said, "Avelina has a story to tell you, John."

John turned to her without speaking, his expression open and intent. He'd become a good listener, John. He wasn't the sort to jump in with questions until he had a sense of what was going on. An unusual trait in one so young.

Alex nodded to her. "Go ahead, Avelina."

"This is probably verra new information for you, so please listen and ask questions at the end. Many years ago, the Queen of the Fae visited me. She told me an evil force had captured the sapphire sword and was intent on using it to overtake the land. My mission was to find the sword and take it back. I was successful, although once the sword was in my power, I had to marry within two moons to preserve its power." She smiled. "I was fortunate to have already met the man I wished to marry. Once I defeated the man who'd stolen the sword, Queen Erena bid me to hide it. She said we wouldn't have a need for it for decades. But she came to me a short while ago and told me the time had come to pass it on to someone else."

John was totally enraptured by the tale. His eyes widened when Alex opened a drawer, taking out a package wrapped in a Ramsay plaid and setting it on the desk. He nodded to Avelina, indicating she should be the one to reveal it, and she unwrapped the plaid and pulling out the sword, its gemstones glittering.

Alex and Logan watched, spellbound, as Avelina set the sword down closer to John. "Erena instructed me to pass the sword along to your grandsire. She said he would choose my successor, and he has chosen *you*, John."

John lifted the sword, rubbing his fingers over the fine gemstones, then glanced up at his grandsire with wide eyes. "'Tis a most fine beauty anyone would be honored to hold. But why me?"

Alex said, "I chose you because you are young and you will protect it well. You have the constitution to think carefully before using it, to always consider what is best for our clan, our people."

John, clearly humbled, set down the weapon. "I hope to make you proud, *Seanair.*"

"There is one other point we must make," Avelina explained. "If you were older, you would have been given two months to find a mate, but I've learned you've already chosen your mate?"

"Aye," he said without hesitation. "Coira."

A knock sounded at the door. Alex smiled at John. "I was certain you'd say that, so I sent for her." Speaking more loudly, he said, "Enter."

The door opened and Coira stepped inside, her golden hair falling to her waist, unplaited but tied loosely back. She'd become a lovely lass at one and ten, but she was still shy unless she was around John.

"Coira, sit down, please," Alex said.

John held up the sword for Coira to see, and she gasped. "Oh, John. 'Tis small but quite beautiful. What is its purpose?"

Avelina gave her a quick explanation, then finished by saying, "Alex has chosen John to be the bearer of the sapphire sword. Legend has it he must marry within two moons, but since he is so young, he cannot do so."

"But could we not become betrothed, *Seanair*?" John suggested. "Would that not complete the legend, make it intact? I'll want no other lass but Coira."

Coira blushed and smiled, clearly pleased by the thought.

Logan jumped to his feet and said, "Works for all of Scotland. Coira, do you agree to marry John when you are eight and ten?"

John smiled and reached for her hand. She clasped it and nodded. "Of course. Naught would make me happier."

"'Tis done, Grant," Logan declared. "John Alexander Grant is the protector of the sapphire sword. You must never let it fall into another's hands, John. You're to use it to eliminate whatever evil is plaguing our land, and once your duty is done, you must hide it and protect it with your life. Do you accept this charge?"

"And you must marry Coira when the time is right," Avelina added.

"I am honored to accept." He tilted his head. "But how will I recognize the Queen of the Fae if she appears to me as she has to you?"

"You'll not miss her," Logan said. "It's a rare lass who appears within a swarm of butterflies." He clapped John on the back. "Now go off and find Chrissa and Drostan with your sire and the guards waiting outside. Be sure to kill any evil along the way. There's something bad out there. I can feel it."

John glanced at Alex, seeking verification of what Logan had said.

"There are guards awaiting you. They'll bring you to your sire. You'll be riding with the Highland Swords, lad."

"You must use it this day," Avelina said, her

voice harsher and more urgent than usual. "In fact, I would urge you not to hesitate. I can feel the rage inside of the sword. 'Tis reacting to evil around us. You'll know what to do when the time comes. John, I've heard of your past success with the spectral power used by the Highland Swords. It has been dormant for a while now. Am I correct, Alex?"

"Not exactly dormant. We had no need for it for a long time. Dyna thinks it will return when necessary. I have to trust her instincts."

"It may be because you needed the last piece, this sword. My guess is your niece and nephews were given their ability to protect John and the sapphire sword. Please consider that, John. The two powers are likely connected. They create the same storm surges. Use the sword well because together, their power could be even stronger."

John, clearly humbled by what Avelina said, squeezed Coira's hand and nodded. "I vow to do my best to protect the sapphire sword, guard it well, and only use it to protect our clans and all of Scotland."

"One last thing," Avelina said. "John, as bearer of the sapphire sword, I suspect you may have some powers of sight. You may get the inkling that something evil is near, that something feels wrong. Trust your gut. You'll learn over time when 'tis real and when 'tis false, but until then, trust all that you feel. I also found that the closer I was to the evil force, the more the sword heated."

"Heated?"

"Aye, the hilt will warm to your touch, much like the spectral swords. Another reason why I believe they are connected."

"I shall do my best," John nodded emphatically.

Avelina gave them each a swift hug, then said, "If you ever have questions, you're always welcome on Menzie land. Both of you. And if you ever feel you're in a bind, please call out to Erena. She will help you."

John nodded before he left, Coira followed, and the door closed behind them.

"I think you chose well, Alex," Avelina said. "I'm glad to turn it over to someone new."

"Now he needs to find the bastard who's out to get half of Scotland," Logan said. "My belly won't rest until he does.

CHAPTER TWENTY-TWO

CHRISSA AWOKE AT DAWN, SURPRISED to find she'd slept through the night. Drostan lay so still it frightened her. She rested her cheek against his forehead and sighed with relief. He was warm, but not from fever. Watching his chest, she could still catch the slight rhythmic rise and fall of his breathing.

She shook him awake, but he didn't respond. His body likely needed more time to heal.

She got up, stretched her sore muscles from all that she'd been through, then left their safe area to relieve herself. The twittering of birds told her there were no major groups in the area that didn't belong, so she thought it safe enough. Following the burn to a spot where it cascaded over a stack of rocks, the water bubbling and gurgling with what could only be described as joy, she cupped the fresh water in her hands, splashed her face, and then sipped and rinsed her mouth. She felt dusty and dirty from captivity, so did what she could to clean up while keeping an eye out for any visitors or movement from Drostan. Finally, she filled the skin and brought it back to their hidden spot in the pines, but a sound forced her to hasten her movement.

Hoofbeats, and from many horses. She hid behind the pine boughs, listening as the force approached.

It wasn't a large force, but it included enough people to pose significant trouble for them. The first sound was from a female voice.

"Where the hell did they go?" one man said.

The woman answered, "I don't know, but we have to find them. This could ruin our plans. I wanted both of them dead to distract the warriors."

"We'll find them after we leave the big event," the man said dismissively. "We cannot miss it. I have to watch the massacre." His voice was vaguely familiar to Chrissa, but she couldn't be sure if it was someone she knew or not. "I've worked hard to get myself in this position. This was my part of the plan. I'll see it to fruition and enjoy every second of the death it causes."

"If your ruse succeeds. As soon as the Ramsays are close enough to recognize the Grants, their attack will halt. And the same is true for the other side."

"Mayhap," the man said, "but they're prideful to a fault. They'll act irrationally to the thought of Englishmen wearing their plaid. Both sides have talented archers. And once they get closer, we'll send our guards into the front lines. Once they start killing, 'twill be madness. The clans will turn on each other quickly enough."

"Perhaps you are right. If so, this could prove to be a brilliant strategy. Between the chaos on the battlefield and the shock of finding Chrissa and her warrior dead, there will hardly be any Grants left in the castle. When King Edward takes Stirling Castle, the English will kill all the savage Scots, and then we can overtake Grant Castle and the sword. Those gemstones and the wealth in the cellars of the castle will make us quite wealthy. We'll leave the bodies outside the gates, and when they're discovered, we can sneak in and let our men in through the back."

"Perfect," the man said with satisfaction. "What a wonderful turn of events that we learned of the sapphire sword. I was pleased to be in the right place to learn of it. We don't have to locate the two ingrates now. They're weak enough that they'll not go far, and I believe one of them was injured. Maybe we'll be lucky and the wolves will take care of them for us. Why not watch the battle and return to look for them afterward?"

She turned to the guards traveling with them, giving Chrissa a view of her face. The man still had his back to her. "We must leave now. Hurry."

Chrissa's hands were shaking.

The woman was Drostan's mother, and apparently she intended to kill her own son, and Chrissa too. She didn't recognize the man, but it was clear their wickedness knew no bounds. They'd fashioned a plan to get the Ramsays and Grants to attack one another.

They had to stop it from happening.

She gathered their things, returning them to the saddlebags before she tried to awaken Drostan. How she prayed he would wake up.

"Drostan?" she said leaning down. She lay down next to him so she could whisper in his ear. "Please, love. Wake up." Shaking his shoulder just a wee bit, she kissed his cheek twice.

His eyes opened slowly, evidence of his weakness, but they did open. She gave him time to adjust, and he turned to her, his hand coming up to cup her face. "Chrissa? Where are we? Were we taken captive again?"

"Nay. We killed Percy and the two guards and we slept out here. But we have to go. I'll explain on the way, but they aim to take over Grant Castle. Please. I'll help you get up."

"Will you help me take a pish because I really have to go," he said as he pushed himself up onto his elbows. "Just teasing you. But I surely am in a weakened state." He tried to stand on his own but stopped as soon as he put weight on his leg. He looked down and cursed. "I forgot, but 'tis coming back to me now. I'll need your help after all. More of your help, I should say. You sewed it up and stayed with me?"

"Aye, please hurry. We'll talk later." She helped him out of their protected area to a spot near a tree so he could lean against it to do what he had to. They made the short walk to the burn, and she sat him down on a rock. "Here. I had one hunk of cheese left that was hidden in my saddlebag. Eat. I'll get everything on the horses, then we must go."

He splashed water on his face while she returned to their spot to gather their furs and plaids. "I think you'll have to ride with me. We can leave your horse here. There will be plenty where we're going."

She'd thought him too weak to stand by himself, let alone move, so it caught her by surprise when he led the horse to a large boulder so they could both mount. Surely that was a good sign, wasn't it?

"Can you mount from here?" she asked after she climbed on.

Drostan struggled, but he managed to climb up behind her on the horse.

"You're sure you can hang on?"

"I'll be fine," he said, though his voice sounded strained, "but I have no idea where we are. Where are we going in such a hurry?"

"We're following the woman who says she is your mother. I'll explain more once we're moving."

They didn't make it far before she heard horses. She reigned in their mount, fearing the worst, and then she heard Alick's bird call. At least, she swore it sounded like him.

She tugged on the reins of her horse, tears in her eyes.

"What is it?" Drostan asked.

"'Twas my brother's call. I think they're ahead." She pushed on, flying through the trees, praying it was indeed her brother. When they finally broke through the woods into a clearing, the most pleasing sight she could have ever asked for sat ahead—her brother and her cousins gathered in a huddle on their horses.

"Chrissa? 'Tis really you?" Alick started to dismount, but she held her hand up and said, "Aye, 'tis me. But we don't have any time to waste. Just tell me where the Grants and Ramsays are meeting."

"Gallow Hill. Why?"

"I'll explain quickly, then we must go. I overheard two of our enemies talking after we got away. They were headed to Gallow Hill." Something dawned on her. "Where are Dyna and Alasdair? Are they hale?"

Alick explained, "They've gone back to bring John along after he was to meet with Grandsire. We're to meet them at Gallow Hill with Connor."

Reassured they were fine, she continued, "The group has two motives: one is to see the Ramsays and Grants massacre each other at Gallow Hill and the second is to overtake Grant Castle."

"They're fools," Els scoffed. "The Grants and Ramsays would never take up arms against each other."

Derric asked, "And why take you two captive? What purpose did that serve?"

"They stole us because they wanted information about where the clans were to meet. Their plan was to kill us and then draw the warriors outside the castle so they could overtake Grant Castle. They believed it possible because they think the Englishmen will massacre the Scots at Stirling." Chrissa gulped, her heartbeat telling her they needed to get moving before they were too late. "They also sent false messages to both sides, hoping to trick the clans into fighting. Their own men will be in the middle to start a battle. We have to get there before anything happens."

Derric whistled and Els said, "Shite. Clever attempt though 'twill fail miserably."

"Wait until Alasdair hears this one," Alick said, shaking his head. "Let's move on to Gallow Hill. Chisholm, can you make it? You don't look well."

"I'll be fine," Drostan said. "Move, lass. How long a ride?"

"I'm not certain, but I think I know exactly where 'twill happen," she said, taking her horse into a nice canter to see if he could hold up.

Alick passed her, taking the lead. "I know where we're going." He glanced back at her, giving her a weighing look. "You wanted to be in the middle of everything, lass. I hope you're ready."

She did too.

CHAPTER TWENTY-THREE

EVERYTHING WAS MOVING TOO QUICKLY for Drostan's sluggish mind. The last thing he recalled was retreating into the copse of trees after his injury. He and Chrissa had decided they'd been set up. Their captors had played a sick game on them. But why?

And hadn't he sent Chrissa off to summon help? He felt sure he remembered that.

Leaning over her shoulder as they rode, he asked, "Tell me again why they took us captive?"

"Aye, 'twas part of their plan. They hope to see many Grants killed, between this confrontation and the battle at Stirling Castle on Midsummer's Day. We are the third part of the plan. They intend to kill us both and leave our bodies outside Grant land to draw out the survivors, giving their men the chance to come over the back curtain wall and overtake the castle."

"And my mother is one of them."

"Aye, and she seemed familiar with the layout of the keep. Did she work inside?"

"She worked in the kitchens for years." It sickened him to his core that his own mother was involved in an attempt to take down all of the Grants. Apparently, she wanted the entire castle for herself. What would the lairds do when they find out? Would he be thrown out? Shunned?

"Well, your own mother wants you dead, so please keep that in mind when you see her."

"Who's her accomplice?"

"I don't know. His voice was unfamiliar to me, but he seemed to think he could get into the castle easily. The guards wouldn't stop him, he said. He plans to let your mother and their warriors over the back wall. Did she take a lover before she left your father? Mayhap he was a Grant warrior who would be accepted back in."

He shook his head. "Not to my knowledge. I don't recall her being overly friendly with anyone." He stopped, thinking over her words. His mind was moving slowly but he had to force himself to stay awake and alert. Do what he could to help. "What about DeFry? Could it have been him?"

"I suppose 'tis possible, but I think not. I didn't recognize the man's voice, and I think I would have recognized DeFry's."

"And Percy's dead, if I recall correctly."

"Aye, he'll not be bothering us again."

About an hour later, Alick and Chrissa both slowed their horses. Chrissa pointed, "They should be on the other side of this hill. I heard them mention this place. Gallow Hill is a common place for the Ramsays to meet with the Grants."

Drostan pointed off to the side. "Mayhap 'twould be best for us to approach the hill through those trees. I don't hear sounds of battle, which is good, but we also don't wish to run into the pair of villains who are out to kill us. Did you not say they'd have their own men here?"

"Go through there," Derric said, pointing to a pass. "'Tis the best way."

She nodded, taking her horse slowly through it. As they made their way through the trees, she gasped at the sight in front of them. A sea of warriors in red plaids, some standing, some on horseback, covered the landscape, banners being held near the front of the line. She could make out her uncle Jamie in front.

Warriors began to shout, pointing at the warriors in blue plaids as they headed toward them. "Look, Alick. The Ramsays are arriving. And another set of warriors will sneak in between the two sides. We have to stop them."

They continued toward the front of the line and ran into Uncle Connor. "You are hale, Chrissa? Your mother will be pleased."

"We're weak but will be fine. I overheard the villains talking. They admitted to sending missives meant to trick our clans to attack each other. We were set up to try to kill the Ramsays. Is Uncle Jamie in charge? I must tell him."

Connor said, "Aye, Jamie's in front with Magnus. We'll stop this before it starts. You and Derric go to Jamie. Alick, Els, and I will go to Torrian and Lachlan."

"Go," Drostan said as she tugged on the reins of their horse and flew forward, heading straight for her uncle.

"Uncle Jamie! Uncle Jamie! Stop! Please listen to me."

Jamie Grant was chatting with Magnus, another of his men, though it seemed more like an argument. "Chrissa?" he said in bewilderment. "I've never been more relieved to see you. You are hale?"

"Aye, but listen to me, *please*."

"Just a moment. We have a serious situation here." He turned back to his second and said, "We'll not raise arms against them. I will not waiver from that."

Magnus barked, "You have to fight or they'll destroy us. It could be a ruse, but to not defend ourselves is asking for a massacre."

"They'll not attack us. I'll not raise arms against Clan Ramsay. No matter what the situation. The missive is probably not true anyway. I can tell from looking at those men, no matter how distant they are, that there's not an Englishman among them."

"What if 'tis a different clan in Ramsay plaids? The missive came from Robert the Bruce. You have to believe him."

"I don't," Jamie roared.

Chrissa dismounted and ran between the two men, shoving her uncle. "I overheard the conspirators talking about this. 'Tis a ruse, but they have two score men who will attack both clans to start a battle. They're here to fuel the fury."

"What?" Jamie and Magnus both stared at her in

disbelief. "What are you talking about?"

"The same people who kidnapped Drostan and me are trying to overtake Grant Castle. There is much more to their plan, but they spoke of this ruse. The missives were lies. They did not come from Robert the Bruce, but there are men here who will start killing your men if you don't defend yourselves. I know not how they're dressed."

"Magnus, gain your horse and go around to meet up with the Ramsay warriors. Tell them what we learned. Looks like Torrian, Lachlan, and Kyle are leading their group."

"No need," Chrissa said. "Alick, Uncle Connor, and Els are over there with them."

Magnus took off without a backward glance.

"Too late. It doesn't matter. What else can you tell me about them?" Jamie said.

"One of them is Drostan's mother. I don't know who the other man is, but their goal is to overtake the castle while our warriors are being slaughtered here and at Stirling Castle."

"In other words, they're counting on the English winning. That's their first mistake."

"I hope you're right. But you have to stop those men from striking our warriors down."

"Magnus will handle it. I've already given our men orders not to raise their swords against any Ramsays. Our warriors will know who to strike."

"And the Ramsays?" she asked. "Did Torrian say the same?"

"Our clanmates are over there," Uncle Jamie said. "If there's one thing you must learn in battle, 'tis to trust your clanmates."

Drostan, who had not yet spoken, said, "The answer to your prayers is coming this way."

"What?" Jamie asked. "Which way?"

"Alasdair, Dyna, and John are coming." He pointed to a line of riders, all dressed in black, entering the area between the two clans.

Jamie's eyes widened. "I know my vision isn't what it used to be, but is that truly John between Dyna and Alasdair? If so, I guess the sapphire sword finally has a new protector. I knew there was a special reason Avelina came with Logan. There's the reason."

"John?"

"Aye," Jamie said. "If my eyes don't deceive me, he's holding the sapphire sword right now. Papa gave me an inkling of what was to come, but didn't say it directly, which meant he didn't wish for everyone to know. But there's proof of it. Avelina brought it to your grandsire so he could choose the next bearer, and he must have made his decision."

Chrissa nodded, a smile crossing her face. "I recall Grandpapa's tales of this, though I didn't believe it to be true. I thought 'twas just a tale, but it really exists. 'Tis an odd size for a sword, though it fits him fine."

"The sapphire sword," Jamie whispered.

Dyna, John, and Alasdair rode toward them, the moment solemn. As they drew near, Alasdair said, "Avelina received a message after she delivered the sword to Grandsire. Said we would be needed here. A small group is trying to take out our two clans.

Chrissa, you and Drostan are hale?"

Chrissa nodded furiously. "There are two score men in hiding who plan to come out and start killing men from both clans, hoping to initiate a clan war based on the false missives they've already received."

"But they didn't count on us being such strong allies," Jamie said with ferocious determination. "They didn't realize that neither clan would raise a sword against the other."

Shouts carried to them and they followed the din. A group of men emerged from the far side of the forest, behind the first line of Ramsay warriors. They started attacking both sides. They wore plaids that were poor imitations of the Ramsay and Grant colors, easily identifiable to any true Scot.

John Alexander Grant lifted the sapphire sword into the sky at the same moment Dyna lifted her bow, and the Grants and Ramsays released their war whoops and went after the attackers. The sky lit up with lightning bolts, hitting nearby trees, killing enemies on horseback, and sending horses into a panic.

They fought the men easily, Dyna and Ashlyn's arrows taking several of them out before they could cause any trouble. Chrissa grabbed her bow and joined in, shooting at men she was sure didn't belong. Thunder roared through the area as more lightning bolts struck, hitting human targets as well as inanimate objects. But this was no natural lightning, for none of the Ramsays or Grants were struck.

The battle ended in a matter of minutes, eliciting cheers from both Clan Ramsay and Clan Grant, whose warriors met in the middle around the dead.

Torrian, Lachlan, and Kyle made their way over to the Grant side, Lachlan shouting, "I've never seen lightning fork out of the sky like that."

"Aye," Kyle agreed, "the power is fascinating to watch."

Connor looked at Jamie, quite serious, and asked, "You are hale? That display did not trigger any memories for you?"

Jamie shook his head. "Nay, I'm fine. I've been over that for a while now. Unless I happen to be the one at the highest points on a mountaintop, I can handle it."

Torrian came up and clasped Uncle Jamie's shoulder. "I don't know who was behind this trickery, but please know my warriors had instructions not to use their weapons against any Grant warriors."

"The same is true of our side," Jamie said. "Magnus got a wee bit nervous, thinking we were about to be slaughtered by a different clan wearing your plaids, but Chrissa came at just the right time."

"And do you know who wrote the missives?" Torrian asked.

"Nay, but we will find out. Chrissa, are you and Drostan traveling to Stirling with us?"

"We had planned to, but Drostan took an injury in captivity. He needs a healer more talented than I am."

"How did you get free?"

Chrissa glanced at Drostan and said, "We're still unsure. Someone left our cell unlocked, and we snuck out. We were followed by a small group led by a sheriff named Percy. We killed them before they could kill us, but Drostan lost quite a bit of blood. He isn't strong enough for battle, and I'm not sure that I am either. We ate little and slept less. I'd like to return to Grant Castle to tell them what to expect." She shot a glance at Drostan. "Drostan's mother is one of them."

Jamie asked, "Your mother? When was the last time you saw her? I thought she left years ago."

"She did," Drostan replied. "Apparently she has some other agenda now, working with some unsavory characters. We don't know who her accomplices are other than Percy, but he's gone. DeFry was there, also. Could he be a spy and be the one who left our cell unlocked?"

"Alasdair trusts DeFry. We'll have to be alert. I'm sorry to hear about your mother, but don't let her actions upset you. 'Twill not reflect badly on you at all."

Drostan let out an audible sigh of relief. Laird Jamie had no idea how much he appreciated that comment. "I suspect she'll go after my sire. I need to warn him."

"Aye, I understand." Jamie turned to Chrissa. "You're one of our finest archers. Go with Drostan and tell our family all that has transpired, but come join us once you do. The Bruce needs you. But Drostan, I'll not have you come with her. You need to stay home until your injury is healed. I want no dead warriors from Clan Grant for any reason."

Drostan hated the thought of sending Chrissa off to battle without him, but Jamie was right about everything. "Aye, I'm not capable of riding a horse into battle."

Chrissa gave him a swift hug, then Jamie lifted her onto her horse. Alasdair and the others were just joining them.

"Well done," Jamie said to the group. "Are you headed to Stirling?"

"Aye, we are," Alasdair replied.

Drostan managed to climb up behind Chrissa. "We'll take our leave. I may not be able to ride a horse into battle, but I can certainly use my sword when on my feet. Once I've improved, we have a score to settle with our captors, and I'll take pleasure in seeing it done. But not until after I see to my sire."

CHAPTER TWENTY-FOUR

CHRISSA COULDN'T HELP BUT SMILE at the reception they returned to at Grant Castle, the reception she'd always dreamed of having one day, but she hadn't expected it to happen so soon. Obviously they'd been missed. Plenty of guards manned the gate and the curtain wall, something else that pleased her. Once they reached the gates, the portcullis was raised, and cheering rose up all around them. Taking her horse inside the wall, she stopped at the gate. "Have you seen Drostan's mother?"

"Nay. And no one has entered that we don't know."

That small reassurance made her feel better. She took her horse directly to the stairs, where her parents stood waiting.

"You're hale, daughter?" her sire called out.

"Aye, Papa. Weak, hungry, dirty, and tired, but I'll be fine. Drostan didn't fare so well. He took an injury and lost quite a bit of blood." Drostan dismounted and nearly fell over, so her father helped her down.

She was pleased to see her father stood to anchor Drostan, whose skin was now pale and clammy. Anyone who looked at him would know he was struggling.

Her mother gave her a quick hug before shifting her attention to Drostan. "You need to go straight to the healer's chamber."

Drostan didn't say anything. He just stood still for a moment, apparently gaining his bearings. "I'll go as soon as my head stops spinning."

"Mama, I'll take him there. Follow along and I'll explain everything."

Her mother gave her a swift hug, then Chrissa looped her arm through Drostan's and said, "'Tis a chamber off the hall. You remember, do you not?"

He nodded, but first he turned to her father. "Watch for my mother. One of our captors was my mother, though I'm not convinced she'll follow me here."

Her father said, "Your mother's been gone a long time. Are you certain it was her? And why would she kidnap the two of you?"

"I saw her, Papa. It was his mother. I also heard them say why, but I'll explain in a few moments.

Fortunately, he accepted that her first concern was Drostan, because he said, "I'll make sure everyone is aware of the situation. We all knew her," Da said, walking off before Chrissa could tell him she already had.

They walked into the hall, conversation buzzing around them, eyes on them.

"Who else dared to steal you away?" Chrissa's mother asked. Plenty of fire danced in her gaze as she said it.

Grandsire sat in a chair by the hearth, but he stood abruptly from his chair as they neared him. Leaning on a stick of wood, he said, "Chrissa, you are unhurt? I can see with my own eyes that Chisholm is hurting. If you gained that injury protecting my lass, you have all of my gratitude, lad."

"Aye, Grandpapa, I'm fine. And he did protect me. Honestly, I'm too exhausted to speak of all that transpired," she said, hoping he wouldn't ask any more questions. She could feel her strength waning and couldn't imagine how Drostan was managing.

"Who? I want names, Chrissa. Tell me who, then go to the healer. Both of you."

"Grandsire, Percy and DeFry were there, along with a Drostan's mother. Drostan killed Percy, but someone unlocked our cell, basically setting us free. Our weapons and horses were waiting for us. Mayhap DeFry is loyal to the Scots after all? We don't know. But I overheard Drostan's mother scheming with a man whose voice I didn't recognize. He said he is known here well enough to gain access through the gates, but 'twas not DeFry. 'Tis the important part for now. I'll explain the rest later. We've already told Papa about Drostan's mother's involvement but keep watch."

Then she led Drostan into the chamber, where he fell into a chair. Her mother and Aunt Gracie came in right behind them. Aunt Gracie took one look at the two of them and said, "Chrissa, get some food for yourself first, then bring something for Drostan before I tend to his wound."

She kissed his forehead then left. Heading straight to the kitchens, she ran into her sire, who said, "Get what you need and meet us by the hearth." Meaning her grandsire.

She stepped into the kitchens, but she didn't make it very far before she saw a chair and tumbled into it. Bending at the waist, she held her head in her hands, letting the tears fall. They'd made it home, she and Drostan were both hale, and somehow they'd escaped captivity. It felt too good to be true, like a dream she wished to stay in.

But there was more.

She was in love with Drostan. Did he remember exchanging those words with her, or had he forgotten, like she'd forgotten their pledge to each other all those years ago? She hoped he did remember—she knew the moment would be burned into her brain forever. She mulled over all that had happened, finally working up the necessary motivation to find some food and goat's milk. After instructing a serving lass to bring the same to her mother in the healer's chamber, she made her way back to the hearth. The two men she loved dearly allowed her to sit and eat before they pressed her for anything.

Finally her father whispered, "You're in love with him, are you not?"

She just nodded, surprised he would ask her that question, but gratified he recognized the new closeness between them.

Grandsire said, "Are you getting married soon?"

He gave her a knowing look, but she shook her head. "Nay, he hasn't asked me, and we did not handfast."

Her father still arched a brow at her.

"Nay, we haven't yet." She blushed, but it was the right answer because she noticed her father let a breath out.

"Tell us everything, lass," Grandsire said.

She told the story as best she recalled it, including the part about the false missives to the two clans. That caused a few questions to be thrown at her. "Who would be that evil? That conniving?" her papa whispered.

Grandsire said, "Should be able to figure it out."

"How?" she asked.

"You said the man had familiarity with Clan Grant. Few around here know how to write. Maddie taught many of our people to read, but not as many are capable of writing. We didn't have the supplies."

Why hadn't she thought of that?

Her mother called her into the healing chamber about a half hour later. She hurried in, hoping they would deliver good news.

Drostan was dressed in clean clothing and looked much better. "Are you leaving for Stirling?" he asked.

"I'd like to head out on the morrow. Still two days until June four and twenty. Do you mind? Are you going to rest in here?" She sat down next to him while her mother and aunt cleaned up the chamber, then they exchanged a look and left.

"I need to see to my sire first."

"I can warn him, if you like. It may push you too far to go out there." Although she wasn't sure which Inan she would encounter—the kind, old-fashioned man, or the drunkard.

"I know, but I'll not rest until he's been warned about Mama. I'll not rest until I see him." His hand reached up to cup her cheek. "You look exhausted. You need to sleep."

A sudden fear bit into her. He'd been so ill… what if he didn't remember what had happened between them? What if he only remembered their argument? He ran a finger down her cheek. "I love you, too. I can read the worry on your face. The way you took care of me…and how awful I felt when we were so upset with each other…it made me realize how much you mean to me. Hopefully, when this is over, I'll speak with your sire to see if he'd accept my suit for your hand. I know I'm not of noble blood…"

"That does not matter, Drostan."

He lifted his gaze to hers and said, "I pray you're right, because you're the only one I want in my life. I'll ask him once the time is right, and I hope he'll approve of me." He brushed his hand across her cheek.

"Of course he will."

"I'll not believe it until I hear it. First, you need to sleep, then help the Scots win this battle. We need to have everything with Edward's son finished. Get the English out of Scotland so we can go on with our lives."

He kissed her lightly on the lips and said, "Go."

So she headed up to her chamber and changed into a night rail. To her surprise, she fell right asleep.

Drostan made his way slowly out of the healing chamber, thanking everyone for their help along the way. Alex Grant waved him over to a chair at the hearth, but he said, "With all due respect, I'd like to accept your offer upon my return. I'm sure Chrissa filled you in on all that has transpired, so I feel the need to visit my sire first."

"Understood," Alex said. "Would you like anyone to go with you in case you run into anything you aren't suspecting?"

"Nay, I'll be fine. My thanks to you."

He hobbled out the door, not surprised to be greeted by Hendrie and Sky.

"My lord, I've taken good care of your pet." He held Sky out for Drostan to pick her up so he did, briefly, though he knew he couldn't take her with him. The last thing he wanted was to drop her by accident. She was still so small.

"Wee Sky," he chuckled as she licked his cheeks. "I see you missed me. Many thanks to you, Hendrie, for taking such good care of her."

"You have a warrior's wound, my lord?" Hendrie stared with huge eyes at the bandage around his leg.

"Aye, seems that I do." He thought of his father and how a wound had ended his warrior days. Would the same happen to him? Nay, he refused to believe he'd allow something to change his whole being. Even if he couldn't fight, he could still train warriors. The thought made him wonder why his father had given up so easily.

The answer seemed quite simple. He'd always blamed his parents' troubles on his father's drinking, but perhaps he'd gotten it wrong. He'd certainly gotten *her* wrong.

"Did you hear that Sky was the one who found you, my lord?" Hendrie said, bringing his attention back to the moment.

"What?" He rubbed the pup's ear, and she promptly gave him a wee yip of approval. "Did you find me, pup?"

"Aye, Astra and I searched for you, then we told her cousins where you were so they all went after you. We helped. I'm sure of it." His face beamed with pride.

"Many thanks to you. I cannot wait to hear more details, but you must save the story for when Chrissa is with us." He rubbed the scruff of beard on his chin while his gaze searched the area. "Have you seen my sire?"

"He came to the warriors' camp the other day. He kept talking about your bravery and your sword skills. Said he didn't fear for you. He was certain you'd escape and save Chrissa too."

"My sire said all of that? Are you sure?"

"Aye, he wouldn't stop talking about it."

Drostan couldn't have been more surprised. "Hendrie, I need to go visit with him, and he's not fond of dogs. Would you mind hanging on to Sky for a wee bit longer?"

"I'll take good care of her, my lord. I'll be in the lists. She likes to be around people."

Hendrie took off and Drostan smiled. He was a fine lad, for certes. Hobbling out to his sire's cottage was not an easy ordeal. Surprised at how quickly he tired, he wiped the sweat from his brow and continued. He had to warn his father about his mother. She would come for him, of that much Drostan was certain. His father had verbally abused her for years…and she was not the sort of person who'd let such a thing go.

His father wasn't a perfect man. Mayhap he wasn't even a good one, but he'd stayed with Drostan. His mother had left without a word, something that had hurt more than he cared to admit. Now he understood the truth: he was fortunate she'd left. Although his father was a miserable drunk, he was no traitor. Nor could he casually talk about murdering innocents.

He knocked on the door, but there was no answer. He opened it and stepped inside, waiting for his eyes to adjust to the darkness. "Papa?" He didn't see him in the main part of the hut, so he moved back into the area that held the bed, not surprised to see his father sprawled across it.

Probably passed out from too much to drink.

"Papa?" he called out softly.

No answer.

When he moved over to the bed, he noticed the blood on his father's tunic. Heart racing, he touched his hand to the man's neck to look for evidence of a beating heart. There was a small pulse there, not strong enough to reassure him.

"Oh, Papa," he muttered, kneeling next to him and listening for any breathing. "Papa? What happened?"

Had his mother killed him so callously? If so, she was more of a monster than his sire had ever been.

"Drostan? Sorry…so sorry… proud of you, son."

"Papa, who did this to you? Was it Mama?" His father's eyes blinked several times, but then he nodded slowly. "Mama. Be careful." He pointed over Drostan's shoulder.

He pivoted so quickly a stab of pain shot through him from the rapid movement on his wounded leg. The sensation was so overpowering, he fell onto a stool, massaging the muscles that were revolting against Chrissa's tight, careful stitches and the sudden change in movement.

No one was there, so he turned back to his father. "Papa, hang on. I'll run for the healer. We'll get you sewn up. Please."

But he could sense the life force leaving his sire's body, could see the blood pooling on the bed beneath him. "Papa?"

He felt for the pulse in his neck again, but it was gone. He hung his head over his father, fighting the tears that threatened to drench his face.

The door opened and his mother stood there, a dagger in her hand.

"Did you clean it so my sire's blood isn't on the weapon you use to kill me?"

She didn't look anything like he remembered.

Oh, it was her, but something in her face had changed. Twisted. And he no longer recognized the woman he'd known. She was thinner than before, too, and she'd changed her hair, wearing it up on top of her head instead of in a plait down her back.

"I knew you'd come back. I had one more thing to do with my life before it was complete: kill you both." She came forward, still brandishing her dagger.

"Why me, Mama? I never hurt you. If anyone was hurt, 'twas me. How could you desert your own child without a word?" And that was the least of what she'd done. He was so upset that he wished to throttle her, leave her for the vultures, yet he struggled. She was his *mother.* Wasn't she supposed to love and protect him?

Did she ever do that? a small voice asked in his head.

He flashed to the memory of Alexander Grant telling stories to his grandbairns at night by the hearth. Of Kyla Grant fighting for her daughter, coaching her, and always, always trying to do what was best for her.

His parents had never been like that. Neither of them.

"Nay," his mother sneered, "because I knew you'd end up just like him. Lads grow up in the image of their sire. By killing you, I'll save your wee lassie the struggle of living with a man who does nothing but drown in his ale every day, ignore her wishes, and force her to live in a cold hut in the mountains. I have a better life now. I'm going to live in London once I get my riches. And I will get them. The Grants don't deserve their wealth."

That lit a fire in him and he forced himself to stand. "'Tis where you're wrong. I've never mistreated a woman before, and I never will. But you don't care about me, do you? You're a heartless bitch."

She came toward him with the knife in front of her. He feared she'd try to use it, but she didn't. "You don't know anything about me."

"I know you left without saying a word to your only bairn."

She sauntered toward him, but then she did something he hadn't expected. "You're right, I did. Here"—she held the hilt of the dagger out to him—"stab me for what I did to you. Go ahead. Do it."

She held the hilt of the dagger out to him, but he refused, recognizing it as a symbol of his family and all he wanted to leave behind. "Nay, I don't want it."

"Take it. Hurt me the way your father did. Go ahead. Take it."

He shook his head and held his hands up. "Nay, I'm not like you or Papa. I'm not going to do something I'll regret for the rest of my life like you have."

She tipped her head back, laughing convulsively.

"You killed a drunk, Mama, but I'm a Grant warrior? Do you really think you can hold me down to stab me?"

She closed her eyes and laughed harder. If he'd

been looking for a chance, he had it. He could have taken the dagger, killed her, and ended this farce, but he couldn't do it.

When her laughter died down, she brushed at the side of one eye. "You make me cry with laughter. I knew you couldn't do it. You're a weakling, just like your father. You'd never be able to kill me." She reached for the knife and picked it back up with intent.

A figure stood in front of the doorway brandishing a dagger in her hand.

Chrissa.

His mother spun around to stare at her. "Who the hell are you? If you take another step, I'll kill him." Recognition dawned in her eyes. "Ah, 'tis you. You've always had a lot of airs for a useless lass. You're nothing." She spat at Chrissa's feet.

Chrissa tipped her head and said, "I'm the woman he loves, and I adore him just the way he is. I'm pleased he can't kill his own mother, his own blood."

"You two deserve each other. Neither of you have the gumption to hurt me." She picked up the dagger and flicked it back and forth in her hand. "Who wishes to be first?"

"Mayhap he can't bring himself to fight you," Chrissa said, "but I can." She flung her dagger and it embedded in the side of the woman's neck, blood spurting everywhere.

She was dead in seconds.

CHAPTER TWENTY-FIVE

CHRISSA RAN TO DROSTAN, THROWING herself into his arms. "Forgive me, but she wanted to kill us both… She was going to…"

"Hush," he said, setting his fingers against her lips. "She was right. I couldn't do it unless she went for you, but she would have killed me first, then killed you. You did the right thing."

He hugged her tightly while Chrissa fought the need to cry. "Your sire?"

"She killed him. Stabbed him while he was drunk. He was still alive when I got here. He…he told me that he was sorry." He stopped to gather himself, a whistle of air traveling though his pursed lips. "He actually said he was proud of me. Words I've not heard often."

"You must be devastated. You lost your mother and your father on the same day. Drostan, I'm so sorry."

He pulled back and kissed her, a tender, loving kiss that nearly brought her to her knees. Then he kissed her forehead and said, "Go. I'll walk you to the keep so we can inform everyone of what happened. In the morn, you must gather your things and go to Stirling to support our king. If I could go with you, I would, but I would be more of a hindrance."

"Before we left for King Robert's camp, you wanted me to stay back. You said you'd be too worried. Why not now?"

"Because I believe in you. I've seen the way you've dealt with everything, from those fools trying to turn our clan against the Ramsays to the way you just protected me when I should have protected you."

"You did protect me," she said, cupping his cheeks. "You saved me from Sheriff Percy. We got away together. We can do anything together. When we're both hale. I wish you could go with me, but my thanks for understanding why I must do this." She kissed him, long and slow, and then pulled back. "I love you. I'll miss you terribly, but I'm going to do as you suggested. I'll leave on the morrow and should arrive by nightfall. I'm going to sleep and will rise before dawn. Come, let's go back to the keep."

They made their way back to the castle, saying little to anyone. Drostan moved so slowly that she worried he wouldn't make it all the way back, but she stayed by his side, knowing she'd never wish to leave him again.

Going to Stirling without him would be difficult, but she would do it. And then she would focus on their relationship. They needed time to get to know one another in a different way, and that she looked forward to, without a doubt.

The serving lass brought fresh water and linens to his chamber, so she helped him clean up, then settled in bed, spooned in front of him. She didn't care what her mother said, she would not leave him this night. The sound of his heartbeat soothed her more than anything could at this time.

It was a sound to be treasured.

When Chrissa arrived at New Park, she was pleased to see so many warriors had gathered to support their king. No one questioned them since they wore Grant plaids, and they were directed over to a group near the back.

"Grants and Ramsays fight in the group with King Robert."

She and the score of guards she traveled with made it to their group in a short time. They'd brought several sacks of food stuffs, so she took the one she'd gathered over to the group where her cousins stood.

"Chrissa, welcome!" Maggie called out. "We need another archer. We'll be fighting from that hill over there on the morrow."

The group was arranged in a circle around a small fire. Alasdair, Emmalin, John, Els, Alick, Derric, and Dyna. A few Ramsays sat with them too: Sorcha, Maggie and her husband Will, and Molly.

"Torrian and Jamie are with King Robert," Dyna explained. "Their warriors are in his band of fighters. Loki brought his warriors, and he is working with the schiltron of spearmen along with Tormod and Cailean. There are four bands of fighters."

"How many total?"

"Around six thousand at last count. There are four sets of spearmen who will go first on the offensive, then a couple of Scottish brigades, then the light cavalry. King Robert is leading the Highlanders and they will go after the cavalry. Anyone who hasn't trained will be last to fight, if necessary."

"So where are the Highland Swords fighting?"

"All the Scotsmen who haven't trained with Robert are in the group behind the hill. We're to lead it. He's saving us for last."

Molly asked, "How is Drostan?"

Chrissa passed out the loaves of bread and cheese she'd brought, then passed around the sack of apples before she sat down on a log and explained what had happened.

Alasdair asked, "So his mother was part of kidnapping the two of you?"

"Aye, she was the one who planned to leave our bodies outside the keep after the battle. The plan was to draw everyone out of the castle so their men could come over the back wall. I've informed Grandsire, and with Drostan's help, I'm sure they'll devise something to stop the bastards."

"You don't think his mother's death will stop it?" Els spoke with his mouth full, which made her laugh, but he got his message across.

"Nay, I heard a man with her, a stranger, but he could be anyone. If you have any ideas, please let me know." She went over what she'd overheard, but they had no suggestions.

"So we battle on the morrow?" she asked.

"Aye," Alick said. "You better stay with the archers. There are too many strangers here who'd be happy to find a wife. They'd love to steal you and take you home to the Highlands."

She glanced at Maggie to see if he was joking. Her Ramsay cousin shrugged. "I can't argue with him. I've seen many who would do just that. Stay with the group. We'll fire whenever we have clear shots."

Alick added, "Our king had an easy time of defeating de Bohun, one of Edward's best men, with just his hand axe last eve. He was the first to advance, but King Robert took him out with one blow. We're going to win this."

They continued to discuss the situation and their chances of victory, but she tired quickly. "Where are you sleeping, Dyna?" she asked at last. "I'll sleep near you."

"Right here, once the fire's out."

Sorcha and Molly nodded to her. "We'll huddle together. Right here," said Molly. "I'm ready to sleep, too." The men were quieting down.

As she drifted off, she thought of Drostan.

Drostan buried his father while other men from the village buried his mother. He just couldn't bring himself to do it. At his request, they'd buried her body deep in the woods. She didn't deserve to be buried with the clan.

His leg still pained him, but he wouldn't let it hold him back, so he made his way up to the keep to speak with Alex Grant. He found him seated near the hearth, lost in thought. "My lord, I'd like to ask for your help. While my mother is gone, there is still someone else out there who could be planning to take over your castle. We don't know how the battle will end, so we should prepare."

"Do you have any idea who it could be?"

"I have some thoughts. But, more importantly, I'd like to set up a device that will guarantee their failure. Would you mind strategizing with me?"

Alex Grant smiled and said, "Naught would give me more pleasure. We'll fix his arse. He won't be taking over our castle, no matter who wins Stirling Castle."

The following morn, Chrissa followed the team of archers over to their spot overlooking Bannock Burn. Part of King Robert's plan was to prevent the English from being able to move in all directions. They intended to restrict them to two directions, which would make it much easier to defeat them.

King Robert started the day with a ceremony to knight many who were to go into battle, then commanded the banners be hoisted up in full view for the English to see. His brother Edward was in charge of the schiltrons, and they headed toward Bannock Burn, the English not far away. After they knelt in prayer, they went on the offensive, something that took the English by surprise. Robert the Bruce had used schiltrons of tight spearmen before, but never in the offensive.

The Highland Swords team hung back with the archers, behind the small folk. Chrissa's uncles had been called up to Bruce's Highlander Brigades, the group that would go after the schiltrons and one other Scottish brigade.

They found a vantage point to watch the battle, in a section of the forests so they'd not be easy targets. The schiltrons were already killing many English. Although Robert had primarily used the tactic defensively, from what she'd heard, it was proving equally successful as a form of offense. "Look," Maggie said, "Edward is putting his archers in place against our schiltrons."

The English archers came from the back of the field and started nocking their arrows, shooting wildly. Robert countered by sending his brigade out. The archers tried but failed to take out the brigade.

Derric rubbed the palms of his hands together with delight. "King Robert will be smiling just now. He'd tell you that if you could see the whites of the Englishmen's eyes, they'd be turning yellow. They're losing and they don't know what to do next."

Screams of death and the grunts of battle carried over the land. Chrissa had somehow thought it would be different. She'd assumed, at least, that the battle would be more difficult. Instead, it seemed like the English were giving up.

They were running away.

King Robert waved his sword over his head and gave a signal to Derric, "Bring out your archers. Kill the bastards!"

Derric helped the team of archers get into position in the spot they'd chosen prior to the battle. Some climbed behind trees while others hid behind boulders. The battle raged on. It was sobering to see Scots fall beside the English, but the English were dying much more quickly.

One hour passed, then another, and the fighting continued. Derric's face hard with purpose, he ran down to the main line.

"Corbett, where are you going?" Dyna called out.

"Going to move this battle along. I can see our men tiring. 'Tis time for us to join it, whether our king wishes to admit it or not."

But something stopped Derric. He froze at the movement behind him, so he turned around to watch the youngest lad in the group.

John stood up, a look of alarm on his face.

"What's wrong?" Alasdair asked.

"Something's wrong," he said, glancing down at his sword. He'd had a hand on the hilt. The next moment he started running toward his horse. "This way," he called over his shoulder. "I can sense something really evil…"

"Mount up, Highland Swords," Alasdair shouted, already following his son. "We're following John." No one objected. They all knew the sword was powerful.

"I'm coming too," Chrissa insisted. After everything they'd been through, she needed to see this through to the end.

"We'll stay back with the archers," Maggie said, waving them onward, Sorcha and Emmalin behind her.

By the time they were all mounted and moving, John was already a distance ahead of them. Alasdair was the first to ride after him, followed by Derric, Dyna, Chrissa, Alick, and Els.

They rode for nearly ten minutes before John finally slowed his horse. It didn't take long for Chrissa to figure out why. Twenty or so Englishmen were dragging King Robert toward a tree stump. Although there were thousands of Scots in the area, none of the other Scots could be of help to him here.

Only them.

One of the English soldiers walked forward, brandishing a large sword, while a few others pushed Robert the rest of the way toward the stump, his hands bound behind him. "We'll end this fight by bringing your head out on a pike," the swordsman said. "Then King Edward will be recognized as the true King of Scotland."

They planned to behead King Robert.

Chrissa's heart leapt into her throat as she rode toward them. Would they be too late? John was almost upon them. Would the English bastards kill him too? She slowed her horse and reached for an arrow, just in case.

The look on King Robert's face told her he had

no fear. "Kill me if you wish, but you'll not silence my brethren!"

They forced him to his knees, two of the men doing their best to force his head onto the stump while the man lifted his sword. The entire group was so focused on what was happening with Robert the Bruce that they didn't notice their arrival until they were nearly upon them.

Then John had ridden into full view. He was only a short distance away from the Englishmen. Lifting his sword into the air, he said, "Free your prisoner."

The Englishmen turned to look at them. Several of them laughed at the small lad on horseback with a sword held over his head.

"John, be careful!" Alasdair shouted. They were almost upon him, but if Chrissa had learned anything from the past several days, it was that terrible things could happen quickly. John was alone for a short time until they were close enough to assist him.

"Free your prisoner," John repeated, his tone lower now.

The ground began to shake, and a bolt of lightning ripped through the sky.

One man yelled, "Kill him quickly before it's too late."

But the swordsman had blanched. "I'm not killing him after that happened. Didn't you feel the ground beneath your feet?"

The other man stepped forward, raising his sword. "Then I'll see it done. Get his head back over the stump!"

The people holding Robert had released him in their shock, but they reached for him again. John let out the Grant war whoop, his bellow surprisingly loud, and brought his sword down, pointing it at the swordsman who had just raised his sword again, readying a strike at the Scot's king. A bolt of lightning struck him in the chest, and the sword tumbled out of his hands before he crumpled to the ground.

The other Englishmen began to yell, some running, some hiding, a few coming at them ready to battle.

John's sword moved from one man to the next, all coming toward them, striking each of them down. Dyna nocked an arrow and shouted, "Chrissa, shoot. Some are turning back to come at us."

Chrissa hit two men who'd spun around to attack while Dyna struck three. John's sword shot out another bolt of lightning that caused the three men holding the king to go airborne before landing on their backs, dead.

Alasdair and Derric dismounted, chasing some of the remaining English down. Then two of the soldiers mounted their horses and headed straight for John, but Alick and Els, still on horseback, took them out before they even got close.

When the English force all lay dead on the ground, the group stopped, panting as they secured the area. Derric raced over and helped King Robert to his feet. "'Tis the last time I try to take a pish in private," the king muttered.

Everyone turned to stare at John.

Chrissa couldn't believe all she'd seen. John had stopped a group of Englishmen from beheading King Robert. What would have happened if they hadn't arrived in time? All would have been lost.

"You are hale?" Derric asked the king.

"I'm fine, thanks to the Highland Swords." He strode over to stand in front of John's horse. "Who are you, lad? And what kind of sword do you hold? 'Tis quite special."

John, clearly shaken by all that transpired, shook his head, unable to speak.

Alasdair moved over to stand next to him. "John is my son and great-grandson to Alexander Grant. This is his first battle, so please allow him a moment." He looked up at his son, patting his thigh. "Well done."

John, who still looked incapable of words, lowered his sword and returned it to its sheath.

"John, many thanks to you and your group. You saved my life. Say whatever 'tis you'd like and 'twill be yours."

John said, "I do have a request."

"Just name it, John Grant."

John took a deep gulp before his gaze scanned the area. "I wish for no one to repeat what they saw here. This must stay a secret. 'Twould not be wise to let anyone know the English were able to reach you."

Chrissa dismounted and moved closer so she could hear everything. She could see the pride in Alasdair's eyes at what his son had requested. She understood exactly why he'd said what he did, but would everyone else?

King Robert looked at Alasdair and nodded, a sly smile crossing his face. "You have a wise lad, Alasdair."

"Wise indeed," Dyna agreed with a nod.

If word got out that John held the sapphire sword, they'd be attacked many times over. They likely wouldn't reach the castle with the sword still in their possession. John apparently wasn't willing to divulge that information to King Robert, thus guaranteeing its fate was in the hands of their clan only.

"Consider it done. I'll not speak of this event, and I order everyone here to make the same vow."

"I will take that vow, except I must share it with my grandsire," John said.

King Robert gave him a slight bow. "Accepted." He moved over to a horse and said, "May I take yours, Corbett?"

"Aye, I'll ride with my wife."

The group headed back toward the camp, and Derric and Dyna broke off from the rest of them to escort the king back to the battlefield, since the sounds carried on. They returned to the group with both horses. Much as they all wished to wave their arms in victory, they could not. They'd vowed not to mention what had just transpired.

They'd done the unimaginable. They'd saved the king from certain death. But there was no time to dwell on it.

When they arrived close to the battle, Chrissa

caught bits and pieces of a conversation between Derric and King Robert, the gist of it being that King Robert wanted everyone fighting. He would hold nothing back after what just transpired.

Then Derric announced with a wave of his sword, "Our turn. The small folk and the Highland Swords will finish this."

Their turn had come.

He charged over to the large group of Highlanders on foot and yelled, "'Tis time to show them what you're made of. Kill the English!" Then he waved on and the Scots tore over the hill. Derric glanced at John and said, "Mount up. Lead the way with that sword."

John said, "I'm ready."

They mounted, nearly ready to go, when John pointed. "Look, many of the English are running."

Indeed they were. Had the sight of the Highlanders on foot been too much for them? "'Tis your cue, lad. Take your sapphire sword and send the rest of them home," Alasdair said. His eyes shone with pride.

They mounted and followed John out behind the force of Highlanders. Once they were all on the field, Alick, Els, and Alasdair yelled the Grant war whoop while John held the sapphire sword up, pointing it to the heavens above.

The ground shook, tossing some English into the air, but the onslaught continued. Lightning flashed on the battlefield, taking out English, as the Highland Swords rushed forward, their swords ably cutting down everyone they could see.

John and his sapphire sword shone above all others as he led the group, his sword lighting up with each bolt of lightning.

What followed was a massive display of might that sent the English running. Chrissa nocked one arrow after another, sending arrows out over the fighting Highlanders, making sure she didn't hit any Scots.

The battle was long and hard, but each moment brought them closer to victory, and before they knew it, the entire force of the English turned tail and ran. The Scottish force was so powerful the Englishmen began to jump into streams, hoping they'd picked one that would carry them to safety.

Instead, many drowned.

King Edward did escape, but his fighting group was devastated, many of his barons and nobleman killed by the onslaught, even though they greatly outnumbered the Scots.

The battle was done and the Scots were victorious.

CHAPTER TWENTY-SIX

THE CELEBRATION ON THE SCOT'S side continued well into the night. Still, it was not all a celebration. Many of those who'd fought in the thick of battle were so exhausted they fell asleep where they landed. Others were searching for their missing comrades.

Chrissa wandered through the dead with Alick and Els, looking for any Grant bodies they could bury or take home for burial on Grant land. The task was more gruesome than she expected so she forced herself to carry on with her cousins. It was an important task, but her stomach threatened to turn at the sight of so many dead bodies.

This was a part of battle she'd never given much thought to before, and she doubted she'd ever forget it. Horrifying yet sobering, she wouldn't be discussing this part with anyone. She was bending down to turn one man's face over when she froze. A familiar voice, ten body lengths away from her. She was certain it was the same man she'd overheard speaking with Drostan's mother.

The traitor. The villain who'd come up with the plot to have Clan Grant massacre Clan Ramsay. She stood slowly, her knees knocking with the force of the rage that coursed through her.

Her brother touched her shoulder. Speaking in an undertone, he said, "Do not say a word or he'll know you're on to him. I hear several voices, but I think I can guess which one is sending shivers through you. 'Tis verra important for neither of us to react. I'll finish here, and you go speak with John. Tell him 'tis time to put our plan into motion."

Alick was right, of course, so she swallowed her rage and walked away, heading straight for their small area in the camp, well hidden in the trees.

When she arrived, John was packing up items while he chewed on an apple.

"John, he's here."

"Is he?" He took one more bite and tossed the apple to her. "I'll plant the sword just where we planned. On that large boulder near the entrance to our camp. You agree?"

"Aye," she said, catching the apple and taking two bites before she tossed the rest into the fire they had built.

Molly's eyes widened. "You found him?"

"Aye, now we must be patient."

Maggie chuckled, covering her mouth. "Oh, I do hope to be there when this bastard gets caught."

"Oh, we'll all be there. 'Twill happen right on Grant land, in front of everyone." Which meant Drostan would be there to see the bastard caught, too.

She couldn't wait.

Chrissa and John headed back to Grant land, along with the rest of the Grant contingency, Alasdair just ahead of them talking with Els.

"Do you think 'twill work?" John asked excitedly.

"Aye, he took it. I can't wait to get back and catch him in the act."

Before the battle, they'd secured a small sword from the Grant armorer. Similar to the sapphire sword in size, it was a stunning weapon, although not of the quality of the sapphire sword. Still, to someone who didn't know the difference, it was a passable fake. Grandsire had come up with the idea.

Sure enough, the sword John had left on the rock outside their camp had been taken. The bait was in their enemy's hand, and if he did as they suspected, he'd take it back to Grant Castle, thinking he could use the weapon's power to secure the castle. They'd left camp early, before daylight, wanting to get home in time to catch the villain in his treasonous act. John had left the false sword where he could steal it while Chrissa and John slept.

"You're sure he was the one you overheard?"

"Aye, absolutely."

They rode on in silence for a few moments, and John was the one who broke it. Without going into any great detail, he said, "I cannot believe this battle was so successful. I think 'twill be talked about for years to come."

"I hope you're right," she said. "I hope 'tis really the end of the incessant plague upon our people. King Edward needs to stop and give us the freedom we've requested. We are capable of managing our own affairs."

"Aye, I'm sure 'tis so. 'Twill be called the Battle of Bannock Burn," said John. "I'm quite sure 'twill be talked about for decades as the battle that finally defeated Edward II. I've listened to Papa, Grandsire, and all the others speak of so many battles, but this one was different. The amount of time it took, the number involved, the strength of King Robert's different groups…"

"And the spectral swords?"

"Aye, but the power was hardly noticed in the middle of the battle. What will be remembered is how the English ran as soon as the Highlanders, or the small folk as some called us, came across the hill. That was a sight to see. I can't wait to tell Grandsire all about it."

"And I can't wait to see our enemy caught."

Drostan waited in the great hall for the group to return from Stirling. Word had already returned to them that Edward had run home with his tail between his legs, though not until after a long battle. He prayed Chrissa and the other Grants were all right.

The first group arrived and he hurried out into the courtyard, eager to see the group that had returned first. If not for his wound, he'd have gone to the stables, but he'd already been sewn up twice and didn't wish to endure it a third time. To his surprise, Sheriff DeFry and Father Dowall were the first two to approach the keep.

Alex came out the door, waiting not far from him.

DeFry strode directly to him while the priest went past him to greet Alex. "Look, I'm sorry for what you had to go through, but as a spy for the Scots, I had to pretend to go along with them."

Drostan's temper flared, but then he reminded himself that Chrissa had said the voice she'd heard was not DeFry's.

Alex joined him while Father Dowall went inside. "You took part in my granddaughter's kidnapping. If you wish to take another step, you'll explain yourself now. Otherwise, I'll have you flayed for your part in it." Some of the rage slipped out of his expression. "I must admit, I suspect there's more to the story than I heard, so I'm offering you this one opportunity to tell the truth. Don't be foolish and abuse it."

DeFry looked earnest, although he'd appeared as such during his interrogations of Drostan. "I was spying, but for the Scots. I'm the one who went to Alasdair and told him they'd been set free and they could head to Gallow Hill. I knew they'd be needed there. Believe me, I didn't know anything about his mother. Percy brought me in after he'd made his plans with her and another man. He trusted me, though he shouldn't have. But he got his just due."

The words ran of truth, and yet…

Alex turned to Drostan. "What say you?"

"I'm not sure what to think. He was there, but Chrissa insisted the voice she heard belonged to someone else."

"I allowed them to escape. I left the door unlocked," DeFry pressed, his face covered in sweat. "I even left their weapons and horses out for them."

Alex looked to Drostan for confirmation, and he nodded. "True. Everything felt much too convenient. I thought we were being set up because it was so easy. Percy followed us with two of his goons, but DeFry was not there. No one else came for us."

"So who was working with your mother?"

"I don't know for sure, but I have my suspicions."

They looked to DeFry, who shrugged his shoulders. "I'm not certain either. I wasn't involved in their conversations, but I know there's a third person. I have my suspicions, too. I fear he may still try to enact their plans, even though he's the only one left standing and the battle didn't go as he hoped."

Just then, Chrissa arrived with her cousins, and she jumped off her horse and raced over to Drostan, throwing her arms around his neck, kissing him heartily, and saying, "'Twas wonderful. Long but so worth it because we won! The English will not be back for a while. And I figured out who was with your mother."

"I think I did, too." He hugged her tight, knowing

he needed to know she was safe, that she'd survived, and they did indeed have a future together.

Alex cleared his throat.

Chrissa jumped away from him. "Sorry, Grandsire." She hugged Alex and then stood back, blushing.

Alex said, "You're forgiven. I remember being in love like that."

Chrissa gave him a look. "You were *always* in love with Grandmama. Do not try to tell me otherwise."

"True, but young love is when you notice naught else but that person. When love matures, it changes, and you can notice the world around you again. You just proved my theory." He patted her shoulder and smiled. "I'm pleased you've chosen a fine man."

"So who is it?" Drostan asked. "If 'tis the same as my man, he's already here, and I suspect he's in the back, letting his men in."

"We must stop them!" Chrissa shouted.

John joined them and asked, "Is he here yet?"

"Who is it?" Alex asked.

Chrissa and Drostan answered in unison. "Father Dowall."

"He just went into the hall," Alex said, turning around to follow him. "Wee bastard. And I doubt he's tied to the church. The costume is a great disguise that fooled many."

"Don't worry," Drostan said. "He won't go far."

Chrissa looked at him, her face a question. "What did you do?"

"Come, you'll see."

Drostan took her hand and led the group that had gathered out front around to the back of the keep. Alex, John, Connor, Alasdair, Emmalin, and Els all followed.

When they opened the door, they were all shocked, but then they broke into gales of laughter. About forty guards had come over the back wall, only to find themselves stuck in something. They struggled to get free, only to find themselves caught in another spot.

Father Dowall was also stuck, but his mouth was going as fast as anything they'd ever heard.

"I don't believe I've ever heard a priest curse so," Alex said. "Have you, Connor?"

Connor just crossed his arms and laughed.

Father Dowall took off his robe and his collar, flinging them away from him, then took something and unwrapped it. "You can laugh all you like, but I'll free myself right now." He took out a sword and held it up in the air. "I have the power!" he bellowed.

The laughter grew even louder. Chrissa squeezed Drostan's hand and said, "Tar? 'Twas a brilliant solution, Drostan."

John yelled over, "'Tis a phony sword, Father, though I guess you're no priest. No matter, I've already hidden the sapphire sword, and no one will ever find it."

Connor said, "Well done, Drostan. I think we'll leave them like that for a while."

The cursing continued, and they all turned

around to go back inside.

Drostan leaned over the parapets, watching the woman he loved in the courtyards. Tears filled his eyes, something that hadn't happened since he lost both of his parents on the same day and fallen more deeply in love with Chrissa. He'd also been kidnapped, stabbed, and put into an impossible situation by some evil men.

And one very evil woman.

He'd come out here to leave that awful day behind, hopefully, and start a new life with Chrissa. If her family would allow it.

Alex leaned over the parapets on one side of him while Finlay and Kyla were on the other side. "Now, lad," Alex said. "Captivity makes people do things they'd never do outside of captivity."

"'Tis true. Listen to my father. He knows," Kyla said.

"The thoughts I had in that dingy cell would frighten anyone. My mind kept traveling to strange places and thinking verra odd thoughts." He scuffed the ground with a boot. "And to think the reason I was there and went through that was because of my own mother. I am so sorry for all of the trouble she has caused. I wish to apologize to all of you, but I don't know how to do it properly. If you wish for me to leave the clan…"

Finlay interrupted him, clasping his shoulder. "Enough of such nonsense. You had naught to do with it. Your mother had her own twisted leanings, and you're not to blame for her actions. Think no more on any of it."

He looked at Chrissa's father, appreciating his words. It was as if Finlay had peered into his soul and seen all of his fears. Now if he could just believe them to be true. "I do love your daughter, but if you wish to send me away…"

Alex said, "Enough of that. Why did you come up here?"

Drostan took a step back from the parapets so he wouldn't be distracted by Chrissa. "Because I knew the three of you were here and I'd like all of your blessings. I wish to take Chrissa as my wife, if you will all allow it."

Kyla rushed over and hugged him, squealing.

"Is that approval?" he asked, looking at Finlay's wide grin behind her back.

"Aye, we would love for you to marry Chrissa. Wouldn't we, Papa?" Kyla asked, leaning toward her father.

"Aye, 'twould please me to attend one more wedding festival before…"

Kyla practically shoved Drostan out of the way in her haste to get to her father. "Don't think you're leaving me. Not yet, Papa. Do you hear me?" She gripped her father's shoulder, staring into his eyes, before she spun around abruptly and said to Finlay, "I have to go or I'll start sobbing." But she paused for long enough to call out over her shoulder, "Never, Papa. Never!"

Finlay and Kyla left, leaving him alone with Alex Grant. Drostan looked at him from the side and asked, "Before what? Was she right, Alex?"

"Nay, she has no idea what I meant." Alex stared out at the group beneath them and mumbled, "Actually, neither do I."

CHAPTER TWENTY-SEVEN

CHRISSA STRODE BACK FROM THE archery field. She was the last to leave. Practice was a distraction, and truth was, she missed her cousins dearly. They'd all left a few days ago.

She took a deep sigh when something dropped out of a tree in front of her as she walked beneath it. A single white rose. She bent down to pick it up and then jumped as Drostan dropped out of the tree too.

"I didn't think roses grew in trees, Drostan. But surely warriors don't either. This rose is most lovely and has such a sweet scent." She inhaled the aroma and smiled, then stood on her tiptoes and kissed him. Pulling back, she teased, "Only one though? Several would have been much sweeter."

"One rose represents you. You are the only one I'll ever want or need, Chrissa. You are my one rose."

"Oh, you're sweeter than this rose."

"And I'm here to ask you to marry me. I've gained the approval of your parents and your grandsire, which I found more daunting than any task I've faced as a warrior. Chrissa Grant, will you please marry me, be with me forever and ever? Promise never to leave me?"

She squealed and threw her arms around his neck. "Aye, of course! I love you, Drostan, and I'd never walk out on you like your mother did. I hate that you felt the need to say that." She lifted the rose to her face again so she could breathe in its sweet aroma.

He kissed her then, a deep kiss that sealed the moment for her. When he ended the kiss, he whispered, "I love you more than I ever could have guessed. And I'm so happy you'll be mine forever."

He wrapped his arm around her and they sauntered back toward the keep.

"So was this your plan all along? To ask me just like when we made our pact together so long ago?"

He frowned. "Pact?"

She nudged her elbow into his side. "You forgot already? Do you not recall what your father said about us? That when I fell out of the tree, you helped me, stayed with me, and we made our pact to marry someday."

"Ah, that pact. When *you* fell out of a tree." He grinned and tipped his head back. "I wish I could tell you so, but I just wished to surprise you."

"I'll always remember your sire for that," she said, wrapping her arms around him and squeezing. "Did my sire give you any trouble when you asked for my hand?"

"Nay. I thought they would, but your mother

was actually excited."

"Good. I'm glad they didn't make it difficult for you."

They strode back to the keep arm in arm, both smiling.

To her surprise, her mother and father were waiting in the courtyard as if they'd known about his plan. "Mama, we're betrothed!"

"I know," she said. "Congratulations. We couldn't be any happier for the two of you."

Her father gave her a squeezing hug, then her mother.

"So can we marry on the morrow? The next day? I don't wish to wait." She glanced up at Drostan to see if he agreed, but he had a stoic look on his face that told her nothing.

"You're waiting," her mother announced, crossing her arms in front of her.

"What do you mean?" She glanced from her mother to Drostan.

"Look, Chrissa," her mama said. "I'm sure you can see that your grandsire will not be around forever. This could be the last family wedding he'll be able to attend. I want to bring all of our allies here. I want a huge wedding."

"What about what we want?"

She was prepared to launch into an argument with her mother, but her father said, "Hear your mother out this time, sweetling. Her idea is wonderful and I expect 'twill suit you well."

She looked up at Drostan and said, "Are you going to stand with me?"

"Nay."

She stared at him, wide-eyed. "Why not?"

"Do you not remember what you made me promise all those years ago? You wanted a big festival for our wedding, but it would only happen if I worked verra hard in the lists. Well, I did my part, now you have to do yours. Let your mother tell you what she has in mind, and I think you'll accept her terms."

"But..."

"Come to the garden so no one listens," her mother directed.

She gave in to the three people she loved most in the world and followed her mother into the garden. "Go ahead. Explain your idea to me."

"I'd like for you to marry in late summer, a moon from now. We'll have a big festival before the wedding, with plenty of contests. Grandsire and Uncle Logan can serve as judges. We'll have archery, sword skills, dagger throwing, horseback riding, even a diving contest in the loch." She grinned. "We can even have a fruit tart contest—who can eat the most. Whatever you want. And I want to include all of the allies Papa has built over the years: the Ramsays, Camerons, Menzies, and Drummonds. They can all take part. And we'll have an entire month to plan it and sew you a beautiful gown exactly to your liking."

"That does sound wonderful." There was only one problem. She wanted to consummate the marriage, and she didn't wish to wait. Of course, she didn't quite know how to say that to her mother and father. A glance at Drostan told her he felt the same way.

To her shock, her parents exchanged a look and started laughing.

"What's so funny?" she asked.

"We know why you hesitate," her father said. "We were young once too. Your mother and I have set up a cottage for you. On the morrow, we'll have food sent there, and 'tis yours for the weekend. You'll be alone to do as you wish and no one else has to know. No checking the linens like some clans do. No bedding ceremony for the wedding. You know Grandsire prohibits them. We'll tell everyone you've gone off to visit a friend at Loki's castle. Use it for the month when you think you can get away unnoticed."

"The only one who will suspect will be Grandsire," her mother continued, "but I'll tell him you two handfasted and that will satisfy him."

As soon as Chrissa was able to form words—when had her parents last shocked her speechless?—she said, "You're sure about that, Mama?"

"Your grandsire allowed Brodie to handfast with Celestina when she was already betrothed to a Norse nobleman. And he also allowed Aunt Jennie to handfast. He'll accept your decision."

She couldn't believe what they offered, so she glanced at Drostan again to see his reaction was.

He nodded, a sly grin on his face that he was fighting to make look innocent.

"Hellfire, aye!" She clasped her hand over her mouth as fast as she said it, simply because she hadn't planned to be so honest.

Drostan chuckled and peered from one parent to the other. "'Tis the way of my wife. She's blunt."

Drostan couldn't believe that Chrissa's parents had arranged this for them. They were finally going to spend the night together, in their own hut.

Nay, *two* nights together.

"You know we're basically handfasted now, do you not?"

"Aye, I agreed and so did you," he said, pleased the evening was a lovely one. The temperature was pleasantly warm since it was the middle of the summer, but a cool breeze blew through the trees, the sound of the wavering branches quite soothing. The chatter of the squirrels told him the wee beasties were as pleased with the night as Drostan. They rode one horse out to the place her mother had told them about, surprised to find it well-hidden among the trees. "I had no idea this was here."

He hopped down from the horse, then helped her down before he tied the horse's reins to a tree so the animal could graze while they were inside.

Chrissa hesitated next to the door, looking at him over her shoulder before she opened the door. He didn't care what the inside looked like as long as there was a bed, but he knew it would matter to her. Alexander Grant had advised him the other night, "Never dismiss a lass's needs. They are as important to them as our swords and daggers are to us."

She opened the door wide and took two steps inside, then brought both hands to her chest. "Look, Drostan. 'Tis beautiful."

His idea of beauty was the woman in front of him, not any inanimate objects in the hut, but he nodded readily enough, happy she was pleased. "Aye, your mother did a fine job preparing it for us."

The cottage had one large chamber, separated by a partition that looked to have been added in later, after the main structure was built. To the right sat the large hearth, with a kettle already cooking over the small fire. The smell of roasted lamb caught him. He peeked inside when he walked by it, pleased to see it was a lamb and carrot stew, thick with gravy.

There were candles everywhere, and some flowers arranged in various places, though he had no idea what kind they were except for one vase of white roses. That much he recognized because he'd asked her mother if she could place some inside.

The bed behind the partition was piled thick with furs and soft pillows, plenty big enough for both of them. A platter of fruit and cheese sat on the table in the center of the cottage, and a bottle of wine stood next to the platter, a luxury for certain. There was also a pitcher of ale on a shelf, along with various dishes and utensils and a large basin of water.

"I think they thought of everything, lass. What say you?"

She stopped and threw her arms around his neck.

"'Tis perfect. I love it and I love you."

He kissed her and said, "What shall we do first?" He would leave it to her to set the pace. He had some sexual experience, but not much, so he felt almost as new to this as she did.

"Drostan, I know you probably would prefer to go right into the bedroom, but do you mind if we have a goblet of wine first? I admit that I'm a wee bit nervous."

"Great idea," he said, pulling out a chair for her. The table was too close to the hearth for him, or mayhap he was heating up at the thought of climbing into bed with her. Either way, he had to doff some clothing. "Do you mind if I remove my tunic? 'Tis suddenly too warm in here."

"Nay, do as you wish."

He removed his tunic, leaving his chest exposed, and sat down at the table. As soon as he was seated, he got to work pouring each of them a goblet of wine and cutting off two pieces of cheese, which was why it took him so long to notice.

Chrissa was staring at his chest, her cheeks turning a lovely shade of pink.

His Chrissa had never been afraid of a challenge, so he lifted an eyebrow and said, "Are you warm, lass?"

Her eyes, suddenly full of mischief, shot back up to his. "Aye, I find that I am."

"Feel free to do what I've done," he said with a wide grin. "It definitely helped me."

She removed her tunic, moving slowly so as to tease him, revealing the most glorious breasts he'd ever seen sat in front of him. She leaned forward and the two perfect globes rested on the table. "You're right. This is quite freeing," she said, winking at him with a grin.

He picked up his goblet and drank the rest in one gulp. Hell, but she was perfection. Her luscious light brown nipples stared at him.

He forced himself to look away. "Are you ready yet, Chrissa?" How he prayed she would say aye.

"Nay, I still have quite a bit of wine left. Is something wrong? Can you not find something to do while I finish?"

He almost choked on nothing, but he recognized the look on her face. She was teasing him again.

He stood up, leaned over with a growl, and lifted her from her seat. She squealed in delight as he settled her on his lap. "Naught wrong at all. And I thought of something to do while you finish your wine. You didn't really think I could look and not touch, did you?"

She laughed, throwing her head back and saying, "Go right ahead. Touch all you like, but I am finishing my wine."

He locked his gaze on hers and cupped both of her breasts in his hands, rubbing each nipple with his thumbs. "You are beautiful, Chrissa. Sheer perfection." Something in her gaze changed at his comment—a new vulnerability appeared.

She had worried he wouldn't like her body.

"I am?" she said softly.

He continued his light ministrations, her nipples now peaked, and she arched against him. His arousal was almost painful.

"Aye, you are. Every part of you is beautiful. Do you want to know what will feel even better?"

"Aye," she answered, her hand gripping the back of his neck.

He dipped his head and took one nipple in his mouth, swirling his tongue around the tip, then suckling her until she moaned. When he switched to the other soft swell, he continued to knead and massage the first breast, rolling her nipple between his thumb and forefinger.

"You're quite talented that you can do both at once."

He laughed, lifting his head and asking, "Are you done with your wine yet?'

"Nay, continue," she said, taking another deep swallow.

His hands went to her backside and she started. "What are you doing?"

"Getting you out of those leggings."

"Why?"

"Because I wish to feel all of your skin."

"All right," she said, wriggling her sweet arse until her leggings lay in a heap on the floor.

He took her breast in his mouth again while he moved his hand to her thigh and around to the vee between her legs, though she had them locked tightly together. He started caressing the curls at the juncture of her thighs, and her legs moved apart of their own volition just far enough for him to find her nub. He rubbed her softly there, and she took another long swig of her wine. His thumb continued to pleasure her until she moved her legs far enough apart to give him free access. They said nothing, just enjoying each other's closeness, learning more of each other. Her hands moved to his shoulders and down to his upper arms before they found a way over to his nipples, teasing him much the same way he'd teased her.

He wouldn't have guessed that she would allow him such a slow exploration of her body, but he enjoyed it more then he would have expected.

When he thought she was ready, he easily slid a finger inside her, and her wetness made him moan loud enough for her to hear.

She took another sip of wine, then tipped the goblet up and set it down. "No more wine." She pointed to the bed.

He carried her over to it, reveling in the softness of her skin as he settled her on the furs and pillows. Then he stood back and dropped his plaid.

"Oh, Drostan," she said, looking at his sex as he climbed in beside her.

He settled himself over her and said, "Are you sure you're ready for this, lass?"

"Aye, I do want this, but please do it quickly and don't talk about it. I know 'twill hurt the first time."

He did as she asked, putting his weight on his elbows as he slid into her slick entrance, waiting for her to accept his invasion. He felt her barrier but waited to see if she would relax a bit more, stroking her everywhere he could, slipping in a bit deeper whenever she loosened against him.

"Just finish it, Drostan."

He was perfectly positioned at her entrance so he gave one quick thrust and plunged inside of her, breaking her barrier. She tightened on him and all he could think to say was, "I'm sorry."

He stopped to wait for her, to let her adjust to him being inside of her. She'd lost her maidenhead with that one swift motion. It was only right that he give her control of what happened next. He didn't wait long before she arched against him, teasing him enough that he said, "You are all right? I can move and 'twill not hurt you?"

"Aye," she said with a wee gasp. "I wish to finish. Please, Drostan. I'm fine."

They moved together in the ancient dance, Chrissa naturally picking up his rhythm. She followed his lead until the need pulsating inside her woman's center became too much and she pushed against him, driving him faster, harder, unrelenting until she crashed over the edge, shouting his name.

She brought him with her, and he gripped her hips and climaxed with a roar, giving her his seed. It had been so wonderful that all he was capable of doing was whispering to her how very much he loved her.

A sudden image popped into his mind.

"What are you thinking?" she asked, her finger tracing the line of his jaw.

"Something I've always wanted to do. If you'll allow me."

"What? I'm not fond of surprises."

"You still have your hair plaited. May I undo it? I'll do it in front of the fire so you'll stay warm."

"May I get dressed?"

He shook his head, a sly grin crossing his face. "Nay. I wish to see your hair down around you with no clothing on at all."

She thought for a moment, then asked, "And you won't touch me otherwise? While it was wonderful, I am feeling a bit tender. And I wish to sit on a plaid or I'll be too cold."

"Agreed."

He helped her to the chair in front of the fire and kept his promise.

She, however, did not.

They would have a wondrous life together.

CHAPTER TWENTY-EIGHT

A FORTNIGHT LATER, CHRISSA'S SMILE WAS the widest Drostan had ever seen it… with the exception of the weekend they'd spent together in their cottage.

"Is this going to work for you?" he asked, giving her a playful nudge after picking up his puppy. "Is the festival big enough? Are there enough competitors?" They stood at the end of one of the fields that were to be used for the contests, their clan and family clustered around to watch the competitions.

She nodded with glee and threw her arms around his neck, being careful with the animal he held. "'Tis perfect. Absolutely perfect. Thank you, husband." She kissed him quickly on the lips, then leaned down to rub noses with their pet.

"Do not say that too loudly," he said, even though he wished for her to shout it to the sky. They'd managed to sneak back to the cottage on two other occasions, but no one had questioned them about it yet. "Other than your parents and your grandsire, no one knows we already handfasted." Then he snuggled the puppy in his arms. "Except you, wee Sky."

Sky yipped at him.

She stepped back and gave him a saucy look, wiggling her hips in the new leggings Aunt Gwyneth had given her.

Chrissa's cousin Loki, who was the announcer for the archery competition, stepped forward and held his arms up for everyone's attention. The archers who'd been chosen for the two teams were lined up by the field, and spectators had gathered all around them. Although Drostan and Chrissa each had a group of contestants, they stood together, forming a united front.

"Lads and lassies, join us for the big event, the archery contest! We are blessed with two judges for the contest, and I will provide the third vote if necessary. The judges, seated on the outside, are Logan and Gwyneth Ramsay."

The applause was louder than thunder. Logan stood next to his wife and waved to all the contenders.

Loki continued, "And we thank all the lairds and former lairds of the clan—Connor, Jamie, and Alexander Grant. This is a tribute to Jake Grant, whom we all miss greatly." A moment of silence followed, then Loki said, "Chrissa introduce your team, please."

Hoots and hollers nearly drowned out her voice as she shouted their names: Dyna, Branwen, Molly, Sorcha, Gregor, and Drystan of Clan Ramsay, son of Donnan and Bethia.

Drostan introduced his team next: Ashlyn and her daughter, Isbeil, Gavin, Merewen, and their daughter, Ysenda, and Maggie.

Molly yelled, "We're in trouble! Isbeil is too powerful!"

The battle went on for four hours, but Chrissa's team finally prevailed. He could tell she wished to use her Grant war whoop, but she couldn't, simply because there were Ramsays and Grants on both sides. To celebrate her victory, even though it was against him, he swung her through the air like he'd done when they were small, the crowd hooting even louder in appreciation.

Next up was the sword competition. They'd built a small platform in the middle of the lists, and he climbed up and made his announcement, "Anyone interested in participating in the sword skills contest, please come forward with your weapon. The judges for this contest will be Alexander Grant along with the two Grant lairds, Jamie and Connor." Although he wasn't allowed to compete himself, just like Chrissa had not shot any arrows, he was excited to watch with her by his side. The dream they'd spun together, all those years ago, was coming true before their eyes.

Droves of men came forward to sign up for the contest. Chrissa stood in a group off to the side of several while Drostan helped her uncles plan the sword contest. Maryell, Merelda, Astra, Dyna, and their Ramsay cousins Lise and Liliana stood together, watching all the contestants come forward.

"Lord above, help us all," Astra said.

"What?" Chrissa asked.

Astra lifted a finger and pointed at five men who'd entered the area. Chrissa didn't know any of them. "God's teeth, they're beautiful. They look like Norse gods. Who are they?"

Dyna said, "And they took their tunics off just for us…"

Chrissa said, "Close your mouth, Dyna. You're drooling."

"Who are they?" Maryell whispered. "I must know. Two of them look quite young."

"Lise, Liliana, do you know them?" Dyna asked. "They're wearing Menzie plaids." And the Menzies were connected to the Ramsays by marriage.

The twins turned to stare at the five men who'd just entered the contest. "Oh, those are Aunt Avelina and Uncle Drew's three sons, Tad, Tomag, and Maitland. And the other two are Tad's sons."

Merelda said, "One for me, one for you, sister."

The competition began, and so many had entered it took two days to get through all the contestants, but it came down to a contest between two people—Alasdair and Derric.

Dozens of other contests were held for the enjoyment of all: a horse obstacle course, a diving contest in the loch, a dagger throwing contest. They even held a contest for the best leggings for archery.

The winner? Tora, who clutched a miniature toy

bow.

They also had contests for hunting and fishing, and so everyone feasted for the entire sennight.

But for Chrissa, one other part of the festival pleased her more than any. It was something she hadn't expected. Grandsire came into the middle of the group on horseback at the end, something that silenced the crowd instantly.

"I'd like to acknowledge something that was overlooked with all the excitement over the Scot's win at Bannockburn and the villains who tried to overtake Grant Castle. And that is the part of two young people who helped us find my dear granddaughter.

"Astra and Hendrie, please come forward."

Chrissa had heard about what they'd done, but with all the excitement over the wedding, their achievement had been overlooked. Leave it to her grandsire not to miss it.

"Many of you don't know this, but Astra has an amazing ability to draw maps along with a spatial understanding that many people lack. She and Hendrie set out to find Chrissa and Drostan and they were successful while so many patrols were not. I understand they had a bit of help from a wolfhound named Sky, but I don't wish to ignore their achievements."

Astra and Hendrie now stood in front of Alexander Grant, quietly listening. When he finished his statement, he nodded to a group of warriors who came up and encircled the two young warriors.

Loki stood in front of the group and set his sword

down on the ground in front of the two. The rest of the group saluted the two with their weapons, then rested their swords on the ground, too. The entire crowd applauded and cheered for the two.

Hendrie hugged Astra and was nearly in tears. "It happened, Astra. My dream is complete."

Chrissa couldn't stop herself from rushing forward to hug both of them. It was the culmination of a wonderful festival.

All that was left was the wedding.

Chrissa woke up and raced to the window, throwing the shutters back and hanging out the window.

Maryell mumbled, "Well?"

"'Twill be a most glorious day. Not a cloud in the blue sky. A perfect day for my wedding!" she declared, throwing her arms up over her head, as giddy as any lass on her wedding day. "I wonder what Drostan is doing."

"Yelling at someone to let him sleep," Merelda mumbled, her face hidden under the covers.

A knock sounded at the door and Chrissa giggled. "You'll not sleep another minute, and you know it."

Her mother entered with a tray of fruit and cheese. "You have half an hour to eat," she said, setting the tray down, "then Mama's bathing chamber is yours. We'll get you dressed and then Aunt Avelina, Lise, and Liliana will weave the flowers in your hair." Her Ramsay aunt and cousins had a way with flowers, and everyone in both clans were always clamoring for them to fix their hair.

"My thanks, Mama." She hurried over, hugged her mother, and said, "And now I'm glad we waited. Everyone is here and I'm so excited. Everyone!"

Her mother turned to leave before glancing back, eyes narrowed. "You'll not be late for anything. Do you hear me?"

"Aye, Mama. You'll see how perfect it will be. All of it."

Perfect wasn't exactly how it all went, but she did survive the day. Even through all of the following:

Two of the roasted pheasants burned and sent smoke traveling all through the keep.

Chrissa tripped on her dress and rolled down several stairs, though fortunately she didn't break any bones.

There were so many tents and banners outside that all her cousins had to go out and have everyone move for the ceremony.

It rained late in the morn, soaking everyone.

Two trays of fruit tarts went flying through the air when Maeve screamed upon seeing Daniel and Constance and all their bairns come inside, just because she'd always loved Daniel.

Daniel, always the talented one, caught two tarts flying through the air with his one hand.

The dogs all ate well between the pheasants and the fruit tarts.

But they laughed through it all, and after the rain stopped, tables dressed in ribbons and flowers were arranged in the courtyard and in the hall.

They'd invited so many that the set up overtook the entire archery field and the lists, where there was no parrying allowed. Her procession was to start out near the lists and would end at the chapel in the courtyard. Chrissa started out so far away that many would miss the beginning, but with the rolling hills, they'd see her once she reached the meadow.

And so it began.

Chrissa, mounted on a white horse, was led down a path lined with Grant warriors by her wee cousins, Grant bairns bedecked in their feast day finery. The bairns led her to the base of a hill, where her grandsire and parents waited on horseback. The plan was for them to climb the hill until they reached the meadow, then stand and wait, overlooking all of their guests, until the ceremony began. The meadow was full of clanmates and others who came to watch from far and wide. Menzies, Drummonds, Ramsays, Camerons, they were all there.

As soon as Chrissa reached the base of the hill where her parents awaited her, she nearly lost her composure. One look at Alexander Grant in his fine leine almost brought her to tears. He was such a handsome man. And her mother was absolutely beautiful in a dark red gown with a bodice made from the Grant plaid, her handsome father next to her.

Chrissa wore a white under gown with the red Grant plaid draped in folds and pleats over her. She wore her grandmother Maddie's pearls, and a gold belt rested on her hips. Lise and Liliana had decorated her hair with flowers of red and gold.

"You are beautiful, lass," Grandsire said. "Grandmama would be proud. The pearls are lovely." He held his hand out and she took it, the two climbing to the pinnacle hand in hand on horseback, her mother and father riding on either side of them.

When they crested the peak, the crowd beneath them exploded in cheers and applause. Here the wee bairns of the clan stepped back, making way for each of Alex Grant's living children, who rode up the hill from the keep and stopped in front of Chrissa and her grandsire on horseback. Jamie, Connor, Elizabeth, and Maeve looked splendid in their finery. They led their horses in a bit of a show as they turned in unison and then led the procession while Chrissa's siblings—Alick, Broc, and Paden—fell in behind their elders.

"Do you think Mama is watching, Papa?" her mother asked, her voice choked with emotion.

"Indeed I do, daughter. And Jake and Aline."

They nearly reached the portcullis to deafening cheers, but she was surprised at what she saw. The chapel had been moved to a position a good distance in front of the gates at one end of the meadow.

In front of the chapel at the end of the meadow was her beloved. Drostan stood with Magnus, his mentor of sorts in the warrior camp, and the priest. Her husband looked so handsome she nearly cried over that.

Jamie and Connor stopped them just in front of

the chapel, then turned awaiting someone.

All the onlookers had to step back to allow the newcomers to join them.

Chrissa and her sire were still at the rear of the procession, but they turned to watch the ceremony, and what a sight it was.

Two rows of Grant warriors in full dress joined them on Grandsire's right side.

On the left, led by Logan and Gwyneth Ramsay, they were joined by Aunt Brenna, Torrian, Lachlan, and two rows of Ramsay warriors.

To the right of the Grant warriors came another group, Clan Cameron warriors led by Aedan and Jennie, all on horseback, and two more sets of warriors approached them on Logan's left. First the Menzies, with Avelina and Drew leading, and then Diana Drummond and Micheil Ramsay leading the Drummond warriors.

The last group to join them was led by Loki and Bella. Their warriors, also in Grant plaids, fell in on the other side of Clan Cameron.

Chrissa had no idea they were all to appear. She peeked up at her grandfather and whispered, "Grandpapa?"

"'Tis to let all in the land know that Clan Grant does not stand alone," he said proudly, and she could swear his eyes were misting as he beheld the gathering. "Nor do any of the others. The Ramsays, Camerons, Drummonds, Menzies, Grants. We all stand together. We'll not be put asunder easily. Stand fast, stand sure, and stand together."

Once the procession had finished, the horses

moved back to allow the onlookers to move in closer.

Drostan placed his sword on the ground in front of Alex, Jamie, and Connor Grant. He gave each of them a nod before he came to her, his grin wider than his face, it seemed, and assisted her down. He whispered in her ear, "You are gorgeous. I'm so pleased our day is here."

Chrissa stood next to her betrothed, soaking him in with her gaze simply because she loved his handsome profile and the many colors of his eyes. He squeezed her hand as the priest continued on in Gaelic.

How she adored this man. Even though there were probably thousands observing them, it felt as if it were just the two of them, the sun shining down on them. When the priest finally said the words, it seemed as though she'd missed the entire ceremony.

Drostan kissed her, his arms wrapping around her, and leaned her back to a bevy of hooting from the onlookers, but he ended it quickly and whispered, "Finally, we've both kept our promise."

Drostan couldn't believe it had finally happened. They were married.

Chrissa was so beautiful she nearly took his breath away. Her hair, the gown, the flowers, everything about her was beautiful, but nothing caught him as her smile did.

Her eyes lit up with joy, and her smile told the

world she couldn't be happier.

They turned around and he held her hand up in the air as a symbol they were married, their hands entwined with a piece of Grant plaid. The sea of plaids was impressive—blue and black, purple and gold, brown and gold, and many different shades of red plaids. To their surprise, her family moved their horses off to the side a wee bit while the other clans moved to new positions. Chrissa and Drostan faced outward with the lairds and her aunts and uncles. The clans in their finery faced them, still maintaining their lines.

Once they'd all established their positions, Connor and Jamie issued a loud Grant whoop, and the horses all began to move.

The riders from the different clans all began to move in an intricate choreography, some carrying their banners, some just in the clan colors. They continued weaving in and out and around one another.

Drostan leaned over and whispered, "What are they doing?"

Chrissa laughed and said, "I don't know. Grandpapa told me they were all here and in the procession to show the land that we stand together. Not one of these clans is alone. We will all support each other…"

"In case evil tries to put us asunder again."

"Aye," she said thoughtfully as she stared across the crowd. "The fools thought that pitting Clan Ramsay against Clan Grant could put an end to us. They were wrong."

"And they forgot about all the other clans who support us."

"Exactly. Look," she said, pointing.

The horses had stopped, all the clans mixed together so that one could not identify any one clan over the other.

"'Tis beautiful, Drostan. Now it looks as if we truly stand as one."

Then the horses spread apart, making way for one more group to come forward.

John rode a horse with Coira in front of him. Then came Alasdair and Emmalin, Alick and Bran-wen, Els and Joya, and finally Dyna and Derric.

John came forward and announced to all. "We fight for all of Scotland."

Then he pulled out the sapphire sword and held it up to the sky, each member of the Highland Swords doing the same with their own weapons. The sky filled with bolts of lightning, a show of brilliance and power.

CHAPTER TWENTY-NINE

JOHN AND COIRA STROLLED THROUGH the forest together, not touching, but talking. John told her all his thoughts of the battle. How powerful the memory of the dead affected him. How he'd talked with *Seanair* and his father on learning how to handle such tragedy and loss, even for a good cause.

When they arrived in the middle of the forest, a sudden swarm of butterflies appeared around them, enough that Coira moved next to John and he held her hand, tugging her close.

"You need not fear them. They are my friends and yours, too. They can be everywhere without anyone noticing." Erena appeared in front of them, floating down from the treetops, wearing a mint green gown with purple threading and a purple bodice. "'Tis lovely to meet you, John and Coira. You are one of our youngest, but I think this could be a wonderful thing. You did a fine job with the sapphire sword, and we all thank you for helping to rid Scotland of evil for now. There will be no more battles for a while, and your prediction will prove true. King Robert the Bruce will be remembered for his Battle at Bannockburn forever."

"What shall we do with the sapphire sword, Erena?" John asked, still holding Coira's hand.

"Hide it somewhere where no one else will find it. I'm sure the two of you will find a fine spot. Avelina and Drew hid it behind a stone near a waterfall. But please make sure you'll remember where you've hidden it." She started to float away from them, all the butterflies alighting on her arms. "Have a lovely life. You have earned it."

"Wait, Erena. May we ask a question?" Coira whispered timidly.

"Of course. Do not fear me, lassie."

"What if something were to happen to one of us? What would happen to the sword? Or if something happened to John, what would I do with it?"

"Do not worry, lass. It is part of the beauty of being the bearer of the sapphire sword. Nothing will happen to either of you until I return and tell you to pass it on. It will always protect you. And now I will say good-bye."

And she flitted off as quickly as her butterflies.

EPILOGUE

ALEXANDER GRANT SAT IN FRONT of the hearth and whistled, an ear-splitting noise that all the wee ones in the clan had learned to listen for a long time ago. He smiled as they gathered around him. John considered himself too mature to sit for bedtime stories, but Alex noticed he never stepped too far away, lingering at a nearby table close enough to overhear whatever tale he told that eve, Coira nearby.

Dyna and Derric's two daughters, Els and Joya's daughter, Alick and Branwen's two sons, and Alasdair and Emmalin's two young sons sat waiting patiently for *Seanair* to begin the telling of this eve's tale. The new lassie was cradled to Branwen's chest. Other bairns gathered round to participate in the wee ones' favorite time of the eve.

Ailith came up to her great-grandfather and leaned on his knee, looking up at him with her odd insightfulness. "*Seanair,* do you cry? Why?"

Alex patted her head as he thought on the story he planned to tell in his mind, knowing some of the memories would rid him of the odd pricking of tears in his eyes. "Och, wee lassie, you imagine it. I'm not crying, just thinking hard about which tale I'll tell."

"The swordfight against Grandmama's betrothed," one of the ladies suggested.

"When Growley and Loki saved Gracie."

"Nay, the battle to save Aunt Kyla," another offered.

"I love the one where Aunt Jennie believed Uncle Aedan died. Such trickery!"

"When Maddie saved Claray."

Loki sat in a chair not far away, a bairn in his lap, and nodded to Alex. "'Tis a night for the telling of the Battle of Largs, my laird."

He glanced over at Loki, who was as much kin as if he'd been born a Grant. "I believe you are right. I'll tell the tale of that battle. Then I'll tell you one more tale about a fine lass who came to me long ago and will come again someday."

The youngest bairns knew not what he spoke of, but he noticed his grandchildren moved closer as did all his nieces and nephews, his brother Brodie, his sister Jennie, and so many others.

As if they knew what he knew.

Out of nowhere, Dyna, Astra, and Chrissa joined the circle, their faces as rapt as if they were still bairns.

It was time.

Alex had clung to life with everything he had to see this end, to leave his sons and daughters, his grandsons and granddaughters, and his great-grandbairns with what they deserved most—freedom.

Finally, thanks to Robert the Bruce and the guts, gumption, and tenacity of the Scots, they had prevailed against the English bastards. They had sent Edward running.

Now he could rest at peace, knowing his clan, his people, were led by a Scot. The sudden surge of exhilaration he'd felt this eve would carry him through this tale of the Battle of Largs. He wished to make sure the courage and strength of his clan and his brothers would not be forgotten.

"It was a dark day in the history of the Scots when the Norse thought they could bring their multitude of galley ships up the firth and attack our land and our people. They came out of their galley ships, swarming the beach near Largs, swinging their swords against us, but they couldn't defeat us. Robbie was there with a strong force of Highlanders he'd been training for quite a while. Brodie was there, fighting harder than anyone I've ever seen.

And then there was a lad with a slinger who took out Norseman so slyly the victims never knew what hit them."

His praise of Loki's talent sent the lads he'd mentored—Gillie, Thorn, and Nari, and his adopted son Kenzie—into gales of laughter as they shouted his name.

"But it was the Scottish people who prevailed in that short battle. Our enemies got back into their ships and sailed away. Our fortitude and loyalty carried us through, much like in the Battle of Bannockburn, which is sure to be remembered as the fight for freedom for many, many years.

"Of course, some think we have gained much from the Norse's visits because many stayed, giving us the gift of their strength and culture, not something to be overlooked." When he made that statement, he gave a pointed look to his son Connor and his half-Norse wife, Sela. Then he reached down and took Dyna's hand. "You've enriched our lives in many ways."

He heard Sela sniffle at the end of the tale, but he wouldn't allow it, instead moving on to his next tale.

He told of the young blonde lass who'd been mistreated by her own brother but lived on to be one of the strongest women he'd ever known.

While he spoke, he heard whispers about Great-Grandmama, Maddie, or other enduring terms for his dearest wife. They all knew the story of how she'd been shunned by this very clan in the beginning because of cruel rumors spread by an evil man, her former betrothed. The tale was of a strong woman who didn't allow adversity to destroy her. She continued to create story books to entertain and delight the children of Clan Grant, and to live an irreproachable life—all while she was mistreated.

How he'd chastised himself for not noticing. As laird, he'd focused his efforts on protecting and defending the clan instead of what was happening right under his nose.

He continued the tale of how Maddie had

tricked all his guards to look the other way while she jumped into a hole that had formed in the earth, risking severe injury, to save two dear children. Out of the corner of his eye, he caught the sobs of his sister Jennie, who'd been one of the bairns. She had been stuck in the bottom of the deep hole with a gash on her head, watching over a wee lass who'd hit her head and fallen into a deep sleep.

Maddie had broken her arm in the fall, but the pain had meant nothing to her compared to her worry for the innocent bairns.

Alex had awakened to the truth of the situation. He'd learned to listen, to consider others' feelings, and to love without holding anything back. He'd married the lass, knowing he'd never regret marrying someone with such strong conviction. Knowing she'd gift him with strong sons and daughters.

And she had—five of them.

She'd given him more in their many years together than he'd ever deserved. He spoke of their challenges, their joy at each of their children's births, of their wonder when their three grandsons—Alasdair, Els, and Alick—had been born on the same night, at the same time, and of the wonderful moment they'd adopted Maeve.

He spoke of their arguments, how she quietly taught him the gift of forgiveness, and how together they'd learned to work as partners to consider possible solutions to their many problems. How they'd been blessed by God in so many ways they'd been grateful every day.

When he finished, he stood with a great amount of effort, Kyla handing him his long stick of wood he used for support, Maeve and Elizabeth right behind her, while his sister Jennie rushed to his other side to assist him to his chamber.

He nodded to his two sons, his grandsons and granddaughters, and to his brother Brodie. Then he made his way across the great hall to a quiet rarely heard in the Grant hall. The bairns began to stir behind him, while the others whispered to one another, but he paid them no mind.

Kyla opened the door for him, Maeve and Elizabeth nearby, but he stopped her, leaning down to kiss her forehead, and said, "I love all of you, daughters, and you've always made me proud, but I must speak to my sister privately."

Tears tracked down Kyla's cheeks the way he'd known they would, and he allowed the squeezing hugs that sent ripples of aches through his old bones because he knew they needed it. She and her sisters left him, Maeve wiping away tears, and Jennie closed the door before assisting him into bed, something that took a while.

Once he lay back on the bed, a deep sigh leaving him, Jennie pulled a chair up next to him. She kissed his cheek and said, "Give Mama and Papa a hug for me, and Maddie, and Robbie, and well, you know."

"I know not for sure, but I'm tired, Jennie. My time will come soon."

"You've lived many wonderful years, Alex, and

what you've made here… Mama and Papa will be so proud."

His eyes fluttered shut. He couldn't stay awake for one more moment. He had a vague sense of his sister covering him up with a blanket before leaving quietly. Being a healer, she'd always had an odd sense of when things were about to happen.

He fell asleep quickly, hoping to see Maddie. His need for her had become more than he could bear.

One moment he was thinking of his dear Maddie, and how she'd always carried the scent of lavender, and the next he was riding Midnight, his old war horse, across a meadow full of heather. He found himself in a deep forest, and although he'd never been there before, Midnight led him to a burn where the horse feasted on the cool water. Alex dismounted, realizing at once that he was in the midst of a dream because he carried no pain, no aches. Giddy with disbelief, he pulled out his sword and lifted it overhead, something he hadn't been able to do for a few years. He did it a few times just for the sheer joy of it.

A serene sense of peace fell over him, and his first thought was that he wished he could stay in the forest forever, but for the fact that he was alone. The scent of the pines, the swaying of the branches, and the rustle of the squirrels soothed him. He sheathed his sword and lifted his head to take in the sweet Highland breeze, his long hair lifting off his neck from the wind.

Something made him look up. There, standing in the mist ahead of him, stood a man with dark hair, a pretty red-haired lass a few steps away. "Papa, we've missed you. Our thanks for watching over Alasdair and our grandbairns."

"Jake?" Alex took a few steps forward, his eyes probably deceiving him because the son he missed every day now stood in front of him with his wife, Aline.

"Aye, 'tis me, Papa. We'll spar in a few days, but someone else is here to see you first." Jake pointed to Alex's right, a deep mist swirling around all of them as he disappeared.

Then he saw her.

Maddie stood not far away, radiant as always in his favorite blue gown that matched her eyes, her hair golden in the moonlight, unplaited and glorious with its soft waves.

He said, "Maddie, love. I miss you. How much time have you managed for me this eve?"

His dear wife smiled and opened her arms for him. "Eternity."

He strode over and wrapped his arms around her, burying his face in the sweet scent of her hair. He kissed her softly on her lips and said one word.

"Finally."

DEAR READERS,

I'm sorry! I know I have a group of unhappy readers, but I did this for a reason. It just seemed right. This is the end of Clan Grant, meaning I will go no farther in **time** for this group. I DO plan to go back to tell many of the missing stories from the Highland Clan: Elizabeth, Maeve, Kenzie, Jennet, Brigid, Riley, Tara, and the list goes on.

So that's my next plan. I may even create a new clan in a different time period.

What I won't be doing is continuing on with this group. I don't intend to write books for John, Astra, or any of the others in this new generation. At least, not yet…There are too many of them, and I already have enough characters living in my mind.

I choose to believe that Alexander Grant is happier where he is, and his descendants understood it was his time to move on.

And Maddie? Well, she's ecstatic, but you knew that, didn't you?

Was there really an attempt to behead Robert the Bruce at Bannockburn? No, that was my creation.

Or was there?

Read on! Trust me, there are more! I have no plans to stop writing. Who knows? A new clan could pop up anytime.

Keira Montclair
keiramontclair@gmail.com
www.keiramontclair.com

ALSO BY KEIRA MONTCLAIR

THE CLAN GRANT SERIES

#1- RESCUED BY A HIGHLANDER-
Alex and Maddie
#2- HEALING A HIGHLANDER'S HEART-
Brenna and Quade
#3- LOVE LETTERS FROM LARGS-
Brodie and Celestina
#4-JOURNEY TO THE HIGHLANDS-
Robbie and Caralyn
#5-HIGHLAND SPARKS-
Logan and Gwyneth
#6-MY DESPERATE HIGHLANDER-
Micheil and Diana
#7-THE BRIGHTEST STAR IN THE HIGHLANDS-
Jennie and Aedan
#8- HIGHLAND HARMONY-
Avelina and Drew

THE HIGHLAND CLAN

LOKI-Book One
TORRIAN-Book Two
LILY-Book Three
JAKE-Book Four
ASHLYN-Book Five
MOLLY-Book Six
JAMIE AND GRACIE- Book Seven
SORCHA-Book Eight

KYLA-Book Nine
BETHIA-Book Ten
LOKI'S CHRISTMAS STORY-Book Eleven

THE BAND OF COUSINS
HIGHLAND VENGEANCE
HIGHLAND ABDUCTION
HIGHLAND RETRIBUTION
HIGHLAND LIES
HIGHLAND FORTITUDE
HIGHLAND RESILIENCE
HIGHLAND DEVOTION
HIGHLAND BRAWN
HIGHLAND YULETIDE MAGIC

HIGHLAND SWORDS
THE SCOT'S BETRAYAL
THE SCOT'S SPY
THE SCOT'S PURSUIT
THE SCOT'S QUEST
THE SCOT'S DECEPTION

THE SOULMATE CHRONICLES
#1 TRUSTING A HIGHLANDER
#2 TRUSTING A SCOT

STAND-ALONE BOOKS
THE BANISHED HIGHLANDER
REFORMING THE DUKE-REGENCY
WOLF AND THE WILD SCOTS
FALLING FOR THE CHIEFTAIN-
3RD in a collaborative trilogy

THE SUMMERHILL SERIES-
CONTEMPORARY ROMANCE

#1-ONE SUMMERHILL DAY
#2-A FRESH START FOR TWO
#3-THREE REASONS TO LOVE

ABOUT THE AUTHOR

KEIRA MONTCLAIR IS THE PEN name of an author who lives in South Carolina with her husband. She loves to write fast-paced, emotional romance, especially with children as secondary characters.

When she's not writing, she loves to spend time with her grandchildren. She's worked as a high school math teacher, a registered nurse, and an office manager. She loves ballet, mathematics, puzzles, learning anything new, and creating new characters for her readers to fall in love with.

She writes historical romantic suspense. Her bestselling series is a family saga that follows two medieval Scottish clans through four generations and now numbers over thirty books.

Contact her through her website:
www.keiramontclair.com

Made in United States
North Haven, CT
27 September 2023